NO[illegible] BOOK II)

IN DARKNESS WAITS DESIRE

ELLIOTT ROSE

In Darkness Waits Desire by Elliott Rose

Published by: Cosmic Imprint Publishing

Cover Design: Maldo Designs

Copy Editor: Kerryn Hewson

2nd edition, July 2023

Paperback POD ISBN: 978-0-473-66914-0

Ebook (EPub) ISBN: 978-0-473-66915-7

Ebook (Kindle) ISBN: 978-0-473-66916-4

Created with Vellum

Sometimes all that is needed is to simply trust in your own magic.

CONTENTS

FIELD MAP &
Mountains
(Healing Wat
Dark fae
Fae Dominion
*portal/transference point
Demonic Realm
Soterian Realm
*portal/transference point
caution
Shifter Clan
Vampire Territories
wolv

Exploratory Notes

Living Legend

To accompany field notes
& expand upon as explorations allow
across the realms of the supernatural

Fae

*Notable for pointed ears
A fondness for material possessions
magics to conjure items of golds
and gemstone kind

Vampires

*Strength & heightened senses
*Myst-mysting will transport
vampire/Vampiress to known location
(can be amplified by consumption of
blood for memory access)

witches

*powers of connection to 'source'
Magics of varying elementals
in addition to other gifts bestowed
& beings of self-healing abilities
*Powerful witches may PORTAL
to travel anywhere hence they desire

wolf/wolven shifter
(Werewolf)

*Strength & heightened senses
Transfiguration between animal
form—that of regular being
Gifted with knowing/intelligence

CONTENT NOTES

In Darkness Waits Desire is a paranormal romance novel that contains dark elements, blood, plenty of spice, explicit sex, discussions of sexual assault and grooming (both alluded to, non-graphic), and child slavery/trafficking (occurs off-page).

For more information please visit my website

This novel is Book Two in the Nocturnal Hearts series.

playlist

The Hunted - The Rigs

I Feel Like I'm Drowning - Two Feet

Way Down We Go - KALEO

Very Few Friends - Saint Levant

I WANNA BE YOUR SLAVE - Måneskin

Whole Lotta Love - Hozier

Because The Night - Lúc

Omen - Disclosure, Sam Smith

Love On The Brain - Rihanna

NFWMB - Hozier

Bones - Imagine Dragons

You're Mine - Phantogram

Me and the Devil - Soap & Skin

DARKSIDE - Neoni

Hallow Fate - Gin Wigmore

The Night We Met - Lord Huron

I Want To - Rosenfeld

Wicked Game - Chris Isaak

CHAPTER 1

Blood pounded in Annabelle's ears.

She flattened her back against the stacked wooden barrels and willed herself to merge with the alleyway's long shadows. Ominous, twisted shapes thrown by the night lanterns where they hung in the darkness. The flickering amber light reflected on the wet cobbles below her boots.

She daren't breathe. The slightest noise might reveal her location.

Their presence had closed in on her all week. A menace that drew ever nearer. No matter how quickly she moved on to each new town, the shadows chasing her lingered around every corner.

Tonight she had been so desperately close. Nearly making it to the safety of the tavern when she felt the familiar chill sweep up the back of her neck. Instead she found herself fleeing down this darkened back alley in an attempt to shed her pursuers.

Crimson. Splattered and shining wet. Blood coating her hands. Stuck beneath her fingernails. Clogging her senses with its foul smell.

Belle squeezed her eyes shut. A futile attempt to block out the nightmare from six days ago.

Chilling tendrils of fog swirled towards her ankles. Her heart skittered faster at the sight of it reaching for her, like misshapen claws.

They had come. The fog was their disguise.

Her hand clamped over her mouth to stem her silent scream. Inch by inch she slid her back along the rough brick-work of the alleyway. Body braced to run. It was her only option left.

Might as well face death knowing she had tried every possible means of escape.

She pushed off the wall just a fraction, clutching her satchel tight against her chest. The tavern lay only half a mile from here. She listened intently for any hint of noise above her panicked heartbeat.

Silence, for now.

Time to lay her trust at the feet of the Goddesses.

On the count of three. Don't look back. One. Two. Thr—

She lurched forward into the pooled fog, bolting for the far end of the alley. Adrenaline spiked to urge her legs in a sprint away from the street. Out there she would be vulnerable in the open. Easy prey. These narrow passages behind the brick terraced houses would all connect somehow. If she followed their winding path it would lead her to sanctuary for the night.

The alley disappeared up ahead into a sharp right bend. She threw herself around the corner blindly.

Ooooof. With a gnarly thud Belle collided into something—someone—at full force. A solid frame and large chest towered over her. The wind knocked out of her lungs. A gasp echoed through the dark as she tumbled onto the wet cobbles. Her body sprawled sideways with the force of the fall. Knees hit the ground first. Palms scraped across the grime-covered stones. A sharp sting of broken skin where the ground roughed across flesh. Her satchel flew out of reach with its meagre contents spilling forth into grimy puddles.

NO! Her eyes flew wide. With a painful motion her body dragged itself forward in a half crawl, half limp. She lunged desperately to grab at the leather handle.

"Watch where you're going, witch."

On all fours with her desperation laid bare, Belle stiffened from head to toe at the deep whiskey tone coming from directly behind her.

Did he just say witch?

Her mind desperately wanted to scream for help, but she was too winded to utter a word. Fear drowned out the urge, reminding her that she would be a fool to trust anyone. Her body raced with adrenaline as she carried on a painful crawl forward. Her burst satchel might as well have been an ocean away rather than mere feet.

The stranger would no doubt carry on his way into the

night. This was a cold, cruel world as Belle had found out in the most heart wrenching of ways. You could only rely on yourself.

Fuelled by willpower blazing like a furnace she pushed herself to keep going. Inch by inch towards safety. This moment might be her final breaths, or if she could just keep fighting she might yet have a glimmer of hope to make it through til tomorrow.

A pair of charcoal leather boots came into view—expensive looking but well worn, blocking her from reaching her few possessions.

The stranger crouched down on his haunches meeting Belle at eye level and held her in a fierce stare. Searing aquamarine eyes met hers. Indifferent and cold. Unnatural against the inky grey damp of the night air. No hint of emotion crossed his face. His chiseled features were covered in trimmed dark stubble and thick brown hair, short but tousled, framing his face. The hint of some marking on his skin, tattooed up his neck, reaching from beneath his shirt. A heavy dark coat with a high collar almost moulded him into the night.

Her mouth went dry. She was held immobile as though hypnotised by that preternatural gaze. Like he saw right into her soul.

Suddenly she realised her fingers clutched the cracked leather handle of her satchel. The firm material heavy where it materialised beneath her scraped palms. How had it appeared in her hands? Did she hit her head and black out for a moment?

Belle didn't know how many seconds had passed and right now she didn't care. There was no time. She needed to get out of there. With a start she pushed off her knees, blindly stumbling away further into the night. Leaving the stranger to disappear in the fog behind her.

Don't look back. One foot in front of the other. Keep pushing.

Pain seared up her shins from the fall. Intensifying with every heavy thud of her boots against the cobbles. A limping run was the best she could muster. She reached out to steady herself against the brick wall to her right as she turned into the next alleyway. She winced as the roughness dragged across the fresh wounds on her palm, the gashes opening wider.

The fog whipped around her body. Damp lashed at her skin and plastered the edges of her long dark hair against her face. A chill sunk deep into her chest, boring in with a frightening intensity. *Evil.*

Looming in the fog were dark shapes, visible against the cloak of grey they shrouded themselves within. Ever so slowly and deliberately they closed in.

She had run out of time. The last grain of sand in the hourglass had begun a descent to the other side. A final voyage to the underworld.

So, this is what it feels like to meet with death.

As the fog thinned to reveal the edges of the forms hunting her, a scream caught in her throat at the horrific sight appearing before her.

These were not the men she feared.

This was her every nightmare come to life. Her hands shook uncontrollably. It couldn't be real.

Skeletal creatures, grey skinned, and with sunken black

holes where their eyes should be. Calculated. Efficient hunters. Long claws extending from bony fingers had blackened where they were caked in dried blood.

Two crawled on all fours and two more prowled upright. Somehow human in form, yet ghoul-like in appearance. Four mouths twisted into horrifying silent undead screams. The gaping maws appeared to be sewn closed.

Belle felt her chest seize up as though pinned in a vice. Her face drained of blood. A roaring in her ears hurtled forth as vertigo claimed her in its spiralling clutches.

There was no escaping this fate. She was trapped. Immobile. Frozen.

The first one lunged forward with a shriek and tackled her to the ground. The others followed. Enclosing her with their putrid stench. With a scream she tucked her knees trying to make herself into a ball, desperately shielding her head with the leather bag. Talons swiped at her cloak, shredding the fabric and wrenching it from her shoulders. Another vicious swipe and her satchel was cut to ribbons. She wrapped her head in her arms for futile protection, sobbing at the knowledge this would be it. *No no no no no.*

A savage scream erupted from her throat. Searing pain tore through her side. Razor sharp claws dragged through flesh. Her entire right side felt as though it boiled her alive. Warm liquid gushed down her back where her dress and body had been ripped open.

Her right arm exploded in agony. Screams echoed into the empty night. More lacerations as claws tore open flesh and shattered bone. Red seeped into the blackened pool of water beneath her face, coating the cobblestones in a macabre sheen of violence.

Claws dug into her left calf, piercing the skin and gripping tight, dragging her further into the dense fog. Her arm hung twisted and mangled. With the other she clawed at the cobbles. Crying out in vain.

There was no one. Nothing that could save her from these monsters.

All she had wanted was to live a life of freedom. To one day be her own master. She had dreamed of being able to decide her own destiny and no longer be controlled by another person. Maybe this was all her destiny was to be. A short miserable life filled with heartbreak and hollow emptiness. The girl who had belonged to her wealthy aunt. Presented to the world as though part of the nobility, but in private she was controlled and abused. Enslaved as nothing more than a wretched servant.

Six days ago she had stared into her aunt's lifeless eyes. Shaking as she surveyed the gruesome scene. No memory of what had happened. Perhaps she was a murderer? Perhaps she deserved her own violent end.

But what would it have been to live a life of her own choosing? To have known true happiness. To have loved. To have experienced the love of another.

Her head went limp. Tingling numbness spread through her extremities. A metallic tang filled her mouth, running over her tongue.

This would be her fate. A sadistic and torturous finale.

Her eyes rolled back in her head at the blinding pain from her broken body. The fog encased her and amplified the sickening screeches filling the night air.

Out of nowhere a bolt of blue light filled the alleyway. Jagged lightning crackled through the fog like a whip. She felt the weight of the creature's pressure on her leg vanish. Its claws wrenched from where they pierced her skin. The four figures thrown backwards by an unseen force.

The fog began to swirl and compress into a tight ball surrounding each ghoul, lifting their horrific bodies into the air. Their foul clawed hands scrabbling at their throats as if being suffocated by the very fog they lurked within.

Belle rolled onto her side and pressed shaking fingers against the blood where it seeped through the bodice of her dress. There was too much. It gushed against her hand. Black spots crept in at the edges of her vision.

Charcoal leather boots stepped in front of her hazy vision. Long strides stalked towards the creatures with intent. Reaching under his coat, the stranger withdrew a short blade in each hand. Instead of silver metal these glowed with a bright blue flame.

His tall, broad stature was a towering physique before her. All muscle and a foreboding kind of strength. The kind of imposing power that held a steely facade and potential to strike, if necessary. Masculine beauty disguised a cold beast within.

And he had his prey in his sights.

The ghouls writhed and twisted where they each hung in the air. Grotesque choking filled the silence.

Belle's vision blurred. Unconsciousness dragging her under. It was far too late. But she could die in this moment safe in the knowledge she had been avenged.

The last thing she saw was four severed heads thudding to the ground in a flash of blue flame. Splatters of black blood oozed forth as the decapitated bodies crumpled in a heap behind them.

Then she was gone.

CHAPTER 2

Lachlan of Nocturne was many things to many different supernatural beings. Protector, defender, wise counsel, Guardian. What he was not was a sentimental fool.

From the moment he crouched down to help the girl sprawled on all fours on the cobblestones, he had sensed it. The whisper had come in undeniable and insistent from Source.

She is yours. Your fated mate.

Fuck. No. This would not be happening to him now. After two hundred years his plan had come together and he was not going to allow the fates of the Universe to derail his vengeance.

Vampires, shifters, and fae would most commonly have a *mate* fated to them. An instinctual drive and lifetime bond that could not be denied once awakened. Despite their strength and mystical gifts, it was a weakness that could always be exploited.

Witches had the power to choose, and Lachie chose to go it alone.

He growled to himself as he wiped his blades clean of the snatchers' blood. He turned as he sheathed them in their holsters below his coat. The sight of her mangled body lying in a pool of blood clenched something long iced over within his chest.

She was clearly working as a servant. Perhaps she had been one for the House of Elharean, judging by her ragged appearance. Lachie knew all too well the squalid conditions those in service to the powerful dark witches affiliated with the House of Elharean endured.

The girl—witch—seemed to be running from something or someone.

That didn't mean she was any of his concern. Most definitely not *his*. Certainly not his *fated mate*.

Lachie was regarded as the most powerful witch within his home realm. The chosen Guardian from an ancient lineage of practicing witches. He had been chosen to lead and protect his community. To safeguard supernaturals from the threat of the House of Elharean, a legion of dark witches who sought to enslave both supernatural and everyday people. Their dark agenda fed on the power within all who fell under their control. Lifetimes of servitude taken by force or coercion from all those who pledged their allegiance to the House of Elharean.

All beings here in this world had the potential for magic

lying within them. The vast majority living outside of the supernatural community going about their normal, regular people lives had either forgotten the old ways long ago or their ancestors had deliberately turned their backs on magic.

His elite group of supernatural beings who served as his most trusted were highly trained and skilled in the art of spying, intelligence, and combat. They were also experts in covert operations here in the non-magical world, crossing the threshold between realms to eliminate packs of snatchers. Those ghoulish souls trapped in limbo and commanded to roam the non-magical world searching for newly awakened supernatural beings to deliver to their House of Elharean masters. He'd been tracking this pack, only they had behaved strangely tonight. Usually opportunists and scavengers, he hadn't witnessed such a direct hunting of any supernatural beings before. This was different. Unsettling in the way they had evaded him and managed to attack her before he could intervene.

They weren't going to kill her but their blood thirsty nature wouldn't stop them from savaging the witch before dumping her body with the House of Elharean.

Crouching down, he hovered his hands two inches in the air above her gaping wounds. One above her arm, the other moving over the largest lacerations on her side. Heat gathered in his palms as the healing spell took hold. Knitting bones back together and repairing the slashed open skin. A triage style enchantment would have to do to prevent her from bleeding out. A faint trace of magic still clung to her aura which meant she was alive, even if a mortal might have succumbed to these kinds of injuries by now.

He scowled to himself. He hated places like this. The narrow back alleys where only grime and menace could ever be found after dark descended. His magic roiled around inside of him. The air reeked of misery. No wonder the snatchers were drawn to these places. Where hope had long been extinguished from the vocabulary of the mortals suffering out their lives in overcrowding and destitution.

The last of her wounds closed over beneath his gaze. Porcelain soft skin now covered in gruesome welts. The evidence of untold savagery ran across her torso and arm as angry, red slashes. Back in his realm magic and healers would be able to do the rest now that he could safely move her.

Footfall crunched, moving towards him in the darkness. For a moment he tensed, ready to strike, before hearing a familiar voice call out.

"There he is. The prince of charm himself!" A hand clapped him on the shoulder, "I see you've also enjoyed happy hunting this night."

Ceranthe. A non-magical being—mortal—and a long-standing trusted ally in this strange world. His tussled sandy hair and lazy grin allowed him to move around with an easy charm. A perfect ear to the ground when rescuing supernaturals newly awakened to their magic.

"Oh shit! What happened?" He peered down at the figure twisted on the ground. "Will she live?"

"The pack got the drop on me. Never happened before."

Lachie muttered through clenched teeth. “A witch. I’ll portal her back with me.”

“Aye, and best be soon from the look of those wounds. I finished off two others of the bastards. Found them lurking close to the tavern.” Ceranthe slung his crossbow across his shoulder.

Lachie nodded sternly. “They seemed to be drawn to her. Hunting. I can’t explain it.”

Ceranthe’s brow drew into a frown. “We’ve done all we can here tonight. You best be on your way, Lach.”

“Are you sure you don’t have any magic within you? Dispatching two like that on your own?” Lachie turned to eye his companion sternly. “That was reckless. I’ll not be having you get yourself killed when you could—should—have waited for me.”

“Is it so hard for you witches to believe that maybe I’m just that good? Mortal or not. My aim is true.” Ceranthe shrugged his shoulders nonchalantly.

With a grunt Lachie shifted his weight and with an effortless motion scooped the limp frame of the woman into his arms. She suddenly consumed his every sense. Her soft curves beneath his fingertips. Plump mouth tinged with blue and slightly parted as she drew the shallowest of breaths. The heavy wet dress clung to her, shredded across her waist like a shipwrecked sail. The heavy material might as well have drowned her alive. Long brown hair hung in a single braid with the edges framing her face loose and plastered across her deathly pale cheeks.

Dragging his attention from her body cradled in his arms, Lachie fixed Ceranthe with a glare.

"You'll not do any more hunting without one of us to fight alongside you here. Or watch me come through the threshold to wring your neck myself."

Raising both hands in quiet surrender, yet with eyes crinkling in a smile, Ceranthe knew better than to say anything while Lachie was in this kind of mood.

Lachie tightened his grasp on the body in his arms. The rain and the wet cobbles of the alleyway began to dissolve as though into a thick smoke. It swirled closer around him, billowing and seething as the weightlessness took hold. Lachie drew her in tight, pressing his precious cargo to his chest. Closing his eyes, they both disappeared from the alleyway just as he heard the ethereal words ring loudly through his mind.

Protect her.

CHAPTER 3

The swirling mist parted below Lachie's boots as they landed in the darkened courtyard. It required no effort to carry the witch slumped in his arms. Ahead of him the castle windows glowed bright, illuminated against the dark sky. A faint sliver of a moon hung amongst the vast scattering of stars spread overhead. He strode towards an ornate looking conservatory with fine black metalwork encasing glass panels.

Glancing down he saw her blood had seeped through into his own clothes in the mere moments since they portaled into his realm. *Shit.* Was she still bleeding? Did he miss something?

He burst through the doors and honed in on the gathered supernaturals awaiting him. Crowded around one large examination table were some of the only beings he would trust with his life.

The first to greet him was Nell with her signature calm efficiency. This space was her domain.

"Set her down here." Her voice carried soft but firm across the herbarium. The tall witch with tanned skin and dark hair worked to grind herbs into a paste.

"I'll get started on dressing her wounds." She gestured at the bare surface in front of her with the marble pestle.

"Not your usual cheery self there, Lach. Or do my senses deceive me?" Niall. His youngest brother. Ever at the ready to charm and play the joker. He waved the dagger he held in his hand absently in their direction. Sun bleached hair, tanned skin, and with a similar build to Lachie. Always prepared with a dazzling smile and easy conversation. The bright that contrasted Lachie's dark.

"They got one past you? Spirits, I thought I'd never see the day his majesty was bested by a pack of slime bags." Niall's forearms leaned on top of one thigh where his leg perched casually on a chair. A gifted empath with the power to read and influence emotional states in others. The fierce fighter with a rogue's charm. He always took the opportunity to get under Lachie's cool composure.

To try to at least.

But it secretly grated him no end that Lachie could shield against his powers.

"Not the time." Lachie spat out as he carefully placed the slumped body of the witch on the table.

"Leave him alone, Niall. You know he'll give us all the *look* if you keep poking at him." Lia's familiar voice piped up. The short, curvy witch to his right smirked as she leaned one hip against the edge of the table. Her ankles crossed as she gently swirled glowing embers above her fingertips. The glimmer reflected in her large almond shaped eyes.

"Ignore them both, Lachie. I'm glad to see you returned safely." The imposing shifter wolf standing protectively behind the witch leaned forward and thumped him on the shoulder.

Fehrn was one of his oldest friends and treated him as though a brother even if not by bloodlines. He and his mate, the fire witch Lia, had been inseparable since they escaped from the House of Elharean two winters ago. She had since trained to become an elite spy alongside him and they now posed a formidable team. With his shifter gifts of strength, speed, and instinct from his wolf within, now matched with her powerful manipulation of fire and telepathy. They undertook all their missions side by side.

"Have a little trouble tonight, brother dearest?" His sister sat perched on the edge of the table with one leg crossed over another, leaning back on her hands. Her head of sleek black hair was cut short at her chin, highlighting mischievous blue eyes.

Fuck. This was not good.

"You know you don't need to be here, Brigid." Lachie's jaw clenched.

"Oh, you know I can't help myself when there are innocent lives on the line, no?" Her eyes twinkled as she swung her crossed legs back and forth with childish glee.

Irritation rose inside him. His younger sister, the

Enchantress and gifted Seer. The very reason they all knew to meet him here in the herbarium. She would have detected his impending portal from outside the realm. Most likely she already knew everything that had transpired from just one glance at him.

But that didn't mean she needed to come poking her nose into matters that didn't concern her.

While Brigid's gift of sight wasn't always one hundred percent accurate—she was forever waving her hands referring to something about multiple simultaneous timelines and realities—she had proved right in her *knowing* more times than not.

"Look, you need me here. Whether you want to admit it yet or not." Hopping off the table she waltzed towards him, reaching up to tap him on the nose. "One day I'll turn up unexpected and you'll thank me. I know these things." With a satisfied chuckle to herself she snuggled under his arm and rested her head on his chest.

"Others have lost their lives for less." He growled, reluctantly allowing her to nuzzle her way into his side.

"Are we going to talk about *her*?" Brigid whispered, looking up at him with a smirk across her delicate features.

"No."

"Don't worry. We will soon enough." She cooed.

What could she see that he wasn't aware of?

"Not likely." He let loose a menacing growl as Brigid wriggled out of reach. With a hop she moved to the edge of the table, cocking her head to survey the witch. The problem with having a sister who was a gifted Seer, was exactly that. She was his little sister and she knew the truth of his mind often before he did.

"Who, or what, are we not talking about now?" Niall folded himself into the chair with a bored sigh. Strong arms crossed over his broad chest.

"End of conversation." Lachie shook his head in stern warning as he raked his fingers through his hair.

"Can you get a read on anything from within her mind, Lia?" Nell interrupted as she applied the paste gently to garish, reddened scar tissue. Nimble fingers glowing with golden light as she cast her magic.

Lia placed one hand on each side of the girls head and closed her eyes for a few seconds. Her telepathy didn't require physical touch but it could help intensify the access to memories.

"She's been on the run. Fearful. I can't see the cause of her distress, only that she has no one to go back to."

"No one in her life to return to, you say?" Brigid murmured with twinkling eyes as she snuck a sidelong glance at Lachie. Lia's brow creased into a frown as she continued.

"Hard to tell her age. She seems young in mind but her power signature is potent. She doesn't know she is a witch. Newly awakened to her power. Possibly only since the attack."

His fists clenched.

"You'll see to it that this is fixed, no?" Lachie snapped in Nell's direction where she had finished administering the potion over the raised welts. Her lips moved silently in incantation.

"Of course we will." Brigid stood with hands on hips over the limp body lying sprawled on the table. Leaning down she gently pushed sodden hair from the witch's pale face.

"She is extraordinary. An Ampher, you know."

"Don't care." Lachie said through gritted teeth. But his mind immediately began to spin.

Finding a witch with Ampher powers? That changed everything. This would have serious repercussions for their very existence. They were all now at even greater risk knowing that an Ampher with awakened powers walked among them.

Not my concern. Most definitely not my fated mate.

"There was barely a hint of magic on her earlier." He ground out.

"In magic things aren't so black and white as to obey those strict rules you love so much. Stars, we all know this." Brigid stroked the cheek of the sleeping girl—woman.

"You're the only one of us who can truly protect her. She is special. And she is in more danger than you know."

Lachie's eyes flashed. His shoulders grew tense.

Brigid murmured, as though entranced by the vision in front of her. "There hasn't been one like her, since—"

"I don't want to hear you mention her name." His magic began to swirl with a crackle as it manifested in his clenched hands.

"Lachie, if I may." Fehrn stepped forward to place a steadying hand on his arm, eyeing his fists. "You know Lia and I will protect her with our lives..." A flash of sadness crossed Fehrn's face at a memory long since passed, that neither of them would ever be able to wipe from their conscience. "But we all need to give Nell her peace to complete her healing. Come, we can talk more in the morning."

His jaw clenched tight at the silent knowing passing between them. Fehrn had been there that day when he had failed. However his plan for vengeance would soon be complete. The path he had been destined to walk down these past two hundred years was nearly at its completion. In his sacrifice he would ensure no others would have to endure such suffering again.

Cold, logical, factual. His plan had been refined and calculated. The Guardian ensuring his responsibility to his people was upheld.

Nothing had taken his attention away from that end goal. The plan at the core of his every decision and movement. His icy cold heart protecting itself from further pain.

Nothing that was, until seeing her. Sensing her magic. Feeling that insistent voice within telling him that his path might just lie on a different course to that which he had dutifully followed for so long.

Your fated mate.

Fuck. This was an unmitigated disaster.

CHAPTER 4

Belle stirred, what was that dream she just had? It felt unending.

She bolted upright with a start. Had she been sleeping? It somehow felt so real. Magic. Witches. Savage claws slashing at her spine. Talons reaching out from the shadows to tear at her skin. She kept falling down endless black holes, over and over. Her head pounded like the ominous rhythm of drums of war. She rubbed her eyes to blink away the haze of her dream-like state.

Sunlight filtered through the room. That couldn't be right. She had never slept in a room with windows. She had never experienced waking up with the sun, always up hours before dawn.

Whispers came from close by. Inside the room. Her blood ran cold. Flashes of mangled flesh leapt into her mind.

"Good evening, Annabelle!" A bright tinkling voice filled the room. "We don't mean to frighten you but these things are not easy the first time." An elfin figure bounded onto the bed beside her. Beside her? A gasp escaped her throat. Belle looked down at where her fingers sunk into soft linens draped over the largest bed she had ever seen.

"Now before you start spiralling on me, you're perfectly safe here. In fact, bless the Stars, for I don't know how you hadn't been snatched earlier."

Belle gaped at the woman as though she spoke a foreign language. None of this made sense. She lay in comfort. In a giant bed, with what looked like a real life fairy smiling benevolently at her. Another woman stood over by the windows, drawing the curtains open to let even more dazzling golden light flood the room. Not a sunrise, but the burnt orange glow of a fiery sunset.

Belle struggled to focus. Her head felt stuffed full of cotton. She shielded her eyes against the glare.

"How do you know my name? Am... am I dead?"

The two exchanged a glance among themselves and burst out laughing.

"Of course not. You're in Castle Nitorna of the Soterian Realm. Our protected lands. You were brought here to safety. This is a realm where supernatural beings, including witches like you, can live peacefully." The elf reached over to the small table beside the bed. "Drink this. It will help with the after effects of the healing enchantment. Feels like coming round after a night swinging from the roof on too much Fae wine, no?"

"A... realm?" Why did her head now feel like she was underwater. With a gasp she clutched at her waist. No pain. She twisted around to look down, running her fingers over her arm, expecting to see the mangled gory mess from the attack. But her fingertips only met with smooth pale skin as though nothing had occurred.

Almost as if she hadn't nearly been murdered by a pack of monsters from her worst nightmares.

"I'm Nell. Your healing is physically complete but I would still recommend taking it gently. The wounds within the mind sometimes take a little longer." The other woman—Nell—spoke softly as she moved beside her. In contrast to the pixie creature, this woman was much taller with bronzed skin and gentle eyes. "And this here is Brigid, who could use a lesson in restraint sometimes."

Ignoring her, the elf—Brigid—hopped off the bed. "You're in for a treat this evening. We're going to give you a personal tour. It's about time you got to explore your new home." Her hands clapped together. "But first, some food and desperately needed clean clothes. I hope you don't mind but I got rid of that awful sack-like thing you were soaked through in."

Her eyes widened. "What? How long since—" She couldn't bring herself to speak of the attack.

Nell reached to take the cup from Belle's trembling hands.

"You've been here under your healing enchantment for five

days now." Nell's tone somehow soothed as it floated through the room. Her gentle voice reached out and brushed across Belle's skin like a feather. "Annabelle, listen to me. That life you knew no longer exists for you now. Here there is no danger to you. No servitude. No hierarchy. No enslavement to others. Our gifts and our magic provides all that we need. Yours will too given time."

She really must be dead. "Did you just say *mine* will too?"

Both women nodded enthusiastically. "You're a witch, Annabelle, but your power has only just awakened. Here we can help you learn to harness it and control it. To harmonise with the gift you have from Source."

Brigid disappeared into a large ornate wooden cupboard standing in the corner of the room before emerging with swathes of different coloured material draped across her shoulders.

"Come and try these. I'll not have any witch wearing such hideous garments ever again. The era of the world you came from really does have a long way to go before clothing becomes tolerable."

Belle's feet hit the floor as if floating on command and she padded across the lush carpet. Her head swivelled around the expansive room to take in the finery. Stone walls adorned with beautiful draped fabrics that appeared to shimmer, giving the stone a softness and warmth. Large windows framed by a plush velvet window seat where she could see the sun setting behind distant hills. Through a wide doorway a glimpse of a richly furnished parlour room. Lavish was a description that could never do it justice.

"You're suite is beautiful, no?" Brigid threaded Belle's arms through a soft silk dress as though she were a marionette. A rich emerald colour that wrapped around her waist and tied in the middle. The texture was like nothing she had ever encountered against her skin. Like the first dew drop to roll across a flower's silken petal.

"My suite?" For an intelligent woman Belle sounded like she had lost her brain during the attack. Nothing made sense. The most she could do was repeat back everything the women said to her. But despite her original panic their presence was comforting. This strange place felt strangely familiar somehow.

"Yes, this is yours... for as long as you need until you have harnessed your powers you'll live here in the castle." Another pixie-like grin.

"Does everyone live here?" *Aquamarine eyes. Flashing blue fire across his blades.*

"Not everyone, the realm is extensive. Only newly awakened supernaturals such as yourself." Brigid flashed her a sparkle of a wink. "And our extended family who have been chosen by the Goddesses... those of us responsible for safeguarding the realm."

"The castle tends to be a lot busier during the daytime. Brigid oversees any magical training and education. I look after the herbarium—mostly creating potions and gathering ingredients for spell casting. The other supernaturals you'll see here live in the surrounding towns and villages. Except for during our gatherings like Nightfall or the Equinox balls when others travel here from far and wide." Nell spoke with a soft melody.

The witch knelt down before Belle and moved her feet into the softest tan coloured leather slippers she had ever experienced. They didn't even feel like leather they were so supple and flexible against her skin.

Belle had spent her entire lifetime suffering blisters and aches from the heavy, painful boots of the servant class that were always too small and patched over and over again.

Brigid and Nell both took a step back to admire their handiwork.

"You are breathtaking, Annabelle." A sudden distant look passed over Brigid's face as though her thoughts had strayed far away. "I can see this evening is going to be very... illuminating."

Not having a clue what the enchantress was talking about, Belle suddenly felt a surge of energy. A wave of confidence rushed through her body. It tingled and danced under her skin.

"If this really is my new life, then please call me Belle." She flashed a nervous smile. "Annabelle feels as though it was the part of me that stayed behind... wherever I just came from. Maybe she did die in that alleyway. But I've always dreamt of the day when I could choose my own destiny. It was one of my final thoughts before the..." She gulped. "Before the attack. I think this might just be the moment I manage to have a life that is finally my own."

From out of her pocket Brigid fished a ring set with an emerald gem stone in a wide organically shaped gold band and slipped it onto Belle's forefinger.

"To destiny, Belle."

CHAPTER 5

Belle moved through the castle flanked by the two witches who happily pointed out and explained her foreign new surroundings. This all felt like a mirage. One that would surely flicker and fade just as fast as it had hurtled into her life.

It turned out Belle's suite was located in one of the many turreted towers she had glimpsed through the large windows. Each rounded turret featured a pointed deep-cerulean roof topped with a spire. The stonework was a luminous pale cream colour, that sparkled as though flecked with gold dust in the setting sunlight.

As they wound their way down the enormous grand staircase, Belle ran her hand along the smooth cool texture of the stonework. It felt real enough beneath the pads of her fingertips. Maybe she wasn't trapped in a dream labyrinth after all.

They paused at the base of the steps where they fanned out into a vast entrance hall. Pale cream stonework inlaid with gold stretched out beneath her feet. The flooring seemed to emit a warming glow. Her eyes found themselves drawn upward to take in the ornate vaulted ceiling. She had to crane her neck it was so impossibly high. Decorated in rich purples with white starlight that seemed to shimmer and move of its own accord. As though the night sky lived and breathed a gentle dance through the castle itself.

Tingles of awareness ran down her spine as if the air where she stood reacted to her presence.

"Lachie! There you are, perfect timing." Brigid had a hold of Belle's upper arm and propelled her rapidly forwards. She could have sworn the grip around her tightened a fraction as though to prevent her escape.

One glance confirmed exactly where—or more accurately who—Brigid was intent on dragging her towards. The stranger who had saved her paused mid-stride across the entrance hall. His expression stony despite his sister's cheery greeting.

Her stomach coiled with warmth at the sight of him. Traitorous butterflies swarmed her insides. This man—witch—was even more attractive than she remembered. The kind of roughly hewn, gorgeous appearance you happened upon only on the rarest of occasions. An otherworldly magnetism radiated off his broad chest.

Shit. Close mouth. Stop staring.

"Belle, I believe the two of you have already met." Did Brigid just wink at her? "Let me do the formal introductions.

This is Lachlan of Nocturne, Guardian of the Realm, and my dreadfully overbearing older brother."

What did one do when meeting a Guardian of the Realm? Especially one who had apparently saved her life. Was she supposed to curtsey? Drop a bow? Belle gaped like a fish out of water. Everything she had known in her normal world no longer applied.

His gaze swept over her body taking in her radical transformation from mangled corpse to silk clad witch. Belle's face flushed under his silent assessment. But he gave no hint of emotion, other than that penetrating *look,* followed by an incline of his head in stiff greeting.

An odd prickling sensation built like a static charge surrounding her skin. *Spirits.* A flush of heat erupted across her chest, matching her cheeks at the way her body seemed to respond without intending to do so. His was a kind of rugged beauty that you never expected to see in the flesh. The type only whispered about in tales of fantasy. The most handsome man she had ever seen. Yet there was something entirely otherworldly about him that she couldn't put her finger on.

His scent of faint woodsmoke, cedar, and leather filled her senses. Vague awareness pressed against her thoughts... she should be trying to move... but her body was enthralled. Trapped in place. All of a sudden every sensory input magnified in intensity. New interactions with the world surrounding her pinged at the edges of her aura like starbursts of light. A buzzing sound filled her ears. The cool drifted up around her ankles from the flagstones beneath her feet. The musky scents of horses drifted in from the courtyard. Electricity danced and tingled in the air around her as though she could see the ether itself moving.

"Beauty before age, Lach." Brigid's laugh jolted her back into the room. She looked down to see where the witch had threaded her arm with Belle's and now dragged her through a large stone archway towards the sound of music and chatter.

Eyes wide, Belle felt as though everything had been jolted inside her, awakened somehow, with a trail of heat spiralling straight to her core.

She swung her head around to look over her shoulder and saw to her surprise, that he followed silently. Stalking directly behind her. Like a cold hunter after their prey.

Goosebumps ran up her neck at his closeness and that strange sensation rippled through her insides once more. *What was that?* This entire situation was too overwhelming. Closing her eyes briefly, Belle inhaled long and deep through her nose.

She prided herself on being a positive, happy, friendly person. Someone that others warmed to in an instant. Her natural charm had always been a cause for punishment from her Aunt who saw it as insolence, rather than a desirable characteristic.

It's just nerves, they will surely pass soon enough?

Sweeping her through the impossibly large doorway with an impish grin, Brigid threw one arm wide to take in the hall laid out before them while holding tight to Belle with the other.

"The castle provides for those of us who are in protection of the realms. Along with any supernaturals like yourself who are in the early stages of learning to master the basics of your magic. Think of us like a rather eclectic menagerie, complete with spells and swords... or claws and fangs." Brigid purred a *rawr* and raked her fingers through the air pretending to swipe at Nell beside them.

Within the banquet hall long wooden tables were occupied by small groups of supernatural beings gathered together. Others mingled within the grand room. *No servitude here.* As they wound their way towards a table a blur of introductions swirled in her direction. Shifter wolves with penetrating eyes sniffed the air as she passed by. Mesmerising vampires, easily distinguished by their razor sharp cheekbones, nodded in greeting. A scattering of fae discerned by their delicate pointed ears and luscious hair shaved down one side of their heads. Other witches of any manner of shapes and sizes. All of whom it transpired lived either in or around the castle.

Brigid sat to her right, Lachlan to her left. His shoulders set stiffly, yet he continued to ignore her. The Guardian dropped quickly into a hushed conversation with the shifter wolf Fehrn and fire witch Lia who sat across from them. Belle shot a quick glance where the couple's fingers intertwined, the shifter traced over the witch's pulse point on her wrist absently as they spoke.

A pang of jealousy twinged in her chest. What would it be like to experience that kind of affection from another? To know the soul deep connection of a *mate.*

Her fingers rubbed the hem of her sleeve. There was too much to take in. These supernaturals had lived this life for hundreds, if not thousands, of years. Here she was a mere weed among the cracks of cobblestone. She was sure to be trodden into the dust at any moment.

Brigid flicked her wrist casually without breaking stride mid-conversation with two impossibly beautiful fae. Within a blink of an eye a sample of foods appeared on an ornate silver dish before her. The mouth watering smell wafting through her senses. It was like nothing she had ever seen or tasted before. Amid the conversation she saw other supernaturals each had unique appetites catered to with magic. Vampires with crystal decanters of blood wine. Shifters with platters of meats and berries. Witches with evidently whatever their taste buds desired. She sipped at the delicately carved crystal goblet of wine before her, eyes widening in delight as it caressed her lips as though it were honey.

"Belle here is an Ampher. We've got our work cut out to try and uncover more about her unique magic." Brigid nudged her thigh with her own, dragging her attention back towards the conversation.

The fae cooed with delight. The chatter flowed around her as she did her best to smile, nod, and laugh along when she hoped was just the right moment. Yet, she fidgeted in her seat. Her every sense collided in a constant stream of noise, smells, and sights. She could hardly make out what anyone was saying, it all just felt... too much.

Twisting the beautiful ring Brigid had given her, she realised with relief that the others seemed to be engrossed in conversation long enough to forget she was there. A final big gulp drained the last of her wine and she sat the goblet down on the table. Her head swam from the intensity of the room surrounding her. Time to quietly slip away back to her rooms when no one might notice.

She pushed against her seat to stand and at the same time felt the cool metal band slip from her finger. A flash of gold winked at her as the ring dropped to the floor. Belle gasped and made to snatch at it before it rolled right under the middle of the table. Lunging forward her fingers closed around the ring just as her hand was enveloped in a powerful hold.

Belle flicked her wide eyes up with a start to find herself leaning over Lachlan's muscular physique. Except rather than being eye to eye he was crouched on the stone floor, positioned directly in line of sight with her breasts. Time slowed to a standstill as she became lost in the intensity of his stare. Without letting go of her hand his eyes flickered from where they had been locked on hers. She watched his dilated pupils drift to her lips where they lingered for a long second. Then the molten trail of his stare slipped further down. Her body immediately betrayed her. *Fuck.* She felt her nipples harden through her silk dress and his eyes darkened. A look filled with the deep blue grey of a raging storm as she stiffened under his gaze.

Woodsmoke, cedar, leather. Every sense felt more alive than she could ever recall.

There was nothing she could do but watch as he traced the length of her finger with the pad of his thumb. Belle felt like she might combust in a raging inferno right there on the spot. A pulsating heat wound inside her at his sensual touch. She dragged her teeth over her lower lip as strong hands gently and ever so deliberately slid her ring back onto her finger.

Shit. She burned under his torturously slow caress. A tempest that threatened to engulf her. Her every nerve ending felt like it was awakened as the seconds dragged out endless and devoid of air. His jaw ticked and that small movement broke whatever magic had held her in place. She jerked her hand back.

Without a backwards glance, she fled.

The cold flagstone floor blurred beneath her feet. An unknown beacon of sanctuary calling her back along the corridors that led to her rooms. Powerful magic indeed lay within these stone walls. Without a clue how to find her rooms, the castle led her exactly where she desired to go. Her hands and knees shook as she tumbled through the door of her suite. She leant against the closed door, gulping down deep breaths.

She could see it so clearly now. Lachlan's intensity trapped beneath that exquisitely cool exterior. And apparently her body wanted to find out what it might be like to be inside his storm.

CHAPTER 6

The clash of metal against metal rang across the clearing. Lachie's muscles burned under the jarring impact. Over and over he blocked himself from his opponent. Sweat dripped down his forehead, blurring his vision. The muscle memory of hundreds of years of training took over where his eyes couldn't see clearly. Over his shoulder the second attacker loomed closer. He kicked out with his heel to propel them backwards, pulsing a shock wave of magic into both assailants to give himself space.

With a deft movement he backed out of reach of their blade as it scythed through the air. In each hand he held a short sword which he spun in a fluid motion. Blue flames flared along the razor sharp edges to mirror the magic that thrummed through his veins.

Lachie grunted in defiance and bared his teeth. A dare to them both to risk coming closer.

"Yield, old man!" Niall shouted. "You can't outlast the both of us."

The untamed scent of humidity, damp earth, and sweat hung in the air between them.

"Not before you're on your knees begging, princess." He spat the blood that had pooled in his mouth. An early blow from Niall had landed on its mark. Lucky shot.

Bringing his right hand up he pointed with the blade directly towards the chest of the other man with an accusing thrust.

"You. You're pulling your punches today, no?"

Rowan. His other brother, aged between him and Niall. A witch gifted with the blood of ancient warriors and hunters. He had an affinity for weaponry like no other and had been training his brothers in combat since they could walk. If Lachie was rumoured to be a dark prince then Rowan was the black knight of the Nocturne brothers.

Brooding. Solitary. Deadly with any weapon.

He chose to live out here in the forest far away from others inside the castle. Rowan described it as his sanctuary but Lachie really knew it was his own private fortress.

And he was always prepared for war.

"You idiots have been at it for hours. Enough already. My bones are aching and I'm ready for a hot meal and a soak in the tub." Lia stood from where she perched on her haunches at the edge of the clearing. With a deft movement she sheathed her blades in her back halter.

"Is that an invitation?" Fehrn waggled his eyebrows at his mate from where he reclined against a tree. He sharpened his extended shifter claws on a flint with a wicked gleam in his eye. "I know just the spot to ease that ache of yours."

Lia flushed red and shot embers in Fehrn's direction.

"Don't want to hear about ... that." Lachie grated out, waving his outstretched sword to gesture between the two of them. While he was truly happy for his friend, and adored Lia as part of their extended family, he wasn't in the mood for their constant flirting. Spirits save him, the two of them seemed to barely keep their hands off each other when they weren't dispatched on missions.

Protect.

If that wasn't enough, the damn ethereal voice in his mind had continued to needle at him over the past few weeks. Ever since Annabelle—Belle—had landed with a thud into his world. But there were ways to *protect* the witch without getting involved. He'd made sure she started straight away with lessons to harness her gifts. As an Ampher she was a witch with the power of amplifying the magic of others around her. Which made her potentially the most powerful witch across multiple realms.

And potentially the most deadly.

He'd been reluctantly impressed with how easily she had taken to life among the supernatural community. That ridiculously bright smile seemed to light up the room wherever she went, and she had already become firm friends with Nell and Brigid who guided her well. The more occupied she was with training and nurturing her magic the better. She would learn to protect herself. That meant Lachie could return to focusing on his responsibilities as Guardian. He needed to stay on track. His plan for revenge was drawing ever nearer to completion.

Focus.

That meant *not* spending time hanging around the court-yard where most witches trained and practiced with their gifts.

It definitely meant *not* visiting his sister multiple times a day in her study where he knew Belle would be pouring over ancient texts.

It certainly meant *not* replaying that first night in the banquet hall over and over in his mind. Images of her porcelain skin beneath emerald silk. The sight of her nipples tightening into perfect buds as he drank in her essence. The feel of her soft skin. How his tongue might have run along that perfect finger. What it would be like to run his tongue across—*Fuck.*

He looked down and saw the rocks scattered around the clearing were levitating around his ankles. A torrent of blue tinged electrical charge crackled from his hands where they gripped his blades.

"We know you love to hone your grumpy attitude, your majesty." Niall rolled his eyes. "But you can drop the pissed off at the world routine for one day."

His youngest brother never missed an opportunity to keep him grounded. Being Guardian of the Realm wasn't a royal title or an elected position, but a responsibility chosen by the ascended masters from beyond the veil of Spirit. A blessing given by the Goddesses themselves. He knew Niall was immensely proud of him for shouldering the role for so long. But after two hundred years the idiot still thought he was hilarious with the 'your majesty' jabs.

Lachie grunted. "For the record, I'm still waiting for the day you manage to best me, princess."

He dragged his shirt up over his head and wiped the sweat from his eyes before tossing it at Niall's face. Determined to push all thoughts of a certain witch, her long dark hair wrapped around his fist, running his tongue over her nipples, from his mind. He strode out of the clearing bare-chested. Stomping his way though the dense tree cover towards the castle.

He moved along the forested trail to the beginnings of the castle grounds. He could see the pale cream stone surrounding the courtyard in the distance up ahead. The shimmering effect of the castle's own magic giving off a glint in the sunlight. Sparks, swirls of smoke, and columns of water could be seen rising into the air from behind the walled courtyard. He wondered what Belle had been able to achieve from her training today. She had made fast progress understanding what it meant to connect to Source and work with those invisible forces that were always present.

Most witches had one particular gift that was theirs. The Goddesses may bestow other blessings, but it was rare to have the capability of all threads of magic. In Lachie's case he posessed the exceptional ability of multiple gifts —and the power to use them simultaneously— as an elemental witch. Whereas Belle as an Ampher was able to draw upon and use magic possessed by the witches surrounding her like a siphon.

It explained why their first interactions had been so highly charged. *Not* because they were fated mates, but because she had unknowingly amplified Lachie's magic. Her gifts had been wild and newly awakened. Untrained. That explained why the sensations he had felt were so much more heightened and uncontrollable than usual.

Blood. Screams. No control. His jaw clenched at the distant memories. The familiar feeling of his throat closing and heart beginning to race. He hadn't been able to stop it.

Squeezing the handles of his blades until his knuckles turned white, he realised he had wandered straight to the courtyard. *Shit.* Not supposed to be here again. He couldn't help but scan the space for that familiar long dark braid and perfectly curved figure. Instead his eyes came to rest on the elfin grin staring back at him from her perch on the stone wall. *Shit. Shit. Shit.*

"You're becoming quite the regular here, brother. Don't suppose you're here to train yourself, no?"

"Brigid." A low warning growl.

"Before you ask. I haven't seen her."

"What do you mean?" His heart clenched with a rapid pulse.

A nonchalant shrug from the infuriating pixie. "She's been missing all day."

"Missing?" Something lurched in his stomach.

"She's probably busy."

"Don't mess around, Brigid. You see all. Tell me where she is." His sister might be an Enchantress and a gifted Seer but she had also sworn an oath not to reveal what she could see. The law of non-interference as it was known among those with her kind of magic.

Which meant Lachie knew he could trust her to keep his dark secret.

But it also guaranteed there were at least ten times a day when he would gladly wring her neck for not giving him a straight answer.

"You'll have to wait and see."

"Not possible. What if she's in danger?"

Brigid let out an exaggerated sigh and looked at her nails.

"Unless she has figured out how to leave the realm on her own what trouble can she have gotten into?" She huffed out a breath then shot him a devilish grin. "Unless she *has* worked out how to leave the realm on her own?"

Lachie was already halfway up the grand staircase inside the castle, taking the stone steps two at a time.

He banged impatiently on the door to her apartments. No sounds came from inside. Panic crept up the back of his neck and clasped around his throat. Barging through the door he found the parlour room still and lifeless. No sign of anyone. The grate in the fireplace was cold. How could she have left knowing how dangerous it was to be away from this place —from him?

The door to her bedchamber was closed. He charged

through the heavy wooden frame. His heart pounded inside his ears and still there was nothing to indicate she was here. Bed neatly made. Everything in place. No sign of a hasty departure. One last door lay ahead of him. Her private bathroom. With a slam he practically tore the door from its hinges.

Belle lay in a swirl of steam and bubbles in the large copper tub in the middle of the room. Naked.

Her dark hair floated loosely around her shoulders and her breasts skimmed the surface of the gently swirling water. Her legs perched on the other end of the tub, baring her flawless skin towards the curve of her rear. Perfect legs disappeared below the surface. Only the barest hint of her pussy hid beneath the water.

Lachie had never seen anything like the vision before him. Flawless creamy skin. Curls that tumbled down framing her face. Cheeks and plump lips flushed from the heat of the steam. Soft curves and a paradise of voluptuous flesh that would be seared into his mind forever.

Relief flooded through him that she was here. *Your mate.* Fury followed quickly on its heels that she had disappeared without so much as a hint of warning.

Blood pounding, his temples throbbed. He stood there bare chested and slick with sweat.

"What. Are. You. Doing." His growl ricocheted around the room.

With a lurch and a shriek Belle's eyes flew open. "Lachlan? What in the Spirits—" She looked down and let out a yelp.

Hands flew to cover her breasts and she dropped her legs under the water with such force half the water hit the floor.

"You can't go missing like this." His voice sounded like it didn't belong to him.

"I'm taking a bath!"

"Supposed to be training." He snapped. "Not disappearing without trace."

"It is hardly disappearing when I am in my own *private* suite." The steam crackled with electricity. Bubbles from the bath began to rise up and float around the room like small puffy clouds. "I didn't realise this was a military operation. You are being ridiculous." Belle tried to shift her hands to cover more of herself. But she only ended up pushing her cleavage higher and making the whole scene even more erotic than before.

Lachie felt his blood heat and flow south. He tried desperately not to notice how her mouth was slightly open. How her breath softly panted. How her chest rose and fell faster. This was territory he definitely should not be crossing into.

"Not ridiculous. This is my responsibility. *You* are my responsibility." Her eyes flashed sparks. "Everyone in this realm is my responsibility." He hastily added.

"Walking in on strangers while they are bathing?" She gritted her teeth. "As far as I was aware I am not a prisoner here to be controlled. Now. Get. Out."

"*Never* disappear like that again."

Lachie stood locked in place. Silence hung in the air between them as the blue crackling turned purple with increasing intensity. Potion bottles and her clothing that had been on the wooden bench-top began to levitate in the air. Her gold ring with the emerald gem stone floated off the stool beside the bath. He stepped forward menacingly. Desperate to reinforce the severity of the situation in the only brutish way he knew how.

So what if he gave her a reason to be afraid? Then she'd know just a fraction of how his heart had scrambled inside his chest on the way here.

With one hand he gripped the rim of the tub as the other reached to grasp the ring out of the air. Lachie now stood stooped over her. Close enough to feel her breath against his skin.

Belle's mouth gaped open at his sudden closeness and he watched intently as her eyes flitted lower to his mouth.

In a fluid motion he prised his fingers from their hold on the bath edge and wrapped her wrist in his hand. His every movement laced with tension as though the very air itself might splinter into a million shards. Lachie pulled her wrist up towards him, leaving her breast bare. With a gentle but forceful movement he slid the ring back on her forefinger.

"You're not to take this off. Ever."

Then he swept out of the suite. Slamming the door behind him.

CHAPTER 7

"Then he said… 'never go off and do anything without asking my permission ever again or I will personally lock you in your room!' like a lunatic." Belle threw the back of her hand against her forehead with an exaggerated flourish and popped the other one on her hip.

"Then what?" Nell giggled uncontrollably.

"Then…" Belle added a touch more theatre. "He banned me from bathing for eternity."

Brigid snorted with laughter. Nell squealed. Lia covered her eyes and shook her head.

"He did not!" Brigid gasped for air, shoulders shaking with laughter.

"He honestly removed your hand from—you know?" Lia peeked out from behind her fingers with a mortified expression on her face. “I’ve trained side by side with the man for two years. I just cannot imagine him losing his cool like that.”

Belle flopped down on the plush floor cushions where they sat gathered in Brigid’s room. “It was utterly mortifying. I can’t believe I was completely naked staring down a livid Lachlan of Nocturne.” She reached for her tea on the table, cupping it between her hands. The warmth seeped through her fingertips.

“He’s one of the few who always remains calm enough to maintain his blocks against my telepathy. Enchantress magic included in that list too, of course.” Lia added with a grin at Brigid who was also skilled at deflecting Lia’s telepathic gift. “I’d say you found it a rather... mind-altering experience, Belle.”

“And don’t forget he was near naked too. He might be my brother, but remember I see *all.*” Brigid winked.

Like she *could* forget that. A flush skittered across her chest as the three witches all raised their eyebrows knowingly in her direction.

They couldn’t possibly think—no—she hadn’t been attracted to him yesterday? He’d been a complete ass more times than she could count. Sir Hot-and-Cold had continued to alternate between ignoring her, avoiding her, and then simply staring at her with unnerving scrutiny.

Whenever she was training he seemed to be there silently critiquing her every move. When she researched the ancient texts for any mention of Ampher powers she always got the feeling he was unimpressed with her choice of studies. While Brigid and Nell helped her master the basic elements, circle casting, and the creation of sigils to bind enchantments she continued to feel his unseen presence. Yet he had refused to sit near her in the banquet hall ever since that first night.

That night when he had turned her into a melted puddle of lust with just the slightest brush of his thumb.

"No." Belle pursed her lips. Her gaze scanned the eager faces staring back at her.

"Yes."

"NO."

"Mmmm... Yes."

"But he either ignores me or scowls at me."

Belle gulped back her tea hoping in vain to deflect this entire conversation.

"Look, I don't know Lachie's mind but I can sense yours." Lia smiled coyly.

Nell nodded sagely in agreement.

"And I've never heard of Lachie getting that passionate about... anything. He's always so composed. There's obviously something between the two of you." Lia reached out to touch her arm. "Would it be so bad to open up and let someone in? To put that hurt and pain behind you?" Warmth rolled from her fingertips where her fire magic danced soothingly.

Belle stilled. Her eyes squeezed closed. Of course Lia would be able to hear whenever her fears of *him* rose to the surface. Whenever the hurt of her past came crashing through her mind. It was usually the smallest of things that would bring a flood of unpleasant memories.

"I'm sorry, I didn't realise you would be able to know that

part of me. I don't want to burden you with my past, Lia. Especially after everything you have been through."

Lia had been unknowingly held captive and trapped in servitude for years within the House of Elharean. Belle knew only a brief explanation of what had happened, but it was Lia who saved Fehrn, Nell, and reportedly a vampiress from their imprisonment and torture. The vampiress was so badly injured during repeated abuse that even now, two years later, she was recuperating with supernatural healers far away in the distant mountains.

"Sounds like a perfect opportunity for some training." Brigid popped to her feet with a clap of her hands. "My handsome but ogre-like brother aside, you need to learn the art of walking *with* your fears. As we all do."

"Learn to walk with them? How does that work?" Belle felt uneasy about this sudden change of direction. She was only just wrapping her head around the idea that she might have more than a passing appreciation for Lachlan's chiseled physique and powerful hands.

"As witches we mustn't try to ignore or avoid our fears Belle. But instead we learn to observe them, walk beside them, and eventually choose our path forward from a place of love, rather than fear." Brigid settled herself down on a cushion in front of Belle on the floor.

"This is a lesson on exploring the shadow that lies within. Not to try make you feel unnecessary pain, but to recognise that you can be powerful *and* have experienced fears. Magic used from a place of fear can be extremely dangerous indeed."

Belle reluctantly placed her hands palms down onto where Brigid's were outstretched towards her. Spirits, her heart raced like the skitter of a rabbit to elude long talons and teeth baring down upon its tail.

"Close your eyes. Breathe." Brigid instructed softly.

"Trying." Belle clenched her jaw.

A wave of warmth and soft, honey-like sweetness flooded through her veins. She let out a long exhale.

"Niall isn't the only one who can influence emotions in our family." Brigid's laugh tinkled. "Your power comes from Source, Belle. We all connect to it in unique ways. You'll learn to master elements first—fire, wind, earth, water, and energy—which is where most witches end their training. But for you it will grow beyond that. You have something none of us have and a gift that we know next to nothing about. As an Ampher, yours is the ability to take on and amplify the magic of those around you. But don't worry, we'll start with the basics of connection to Source."

Belle felt herself drop away into a feather soft darkness.

"When you draw on Source you must learn to walk with the shadows wherever they might be." Brigid's voice echoed further away with each passing moment.

BELLE'S EYES FLASHED OPEN. *The familiar heavy perfume of lilies irritated her nose. She stared at the room around her in disbelief.*

Her younger self crouched in the corner with a thread and needle. Hands shaking as she reattached the intricate lacework on the dress laid across her lap. Tears tracked down her face. She must have been twelve in this memory. Her arms covered in yellow-green bruises. A freshly purpled ring encircled her swollen right eyelid.

Belle winced at the memory and touched her own face in sympathy for her younger self. That had been from the spine of a book in the breakfast room earlier that morning. Her Aunt's tea had gone cold too soon for her liking. The book had flown at her before she could move.

The scene morphed and changed to a new memory.

Belle saw *herself standing in her Aunt's study, older now. Perhaps sixteen. Her right wrist bandaged. That time it had been strips torn off her by her Aunt's cane for forgetting to dust the bookshelves in the library.*

Although she hadn't forgotten. Belle had been on her way to the task when she'd been dragged into the courtyard and beaten.

"You'll have to cover up that ghastly thing on your arm. We cannot have my luncheon ladies seeing how you continually injure yourself when they arrive today. At least you haven't gone and messed your face up this week."

The snide remarks pierced Belle's heart as she watched on.

Her Aunt waved a dismissive hand. Her mousey coloured hair pinned back in a tight bun matched the severity of her features. A richly embroidered silk dress was garnished with a red feather brooch. The woman wore a red feather everywhere without fail. Bright crimson, like the colour of oxygenated blood.

The symbol had taunted Belle in her dreams as a child. A feather should represent freedom and soaring high, whereas under her Aunt's enslavement it represented a blood debt she would continually bleed out to repay.

A NEW SCENE morphed across her vision. Belle's stomach hit the floor. She had been dreading the possibility of reliving this moment.

SHE LOOKED on at her mirror image from mere weeks ago. Her Aunt sat beside the fireplace. Her pale blue eyes flickered eerily in the firelight. Beside her sat a man dressed in expensive tailored silks. His pale yellow hair tied in a que at the back of his neck. His hand rested on a silver tipped cane. She was being surveyed where she stood in the middle of the room, like a piece of meat on an auction block. Hands clasped tight together. Eyes fixed on the floor.

The Marquis. He exuded sinister power and his depraved fascination with young girls was widely known. Whispers abounded of the innocent girls—each younger than the last—disappearing without a trace not long after their first encounter with the Marquis. Belle trembled where she stood. Of all the abuses she had put up with in her short life under her Aunt's roof this was surely a fate worse than death.

"I'll have the money to you tomorrow. Wonderful doing business

with you." The Marquis stood and nodded. Her Aunt's face twisted in silent, maniacal glee. He stepped towards Belle and shoved the domed top of his cane under her chin. The movement forced her to look up into his beady eyes.

"I'll have my bride delivered to me this evening. My men will collect her shortly."

The horror of the scene wrenched at Belle's insides. It was too fresh. Too recent. She couldn't stay here reliving this memory of the night she was sold to that monster.

She couldn't handle what came next.

THE ROOM LURCHED. Her memory shifted to the moment she woke up later that same night covered in blood.

BODIES OF THE MARQUIS' men who had come for her lay strewn on the floor in grotesque, twisted forms. Her Aunt's frame lay lifeless among them. Blood seeped through the silk dress and thickened on the floor. The red feather in her hair now dripped with evidence of a gaping head wound.

Belle watched as her past self scrambled to escape the house. The race to get away before she was found. Knowing the darkness would only continue to nip at her heels as it hunted her down.

SHE SAT up with panic lodged in her throat. The room now dim and lit by the flickering glow of firelight. A quick look around confirmed she was safe, back in the present. Brigid's impish grin had softened into something more like compassion than her usual playful cheeriness.

"I thought I would let you sleep the enchantment off for a while." Brigid pulled her to lie back against the cushions and gave her hair a stroke. It was just the two of them now in the faded light—Nell and Lia must have left while she slept.

"It gets easier the more often you memory walk. You did really well for the first time." Brigid cooed.

Belle's fingers sank into the soft fabric of the cushion. The touch grounded her in a reassuring caress against her fingertips that she was indeed back in the present. Safe.

"Why does my magic... it only seems to work at random?" Belle stared at the ceiling and worried her lip. This was something she had been wanting to know. But felt too embarrassed to ask before now.

"From what I understand, Ampher magic is attached to strong emotions when you are first awakened to your powers. You'll learn how to control it given time and you'll learn how to shield. Not all magic is going to serve you. Some kinds will try and take hold of you."

Brigid hopped off the couch beside her and began to twirl around the room. Her arms held out for an invisible partner.

"Now. Very important. We have a ball coming up for the Spring Equinox." This elfin witch was going to give Belle whiplash with the sudden change of conversation.

She rubbed her temples.

"I don't think I'll go."

"Oh, don't be silly. You're going to organise it."

"What?"

"There's no one to do it this year. You're an artist and I'm sure you could use a project to occupy your time, no?" Brigid winked.

"But—" She was right. Of course the Seer was so right.

"Lia and Nell are going to take you to find your dress too, by the way." She called over her shoulder as she wound her way around the room. Each bounce and dip as though dancing a fairy style foxtrot.

Belle yawned as she stood up to leave, a little unsteady on her feet.

"Come on, pretty witch. I'll see you back to your rooms." Brigid appeared as if out of thin air with an arm linked through hers.

"Brigid..." Belle stalled as they reached the door. "I know you are a Seer, but how do you know all of this? If Amphers are so rare, I mean. I'm assuming you only see the possibilities of what can happen or what has already happened?"

"You're right." Brigid said. "I knew a girl—an Ampher—once long ago."

Her eyes drifted to some far away place before continuing.

"But, she's dead."

CHAPTER 8

"What's the update on the snatchers, Ceranthe?" Lachie swiped the edge of his blade against his trouser leg before sheathing it across his back. There might not have been any blood spilt today, but there was enough sweat slicked against the metal to make up for that.

His most trusted inner circle had gathered at his request here in the clearing beside Rowan's cottage. Away from the castle they could talk freely without unnecessarily causing concern. The last thing he needed as Guardian was to create panic when he didn't yet know enough on the matter himself. There was something unsettled in the air across the realms. He sensed it. He knew the others could too. Although no one had come out and voiced it.

Yet.

Other warriors and spies in his ranks were scattered throughout the various supernatural lands. They reported to whoever held the position of Guardian. Once he was no longer here, they would be sworn allies to the next being chosen by the Goddesses to take his place.

He didn't need to call them back from their stations throughout the realms. Not while his plan had yet to be completed.

Lachie's attention was dragged back to where they all hung about the clearing. First they had trained. Now they would talk.

"I've been tracking several packs. They seem to be venturing further than we've seen them frequent before. Hard to tell at this stage if it's a new pattern. Other than that, no targeted attacks that I've caught wind of. But I'll be sure to let you know if that changes." Ceranthe leant against a tree at the edge of the forest clearing.

"Do you think this has anything to do with the sorcerer? Morçaeus? The House of Elharean are rumoured to favour him among their ranks. I've heard stories of his involvement with controlling the snatchers. Some say they are his own creation." Fehrn interjected.

"I'm not sure. Still at a loss as to why they hunted and attacked the girl that night. I haven't heard of that kind of thing before or since." Ceranthe mused as though lost in thought.

Lachie's jaw ticked at the mention of that night. Belle's close call.

"And the other Keyholders? You'll contact them?" He deflected to a different tangent. Ceranthe was the longest serving non-magical being within their ranks. He routinely checked in on the handful of other trusted allies who were granted passage into their realm despite their lack of awakened magic. Lachie held no prejudice against people without it. He'd found some of the bravest souls he had ever come across to be the humblest non-magical beings.

"On to it right now, boss." Ceranthe gave a mock salute before he disappeared in a cloud of mist.

"Niall?" Lachie turned his attention to where Niall lay on his back cushioned by the grass. With his ruffled blonde hair and sun-kissed skin the witch might as well have been enjoying a lazy afternoon lake-side.

"At your service, your majesty." His brother turned and gave him a lazy wink.

"The Fae King has been in contact. He's got... concerns. He asked for assistance. There's a chance his court might have been compromised." Lachie eyed his brother.

Fehrn let out a low growl. His wolf rising to the surface.

"The House of Elharean's doing?" Lia interrupted her mate, concern etched across her face. She wrapped her arms around Fehrn in a familiar gesture of calm. The amber glow in his eyes flickered as his wolf settled under her touch.

"I don't want to assume the worst. But the Fae can't afford to risk not knowing. That's why the King has come to us. Their dominion haven't experienced anything like we have when it comes to how the Elharean loyalists operate." Lachie knew all too well the risk the House of Elharean posed when left undetected.

"Oh, well I suppose I can make myself available." Niall stretched out his long frame. "Seeing as I'm not the one having to organise a ball." He winked knowingly at Lia, who promptly kicked him in the ribs.

"Ow. Fehrn, control your fire demon."

Lia flicked embers at Niall with a laugh.

Lachie pinched the bridge of his nose. *Stars, give me the strength not to murder my brother today.*

"How *is* all that going, your majesty? Got your pretty dress picked out and ready?" Niall propped himself up on one arm and fluttered his eyelashes in Lachie's direction.

"Fuck off, princess." Lachie gritted his teeth.

The mischievous twinkle in Niall's tanned face spread wider. He shrugged his shoulders. "I suppose that's my cue then. I'll tell the King you send your regards." With a swirl of mist, Niall disappeared.

The irony was certainly not lost on Lachie that he was required to balance so many responsibilities. Everything from protecting the supernaturals across different realms to concerns of dark witches infiltrating the highest court within the Fae Dominion was all in a days work. And here he was still expected to coordinate and take part in the frivolity of a ball. Some ridiculous tradition passed from Guardian to Guardian over millennia.

Of course, he would do his duty. Even if only begrudgingly so.

Lachie turned to where the silent figure stood with arms folded off to the side of the clearing. Rowan cast a long shadow wherever he went. As per usual he'd listened, assessed, and quietly judged his next move from a distance. A true warlord.

"They've become too bold." Rowan's manner was stern and clipped. "There will be bloodshed. I can feel it. You know it. Brigid has seen it. I can tell. Something is coming, brother."

Didn't that just sum up his brothers. Fucking grumpy and sunshine.

"Lach, I'll gladly mete out retribution for what those monsters did to Lia. To both of us. To countless others. We've got enough to go on—" A heavy wolf-like presence filled the air.

"No." Lachie cut Fehrn off with a swift command. Then softened.

"Fehrn, I know you want to see their darkness wiped out just as much as I." An unspoken knowing passed between them both. Fehrn *did* know. All too well just how personal this was to him.

"But there is more than just personal retribution to consider here. We're talking about the lives of innocent beings —both supernatural and non-magical—at stake here. No matter what realm they reside in." Lachie chewed through his own words.

Hypocrite.

"You both are doing good work out there. I need you safe. Neither of you are any good to me locked in a dungeon or dead."

And that was the deepest secret Lachie carried. His motivation was *entirely* personal. His plan was his and his alone. He could shield his mind from Lia's telepathy, but he knew Brigid had seen his intentions. She knew of his future. Yet her vow of non-intervention would prevent her from stopping him when the time finally came for him to seek his own form of vengeance.

"Anyway, it's time for you both to fuck off back to whatever distant realm you've set up camp in." He shot a glance towards Fehrn. He knew how desperate the wolf within his friend would be to know he had finally avenged his mate for everything she had been through. But that would have to wait.

"Rowan. Anything these two need to be briefed on before they go?" Lachie trusted his brother more than anything, especially when it came to the art of battle.

"Heard reports of House of Elharean sorcerers working more and more with witches. Using mind control to manipulate their captives. Enchantments that distort reality. Rumour is they syphon power. Which might be connected to what you uncovered about the Seal." Rowan jerked his chin in Lia's direction.

The fire witch knew more than any of them about the Seal of Elharean. A place of dark power and a portal capable of tearing through the fabric of reality into other realms that lay heavily guarded within its castle fortress.

Information that had been vital to complete the final missing piece in Lachie's plan. Now that he had the information Lia and Fehrn had provided, he could finally make his move.

"Hexes have been popping up that are impossible to break

once you step inside the circle that has been cast. So your best bet is to only portal to locations you can be certain are safe until we find a counter spell." Rowan tapped his forefinger against his muscled bicep covered in tattoos spanning every visible inch of skin.

"You don't want to portal blindly into a hex. Trust me."

CHAPTER 9

Belle steeled herself for impending warfare.

This was a terrible idea. But she had made up her mind. If she was going to figure out once and for all how Lachlan of Nocturne really felt about her, then she would do it the old fashioned *non-magical* way. Spending time with him.

Unless he threw her out after hearing her proposal. Either way, Belle would get her answer.

No harm in dialling up what charms she possessed. She had picked out her favourite dress of pale grey silk that made her hair and eyes stand out in a way that she loved about herself. After a lifetime of wearing heavy, uncomfortable servants attire Belle was loving the opportunity to express herself through her own choice of magical clothing. Still she was a bundle of nerves that tightened with each step through the castle corridors. Her fingers fiddled with the emerald gemstone ring on her finger.

Never take this off.

She figured feeling her best had to be a good starting point in her attempt to win over Lachie. If she was going to stay here and feel a sense of fulfilment while developing her magic, she needed something to focus her attention. Brigid, Nell, and Lia all had their *thing* that occupied their time and contributed something towards helping others in the realm. Brigid oversaw magic development. Nell ran the herbarium. Lia was often away on missions collecting intel. She needed to find her own direction rather than simply hiding away with her nose in a book.

This could end in disaster. She forced herself to move her feet through the stone corridors towards the heavy wooden doorway that guarded the threshold to Lachie's private study.

She stood in front of the heavy set timber with a hand raised hovering in mid air. The imposing height left her feeling dwarfed. Her brain was still searching for an excuse to simply scuttle away back to the other end of the castle.

Just turn around now. Save yourself the humiliation.

With a deep breath she gritted her teeth and went to knock on the wooden surface, only to nearly tumble forward as the door swung in on its hinges. Lachie stood frozen mid-step with raised eyebrows. His stern expression barely gave any hint of surprise, but she noticed a hasty swallow in response to finding her practically colliding with his chest in his doorway.

Belle didn't know what she had expected from this evening but she certainly hadn't expected to find Lachie dressed not in his usual worn leather slacks, shirt, and blade holsters for training. Instead he wore a tailored dress jacket in deep midnight blue, pristine white collared shirt, polished black boots, and held his long travel coat in one hand.

Shit. This wasn't his usual attire. He must have other plans this evening.

"Oh, I'm sorry! You must be on your way somewhere." Belle jumped backwards. Both feet nearly tangled together. Blush scalded her cheeks at the awkwardness of her almost-stumble.

Shit. Make a run for it.

Her eyes dropped down taking in his full magnificence. The man was incredibly attractive no matter what he wore but seeing him like this had just turned the appeal factor up immeasurably.

Belle's eyes widened. Oh no! He was making an effort to dress up for someone else. Of course he would have a special someone to dress up for. He was the Guardian of the Realm after all. She hadn't given any thought to the notion he might be otherwise occupied this evening. No one had mentioned him being involved in a relationship or mated with someone. Embarrassment burned through her whole body. Uninvited images of Lachie naked and tangled in the sheets with a mysterious woman flashed through her mind.

"Are you... leaving the castle this evening?" Stars, she sounded like a gaping fish.

“I was— just returning.” He said slowly.

Belle blinked and stared pointedly at the coat clenched in his hand.

He looked freshly dressed. Why pretend he wasn’t just about to leave? Her heartbeat quickened with his presence so close where they stood face to face in the doorway.

“Care to elaborate on what this visit is about?” The Guardian’s icy composure descended once more.

“It’s nothing. Don’t let me bother you.” Belle waved her hands aimlessly and turned to leave.

A powerful grip reached out and took hold of her arm. The space now closed between them. His fingers grasped firm against her bare skin. Her heart leapt into her mouth as his touch scorched at the point of contact. It was enough to send a bolt of heat straight to her core.

“Might as well tell me why you’re here.” Lachie still held her arm. The slightest flex of his fingers squeezed gently against her skin. It was as if on one hand he were testing to make sure she was real and on the other ensuring she didn’t vanish into thin air.

“Honestly, it was a silly idea. I just thought I’d ask if I could help with planning the ball... for the Spring Equinox.” She saw him narrow his eyes. “I heard your usual assistant is unavailable. So I wanted to offer to help because I know how busy you are as Guardian.” Spirits save her or swallow her up in the ground right now. She was babbling.

Belle could still feel his grip hot on her arm as she ploughed on.

"I know you don't have a lot of time for these sorts of things and I thought it would be a good way to do something to say thank you for saving me and bringing me here. A peace offering of sorts after the other day with the incident in the bath—Look, I want to help and I want to keep myself busy. Outside of my training, of course." She added with a hasty breath while realising she had been waving her free arm around gesturing at the castle walls. "But I can see you are busy, so I'll just head back to my suite. Forget I even—"

"Don't go." He growled out as he slowly released her arm. "Come in." His head nodded in a stiff gesture as he pushed the heavy door open wider and indicated for her to move inside with his head.

What was happening. "But you were going—"

"Not going anywhere."

Belle moved into his study and tried her hardest not to simply stare. The walls were lined with books. Two simple but large comfortable armchairs flanked a wide fireplace. The ceiling was mesmerising, decorated in the same rippling blue as in the grand entrance hall to the castle and filled with shimmering stars. On the other side of the room was a large couch and table piled haphazardly with pieces of parchment, ancient texts, and leather bound volumes.

The room seemed simultaneously comforting yet also devoid of personal touches. Functional yet beautiful in its minimalism. The strewn pieces of paper were the only indication that somehow below his cool demeanour there was disorder swirling on the inside. She got the impression Lachie didn't allow many people into this private sanctuary.

He hung in front of the closed door seeming just as uncertain how to proceed as she was.

Spying some drawings on top of the pile of papers, Belle was drawn towards them. The page was filled with illustrations of rich colours, patterns, and decorations. Florals, cake designs, and masque concepts.

"Are these the plans for this year?" She flashed a smile as she bent to pick them up. "They're gorgeous." *Just act normal. Focus on the ball.*

"I can't make heads or tails of it." With a shrug he seemed to let out a sigh of relief. "Not my forte, if you could believe that."

Belle sat in front of the mass of papers. "So you do have a weakness under all that fierce armour?"

Spirits, was she seriously going to try and tease him right now?

"Little use for cake during combat." The faintest hint of a smile seemed to tug at the corner of his lips.

"Well, I don't know. There's always time to indulge in pleasures such as cake." Belle said as his gaze locked onto hers and he scraped a hand slowly over his mouth.

"Is this the guest list?" She dragged her eyes back to the largest stack of parchment trying to ignore the heat that had just spiralled low in her belly at that stormy look.

"It is. Dignitaries from other realms. Supernaturals who choose to base themselves in the non-magical world." He moved towards the couch, seeming unsure of whether to remain standing or sit beside her. She pushed a cushion out of the way in an attempt to coax him to sit. He was putting her on edge and she could already feel her heart pounding at the thought of him continuing to stare at her from across the room all evening.

He eased himself onto the seat beside her and leaned forward, resting his elbows on his knees. His eyes cast across the chaos that lay before them both on the table.

"Being Guardian has many responsibilities. All of which I gladly shoulder. But I've never enjoyed organising the frivolity of balls. Not high on my priority list." He seemed weary at the thought.

"Well I'm here and if you'll let me, I am going to help." Belle hoped her voice sounded light and breezy, even though her skin was tingling with his proximity. She could feel her Ampher power already picking up his magic and beginning to charge the air around them. As long as nothing starts floating around the room please, she silently begged herself. *Deep breaths.*

"Let's start simple. Tell me about this." She slid the list entitled *Fae Dominion* in scrawling ink across the table towards him. To her surprise he started explaining the list of names, who they were, and how they were important allies for safeguarding against the House of Elharean. She could see his shoulders visibly relax as he detailed out the dignitaries who needed to be formally invited.

His whiskey voice ran over the names with familiarity and a gentleness that belied his fierce exterior. This role was clearly important to him and the supernatural community he commanded great respect both from and for. Belle allowed her eyes to rove across his muscled physique from where they sat only inches away from one another as he spoke. Stars, he was devastatingly handsome. She swallowed heavily as she saw the neck of his shirt gape open. From here she could see clearer the inked markings stretching up to the lower part of his neck. Belle's mind wondered how far they extended as they disappeared frustratingly below his shirt collar. Her thighs clenched together as he shrugged out of his tailored jacket and began to roll his shirt sleeves up to sit at his elbows, revealing tanned muscular forearms. More inked patterns across bronzed skin. Her stomach fluttered uncontrollably at the sight.

Hours passed as she slid paper after paper in front of him and he calmly explained the information she needed to know in cool, methodical, and logical sequence. The Guardian assuming his duty.

Belle felt her eyes getting tired. Her head swam with long lists of strange new names, the relationships between the different realms, and more magical history than she could have ever possibly needed to know. Yawning she stretched her arms in front of her.

"You don't need to sleep?" Lachie shifted his weight beside her hesitantly as he noticed her movement. She was tired but didn't want to break the spell that seemed to be holding his friendly demeanour in place. This was a world away from the irredeemable ass who had burst in on her while bathing.

"No—not at all, carry on." *Liar.*

She was so intent on listening to him that she didn't notice herself beginning to doze off surrounded by the warm tones of his voice. As blackness gently enveloped her one thought hung in her mind.

How that small hint of a smile had looked so delicious on his lips.

CHAPTER 10

Silence. Shallow breathing. *Fuck.*

Belle had gone to sleep while he had droned on and on. He stabbed his fingers through his hair. Now what in the Stars was he supposed to do?

He'd ended up in exactly the type of situation he had been desperately trying to avoid for weeks. Lachie had spent the entire evening mere inches from her, prattling on about planning for a ridiculous ball just to keep his composure. It had rattled him to unexpectedly find her in his doorway. Now he'd sent the woman to sleep and couldn't bring himself to wake her. He couldn't make her traipse all the way to the other end of the castle in the middle of the night.

Lachie turned over all the options in his mind. He could try and move her into the bed—his bed. But that risked waking her. And he didn't need the entire castle roused by her screams if she awoke to him carrying her.

The only alternative was to leave her here but somehow make her more comfortable. She had curled herself backwards into the soft cushions only now she sat half upright with her feet tucked under her. He quickly decided not to leave her here in his study alone, because that would be even more ungentlemanly, wouldn't it?

Fuck. There was no training to prepare for this kind of shit.

His gaze drifted over her softness, taking in with jagged breath the opportunity to see her up close and unguarded. Details of her beauty that he really shouldn't be cataloguing in his mind. Her long dark braid hung across her shoulder and drew his eye down to where the ends of her curls caressed across her breast. The silk of her dress stretched tantalisingly across the swell of her bosom. The tie around her waist showed off her curves and the softness of her stomach where the silk clung with wicked temptation. His eyes dropped lower, greedy to soak in as many details as possible. Where the material overlapped at the front of her knees it had hitched up onto the couch. The silk gaped open revealing that porcelain skin and an erotic glimpse of her upper thighs. Just as he had seen that day while she was bathing.

Had she worn this dress for him tonight? Knowing how he had responded that very first night when she had dropped her ring?

Lachie clenched his fists to stop himself from reaching out to caress her perfect form. To experience another moment of that heavenly touch of her skin beneath his fingertips. He had replayed that moment of her in the bathtub over and over, seemingly unable to push it from his mind at all times of day—and night. He had fantasised over reaching down that day in the bath to find out just how aroused she had been. He'd seen it in her eyes beneath the shock and indignation at his outburst. He was sure she had felt the same lust building within.

Focus.

Not your mate. Not your problem.

Only right here, right now, she *was* his problem.

Lachie knew he shouldn't be entertaining thoughts of this woman. This stranger who had arrived in his life and brought her pure heartedness and caring ray of fucking sunshine approach to everyone. While simultaneously giving back to him just as good as he was able to give. Her spirit never backing down from a challenge.

Should he have turned her away earlier this evening? Gone to meet Luciana as he was supposed to? Lachie barely tolerated the witch, who was vain and self centred, but who held a powerful position as the leader of a coven living in the non-magical world. Luciana knew her biggest assets were her looks and her position of power—which in most cases ensured she got exactly what her appetites desired—and was always quick to point out that he would be welcome anywhere anytime to spend the night doing less talking and more fucking. In the past he would have needed nothing more than a hint of an invitation to lose himself in that kind of meaningless sex. But that dark time was long ago. Two hundred years. He had his plan to execute and nothing was going to derail him from getting his revenge.

Nothing. Nothing at all.

Unless it seemed, that distraction related to the woman sleeping beside him.

Careful not to shift his weight too quickly in case he woke her up, Lachie manoeuvred the both of them so that she rested her head against the crook of his shoulder as he lay back into the corner of the couch. Her thick dark eyelashes lay against her smooth skin. Her softly rounded cheeks were slightly flushed with the heat from the fire and her full lips pinkened. Unsure where to put his hands, he cradled them behind his head although every fibre of his being wanted to roam his fingers across her hips and brand them into her perfect soft flesh.

Feeling her fingertips flex against his shirt he momentarily stiffened. Not waking but instead sinking further into his body. Her shoulders still rising and falling in slow shallow rhythm.

He couldn't allow this to be anything more. He had his plan. It was closer than ever to being executed.

As he closed his eyes and felt the heaviness of sleep tugging at him he heard the familiar word whispering softly.

Protect.

CHAPTER 11

The scent of cedar and leather flooded through Belle's awareness. She was deliciously warm. So warm. Snuggling her cheek down her pillow felt a little firmer than usual. There was a strange rigidity and a kind of lumpiness that she swore wasn't usually there.

But there was no denying it. She hadn't slept this well in... forever.

She had woken in the midst of the most intense dream. In it strong hands caressed her body with reverence. Lachie's hands. Her every sense awakened and vibrated with pleasure as his fingertips grazed her bare skin. Her nipples hardened as his thumb pads skimmed over the tight buds, leaving her breathless. She arched to get closer under his attentions and moaned —begged for more.

Sunlight rippled against her closed eyelids. She didn't want to leave that sensual state of pleasure. Only a few more minutes and she would drag herself out of bed. She had promised Nell she would join her to forage for some special kind of herb for her next batch of potions. Brigid would be expecting her for more magic training later that morning. She gave a small hum under her breath and stretched like a cat hogging a sliver of sunlight.

A deep masculine cough caused her eyes to fly open with a start. Niall's impish grin swum into focus. *What is Niall doing in my room?*

All of a sudden the mattress shifted and rolled beneath her. This morning was getting stranger by the second. She raised her head and to her horror realised that instead of having her arms wrapped around her pillow they were wrapped around a waist. Lachlan's waist. One hand tucked under his shirt where the material had bunched up. And Spirits save her, the man looked ready to be devoured. He looked decadent in his ruffled morning state.

Another cough stifled a laugh.

"Not interrupting I hope?" Niall had the broadest smirk plastered across his face, eyes sparkling with glee at finding this unexpected scene of the two of them together on Lachie's couch.

"I don't want to keep you from important... business." He cleared his throat, jerking his chin at the scene before him while sipping on a steaming cup of tea.

Belle felt the body below her go rigid. Looking up her eyes

locked straight into aquamarine depths. Eyes that were steely and unflinching. Not a trace of the easy going conversation from the night before.

Lachie's eyes flickered down to where her hands seemed to be glued to his body. Shit. Her eyes widened as she realised that the hand below his shirt was not just touching bare skin but was just above his waistband. She could see the sinfully muscled V extending down from below his waist and a trail of dark hair dipping into his trousers. Her heart just about stopped beating.

A growl reverberated through the expansive chest below her. A warning? To her? Or to his brother? She watched as his eyes flitted lower still and she followed them to where his erection strained against his trousers.

Shit, this was all at once a collision of emotions. Spirits be there to save her because this was simultaneously the best and the worst way to start her day. She was still highly aroused from her dream. At the same time her lust addled state of mind was trying to make sense of this compromising situation.

Finally her brain seemed to start functioning. With a yelp she scrambled backwards, awkwardly pressing even harder against the bare skin of his stomach to give herself leverage. Muscles rippled beneath her fingers. Now was not the time to be thinking about anything but making a quick escape. Hastily gathering up the jumble of papers from the table into her arms, she fled out the door. Her bearings barely holding together to remember the way back to her own rooms.

"YOU WOKE UP WHERE?" Nell's big soulful eyes were wide with surprise.

"Not so loud, Nell!"

They were in the herbarium beside the castle courtyard. Belle sorted the foraged herbs into bundles while Nell rhythmically crushed aromatic leaves with her stone pestle and mortar.

"So? Did anything, you know, physical happen between you?"

Nell was concentrating hard on her magic in front of her, but motioned in circles at Belle to hurry up with spilling the details.

"I don't understand what happened. When I got there last night he was dressed as if he was leaving. Pretended he wasn't. Then gave me the entire encyclopaedic knowledge of all the realms and their dignitaries who would need to attend the ball." Belle chewed her lip.

"And?"

"And then I fell asleep. But he didn't send me away."

"He also didn't leave you to sleep on the couch alone?"

"Maybe he fell asleep too?" Belle shrugged her shoulders in

disbelief. "Then he looked so incredibly cross this morning. I think he's going to ignore me for the rest of the time organising this ball. Maybe into my next lifetime even."

"Belle, his brother was there..." Nell puffed out a breath to get rid of a loose strand of brown hair that had fallen in her face while pounding the herbs. "I'd say his reaction had more to do with Niall having something to hold over him than it has to do with you."

That could actually be true, she realised. From what she knew of Niall he was a loveable rogue and would spare his oldest brother no quarter.

"Plus, remember you ran out the door before the poor man even had a chance to say a word."

Another good point. She'd been so mortified that she'd turned tail and fled without so much as a squeak. She'd even run off barefooted and left her favourite leather slippers behind in her rush to escape with a shred of dignity intact.

It wasn't the thought of being caught sleeping alongside him that was a shock. She'd had enough experiences with lovers to not be a prude when it came to men, but there was something that had her feeling as though he was somehow off limits to her. His world was that of a chosen Guardian. Filled with responsibilities, duties, and safeguarding the lives of supernatural beings across an entire realm.

She was a witch who barely knew how to use her power and was busying herself with coordinating a ball.

Their worlds couldn't be further apart.

• • •

After her training session later that day with Brigid, where she was forced to recount the mornings humiliation and events from the night before all over again—in painfully descriptive detail—she wearily made her way back to her suite. The lesson on sigils and their ability to bind magic when drawn on a being's skin had taken it out of her. She'd practiced over and over, drawing the small patterns from the texts Brigid had fetched for her. Her confidence grew with each new step in her training.

Even if there was much more complex and nuanced magic still lingering beyond her reach.

She was in desperate need of some hot tea. Creating some new sketches would help take her mind off things too.

Muscular, hard, pleasurable things.

Belle pushed the door open to her rooms and dropped her cloak onto the chair beside her fireplace. She used her magic to light the hearth with a pulse of her power. At least she had now mastered control of the basics elements, even if she didn't fully understand her Ampher powers yet or how they worked. Focusing on her teapot she conjured a steaming hot brew perfect to sooth frayed nerves and relieve the tension she carried between her shoulder blades.

Beneath her breath she murmured the spell to fill her bath tub with steaming hot water. As she wandered through her bedroom the sight of her perfectly made bed stopped her dead in her tracks. There perched neatly on the end of the covers were her slippers she had left behind after rushing from

Lachie's study. On top of it was a handwritten note on parchment in Lachie's hand.

"For the next time you feel the need to run away from me."

The next time?

CHAPTER 12

Lachie stared at the stack of papers spread across the desk in front of him. He'd been here for hours and yet he might have wound up with even more duties than when he first sat down.

Distracted didn't even begin to describe his state of mind right now.

Every small noise had his head swivelling around towards the door to his study. Hopeful that a glimpse of long dark hair and soulful grey eyes might appear.

He had written and rewritten his note to her at least ten times. The evidence of each scrunched up attempt sat in the unlit fireplace smirking back at him.

Any attempt to sound casual and lighthearted about returning her shoes had come across... wrong. He didn't want to frighten her off with his stiff Guardian routine. But he didn't want to make her think there was something more in his choice to let her sleep with him on the couch last night either.

Did he?

His fingers shoved through his hair so hard it stood on end.

No. That whisper that kept insisting she was his mate was wrong. He'd already done enough damage. Wrecked the life of one Ampher. He wasn't able to protect her then. He wouldn't be making that same mistake again now.

Lachie dropped his head into his hands. His eyes slid shut. The memories were always present. Ready to reappear and remind him—gut him—like a metronome armed with a knife.

No matter how hard he tried. They taunted him from across the vast expanse of two hundred years.

He ran through the waist high grass alongside her. That infectious laugh rippled on the breeze. The one that made everyone smile. Even Rowan. Her black hair wild and free-spirited framed her turquoise eyes. A shade darker than his own. Everyone said Fiadh of Nocturne was the strongest and the smartest of them. But Lachie knew, even back then as a young child, his twin sister was also the kindest.

"Lach, I got you a gift." She called out to him from across the field. In her palm sat a rough green stone that shimmered with emerald light. She pressed it into his palm.

"I'll find one for Brigid... and Niall... and even Rowan too. But only if he learns to ask nicely." She rolled her eyes. "Don't tell the others I gave you yours first." Her Ampher magic rippled through her aura in the sunlight like a rainbow.

. . .

THE MEMORY FADED into that of a darkened room.

FIADH SAT HUDDLED in the window of her room staring out over the castle grounds. Her knees drawn to her chest. They were both nearly a hundred years old. Gone was the twin sister he knew from their younger years. Now only a sullen and withdrawn shade of the girl he once knew. She refused to talk to him—anyone—about what was wrong.

All Lachie knew was that she had been leaving the realm on her own more and more frequently. Morlana, their Guardian of the Realm, had tried to intervene but Fiadh had accused the Guardian of stopping her from understanding her own power. She'd blamed Morlana for preventing her from being able to fully use her Ampher.

He had felt helpless. If their Guardian couldn't help his sister what good could he do? No one truly knew how an Ampher's magic worked. The knowledge had been lost over millennia. Lachie remembered begging his sister to be patient. They had never seen someone with her power in the realm within living memory.

And yet she disappeared. Over and over.

Their parents knew her power was too great. They couldn't stop her even if they wanted to.

HIS EYES SQUEEZED TIGHTER at the the images as they floated through his mind.

. . .

The ceremony of the Goddesses. Confirming him as the new Guardian of the Realm. Handing Brigid the emerald ring and telling her he never wanted to see it again. He had sworn that day he would tear the House of Elharean apart for what they did. For what they turned his sister into. He would seek vengeance and he would rather die before he let another being suffer at their hands.

Lachie scrubbed his eyes with the heel of his palms. He needed some fresh air. He needed to launch his fist into something. Rowan's face would do. Maybe he could tempt his brother with a late sparring session.

He swung his blade holster across his shoulders and headed out into the castle corridor. Portaling would be quicker, but Spirits he needed to walk out some of this turmoil inside him first.

Between distracted thoughts of a certain witch and two hundred years of guilt wrecking havoc with his mind, he might admit to himself that he was a mess. But that wouldn't be happening.

When he reached the base of the grand staircase the flickering of light from the ballroom caught his eye. The high arched doorway sat ajar. Enough for the sight of who was inside to stall him in his tracks. Belle had crystal orbs of light floating in mid air around her. Yet her face was screwed up in a frown of intense concentration.

The crystals rose above her head in swirled patterns that she orchestrated with subtle movements of her fingers. Each time they positioned themselves she glared harder at the offending decorations.

Lachie felt the tension drain from his shoulders at the sight of her.

Sparring all of a sudden seemed like a terrible idea.

He hung in the entrance hall unable to get himself to move. From where he stood he could observe her unguarded and lost in her own creative expression. It looked breathtaking on her. Like the Goddesses themselves had showered her in an aura so divine it would put the stars to shame.

Fuck.

He scraped his hand over his mouth.

No. No. No. Whatever this was, Lachie needed to lock it away right now. It could not—and would not—be happening.

Belle's hands dropped to her sides and the crystal orbs fell in unison, stopping an inch above the floor. Lachie nearly raced forward to grab her, before he held himself back. This was her magic. She was in control. Surely she couldn't hurt herself.

He watched as she looked around, then called to someone out of sight.

"Gryphon. Can you help me? I just can't quite..." A male witch appeared by her side. Lachie stiffened. The witch practically fell over himself to get close to her. The idiot might as well have drool all over his chin. Belle pointed to show him something in her portfolio.

The witch reached out a hand towards the parchment. His hand moved closer to Belle's.

Was he touching her?

Whatever tie had restrained Lachie to the floor snapped in an instant. He didn't waste any time walking to close the distance between them and portaled straight to Belle's side.

She started back. Eyes sprung wide.

"Spirits, Lachie! You gave me a fright." A hasty swallow tracked down her throat.

The witch beside her paled under the daggers shot from his eyes.

"I'll take it from here. Thank you, Gryphon." The low growl that came out didn't sound like himself.

"Oh! You don't have to. I know you're busy." Belle stammered.

"What do you need?" He ground out, eyeing the retreating form of the witch to ensure he exited the room.

"Umm... I need to create this pattern here. She pointed to the illustrations she had created. Sketched out in beautiful forms across the pages of her portfolio.

"I think I might have been a bit over ambitious for my magic. Might be here all night at this rate." She shot him a shy smile. "But only if you have the time?"

It was the gentlemanly thing to do. At the very least he could clear the air between them after unintentionally waking up with her wrapped in his arms. Especially since she had bolted from the room before he'd had a chance to talk to her.

“As long as you don’t run away and leave me with this mess.” He arched an eyebrow in her direction.

Pink spread across her cheeks and she ducked her head. “No. I mean, of course not.”

His eyes soaked in every detail of her flushed face. Thoughts of what she might look like pinned beneath him with that same colour dancing across her skin crowded into his mind.

Focus. Shit. The Ball. The plan. Assist with the plan.

Lachie stripped off the blade holster from his back and set it on the floor. He cleared his throat. Willing his cock—and all thoughts of Belle spread out on his bed—back under control.

“Fine. Then I’ve got no where else to be.”

CHAPTER 13

"You're telling me that we live in a magical realm, can conjure anything we desire to wear, and yet we have to leave it in order to find dresses to wear for a ball?" Belle stuffed her plans and illustrations back into the giant portfolio with a huff. "Lia, tell me this is a joke?"

"Oh come on, I know you've been throwing yourself into planning. but you can afford to take an afternoon off to find your perfect dress and mask."

Frustration gnawed at Belle's insides as she reluctantly set the papers down. Not at her friends, but herself. There was more to this than just feeling 'too busy'. Something lay deeper behind the easy surface-level excuse of needing to spend these last days on the final preparations for the ball.

She grew more and more concerned about leaving the realm for the first time since her arrival. There had been so much talk about how dangerous it was for her beyond the border to these protected lands. Now she was having to face that fear head on. All for the sake of a pretty dress.

"I'm sure I have something I can conjure from that wardrobe. I'll just stay behind." She waved a hand in the direction of the wooden dresser. Knowing full well there was nothing *ball-worthy* among the magic that lay within.

"I know you've been thinking about how to make a good impression on a certain witch." Lia fixed her with a knowing look. "You'll be safe, you've got me to protect you. I'll make sure nothing can hurt you. Remember. Telepathy." She added when Belle open her mouth to protest, tapping the side of her head with a wink.

"You've worked so hard on this, Belle. You deserve to sparkle." Nell stood in front of her and thrust her cloak into her hands.

Apparently the only witch with the gift of creating the most sumptuous ball worthy gowns lived in the non-magical realm. Many supernatural beings chose to live where they pleased and keep their affiliations neutral all in the name of prosperous business. In the case of Madame Liu it ensured she would be the dressmaker of choice across multiple realms. Dressing everyone from Fae nobility, to witches, to the House of Elharean.

The major reason Belle felt less than enthusiastic about this venture was because neutral affiliation didn't prevent others with evil intention from being present.

"We won't be running into anyone from the House of

Elharean today." Lia responded to her thoughts as she followed her along the castle passageway.

"How can you be so sure?"

"Madame Liu has a neutral ground enchantment that ensures only those who have pre-arranged permission to enter may do so. She's had a thousand years of satisfied supernatural clientele and no incidents."

"Yet." Belle muttered to herself.

Horses were saddled and waiting for them as they exited the castle entrance hall. Both Lia and Nell confidently swung themselves up into their saddles and looked down expectantly at Belle.

"We're going to ride to the non-magical realm?"

"How else do you think we'll get there?"

"Well, when I arrived... I don't remember... but I don't think it involved horseback." Belle felt stumped by yet another thing she didn't know about this world.

"You're right. There are portals that open up a direct link to go between. It takes mere seconds to rematerialise back here when you use them. That magic is very ancient and it takes a long time to master reliably. Even Lia and I have yet to reach that level of confidence in our magic. Now if Brigid were here for example, she could simply portal us." Nell patted her horse's neck as she spoke.

"Shame she's otherwise occupied with the Goddesses. That witch knows all the best spots to portal to." Lia mused.

Belle swung herself up into the saddle of her sleek black

mare. “So most supernaturals simply cross the border themselves?”

“Yes, once you’ve done it once you’ll know how to come and go as you please.” Nell smiled as they moved the horses into a slow walk. “You’re not a prisoner here, Belle.”

“But does that mean anyone can enter if it's simply a border between the two?”

“It’s a little more complex than that. Physically the two are not connected. But energetically they are. Which means if you are attuned to the frequency, or given permission for passage across the barrier, you can enter.” Lia steered her horse beside Belle’s. “When Fehrn first brought us here he was able to grant us passage through the border after our escape from the House of Elharean.”

“The other way is via an enchanted talisman. Lachie grants those to only our most trusted allies as Keyholders, particularly for the handful of non-magical beings who need to be able to cross the threshold regularly. It gives them a safe means of escape if they ever need to disappear from danger.”

The horses wound their way beyond the castle walls towards the dense forest. The lush coolness of the canopy thickened above Belle’s head. The scents of the wild herbs perfumed the air as they crushed beneath each hoof. Birdsong lilted as the women enjoyed a companionable silence.

As they reached a clearing, a set of large standing stones formed a series of circles several horse lengths wide. In the centre stood two taller than the rest, forming a gateway that towered above where Belle sat on horseback.

Supernatural indeed.

These rough hewn black granite sentinels reverberated with a power that grew palpable the closer they drew. Mist swirled low along the ground and intertwined between each stone with an ethereal white glow.

"Just follow me." Lia called out from up ahead. "Nell will go behind you."

The silky black ears of her horse twitched with anticipation.

"At least one of us knows what the fuck to expect." Belle muttered as she reached forward to pat the glossy neck of her steed.

Her horse continue forward to follow behind Lia. She felt the white mist rise up and surround them, cool and comforting. Barely a couple of seconds passed before the three of them stepped into bright sunlight. Blinking and shielding her eyes, Belle realised with a start that they were now moving along a tree-lined path surrounded by rolling fields. Distant rooftops signaled a town up ahead.

No sign of the standing stones or mist. It was like they had appeared out of thin air. A sleight of hand from the cosmos.

"Easy to leave but there's more of an art to finding your way back." Nell laughed brightly at the sight of Belle's mouth hanging open.

A row of pretty pastel coloured terraced houses spanned in front of them. It reminded Belle of her Aunt's high society connections. As much as she was grateful to be free of her servitude, Belle still felt a pang of sadness. The woman was a brute, but she was all Belle had known. The only place she had called home before her world had been turned upside down.

Hitching their horses outside they were ushered in through a pale pink door by a footman dressed in lush turquoise silk livery. Other than his extravagant attire nothing gave any hint of magic being involved. It all seemed very... normal.

They were shown into the parlour where cream, pale pink, and muted silver accents left Belle wondering what could be so special about this place? Everything seemed to be the quintessential high society formality of the non-magical world.

"Ma'am will be with you shortly." The footman bowed as though they were regal and backed out of the room.

"Well aren't you witches just leaving it all to the last second." With a start Belle turned to see a diminutive woman appear beside her on the chaise. She sat dressed in a high-necked black silk dress covered in pink birds that shimmered across the fabric as though flying. Wait—they were flying! Her white hair was shaved down the sides and left long through the middle, plaited and piled in a high knot on her head. The signature of the Fae. Fine wrinkles lined her obsidian eyes, with tanned skin and a rounded face. She was breathtaking and surely millennia old.

"Madame Liu, we want to thank you for seeing us today."

Lia said gesturing to introduce the others. "May I present Nelloix and Annabelle."

"Pretty girls. Come to find yourself a pretty dress for the Equinox, mmm?"

"We would only humbly choose the best." Lia dipped her head with a coy smile.

Madame Liu snorted. "Flattery. I have had a hundred supernaturals here before you three. Perhaps Madame is already tired." She eyed them with an impish look in her eyes. A dance of wits she clearly enjoyed with her clientele.

Lia feigned a mock gasp and clutched her hand to her chest. "You wouldn't force us to wear a monstrosity from Monsieur Dacard would you?"

A chortle of laughter as the woman waved her hand to motion them to sit. "Come here, pretty girls."

With a stomp of her onyx walking cane the pale formal room dissolved into a riot of colour as the enchantment spell dissolved. They now sat inside a tent lined with billowing fabrics of all textures and designs imaginable.

"You. Up." Belle felt the end of the cane jab into her stomach. Nell pushed her over towards a raised dias in the centre of the room and she dutifully stood upon it. Her mouth hung open as she stared at the ceiling, neck craning to take in the walls lined entirely with a riot of colour and texture. Belle couldn't believe the kaleidoscope of fabrics, feathers, beads, and shimmering metals that looked somehow simultaneously rigid and yet also soft and sensual.

"This one is new." A statement, or assessment more like it, from the Fae.

"She's actually the witch who has organised the entire ball this Spring Equinox. Belle here is an Ampher and a talented artist too." Lia filled in the answers to the questions as they rolled through Madame Liu's mind.

"Ahhh, then only the best." Although the woman was much shorter than Belle she seemed to command the space as if she were ten foot tall. From where she sat on the chaise she squinted at Belle as though searching for something. Then with a hmmpf and two taps of her cane, emerald green fabric began to twirl in the air in front of Belle. The material draped perfectly, folding, and melding itself into a gorgeous fitted bodice. An elongated ruffled train began to shimmer as though filled with golden lights. Belle gasped and reached out to run her fingers over the feather-soft texture. Throughout the layers were tiny balls of spun gold thread that pulsated with light. It made the entire dress look like a gemstone glinting in the sunlight.

"Oh Belle, it is stunning." Nell stood and clasped her hands to her mouth.

"I know someone who will be unable to let you out of his sight." Lia smirked as she swirled embers above her fingertips.

Madame Liu's dark eyes lit up. "There is a someone?"

"No, not—"

"Only *the* someone Madame Liu. Lachlan of Nocturne." Nell interjected.

Belle was going to strangle each witch and then dump their bodies in the forest.

"Aiyah, you tell me this now?" Madame Liu threw her hands in the air. "We must start again!"

The threat of her dress evaporating into Fae-dust snapped Belle out of her murderous thoughts.

"No, please don't, I adore it!" She squeaked. "And isn't that much more important than a dress made simply to try and appeal to the eyes of a man?" Belle clutched at the hem of the dress where it hung mid-air for fear it would vanish as quickly as it appeared.

The Fae studied her for a long second. "Agreed. This one is intelligent. Young Lachlan needs someone who can challenge him."

With a flick of her cane the dress was encased inside silver wrappings and a large bow all in mid-air before floating down to Belle's outstretched arms. She cuddled it to her chest lovingly.

"Thank you, Madame Liu." Tears pricked behind her eyes. This was the most treasured thing she had ever owned. Something made for her and only her. A dress made for beauty, elegance, and dancing. When merely a few weeks ago she had possessed only a single heavy woollen uniform.

"You. Up." The onyx staff jabbed into Nell's back this time as silver metallic fabric began to wind its way into the air.

The witches waved their goodbyes and returned to the horses with beautiful wrapped garments and matching masks in tow. Belle's cheeks ached from how broad her smile beamed.

After mounting their horses, the witches chattered and laughed as they headed back towards the laneway where they had appeared when crossing the mystical barrier.

When they approached a bend in the path Belle felt the air shift and change around them. A cold clammy feeling began to inch down her neck and she felt her horse flare beneath her, also sensing the danger. Grey spirals of mist oozed onto the pathway ahead of them. The same as she had seen the night she was attacked in the alleyway.

"Lia—" Belle hardly dared to raise her voice as all sound seemed to evaporate from around them. Nell and Lia suddenly flanked her on either side and she saw Lia's flames begin to manifest over her right palm as she held the reins in her left.

"Nell, on my signal, you and Belle are to head straight for the barrier. You know the marker to look for?"

Nell nodded solemnly. What was happening?

Out of the trees surrounding the laneway came the eerie forms of a pack of the same sickening looking ghouls from the night Belle had been attacked. The night Lachie had saved her. Grey slimy skin. Long blackened talons caked in blood from their victims.

"On my signal..." Lia built her flame to a white hot intensity. Belle could see the flames of her fire magic flickering wildly in her eyes. With a lunge and a fierce warrior cry Lia spurred her horse forward to charge at the beasts while sending a bolt of flame towards each monster. High pitch screeches wailed through the air as the creatures slashed wildly, hissing as they attempted to break through the flames burning their skin.

Nell swiftly grabbed Belle's reins in one hand and had both horses bolting towards the tree line side by side. The woods flew past in a blur. Belle tried to turn and look for Lia but they were moving too fast.

"We have to go back!"

Nell chanted something out loud but Belle couldn't make out the words as the wind whipped her face. Among the trees a white glow appeared. They hurtled towards the space illuminated before them and burst out into a clearing bathed in moonlight.

Shaking uncontrollably, Belle saw her fingers gripping white against the pommel of her saddle.

"We have to go back for Lia!" She cried out.

"Lia is fine." The scent of charred embers surrounded her as Lia emerged right behind them.

"Are you ok?"

"What. Are. They." Belle's heart hammered inside her throat.

"Necēri. Ghoul slaves of the House of Elharean. We call them Snatchers. They roam the non-magical world searching for newly awakened supernatural beings to deliver to their House of Elharean Masters." Nell's face appeared drawn. A shadow lingered over her face that spoke of much more than her words revealed.

There had been mention of Nell's time as a captive at the hands of the House of Elharean. She had been held and tortured long before Lia and Fehrn had rescued her. Though Nell never spoke of her ordeal and everyone seemed to respect her wish to keep it that way.

"I thought you said there was no risk to me leaving the realm?" Belle's head pounded.

"You weren't in any real danger with me there to protect you and singe them to a crisp. But for an inexperienced being on their own, unable to properly defend themselves, well that's what they feed on. Flesh, fear, and magic." Lia shuddered.

"It's unusual to see them this close to our border." Nell mused out loud. "You'll investigate more with Fehrn?"

Lia nodded. "We'll do more perimeter checks and find out what has drawn them this close or whether it was just dumb luck that pack came across us."

On the ride back to the castle Nell and Lia went ahead speaking together in hushed tones. Belle followed behind lost in thought. She realised time must move differently between the different worlds. When they had left Madame Liu it was broad daylight. As soon as they crossed the boundary it had turned to night.

Exhausted and shaken she couldn't help but play over again in her mind how the creatures seemed to have only one focus. She had felt it in their darkness. Sensed the unseen energies clawing at the back of her neck.

They had all been fixated on her.

CHAPTER 14

Keep smiling. Keep. Smiling. Lachie repeated to himself silently through clenched teeth with every mind numbing handshake, air kiss, and clasp of his shoulders.

Being Guardian of the Realm was his sense of purpose and duty. But the tedium of attending these annual events where he was expected to rub shoulders with his guests all evening was almost unbearable. At least he neared the end of the long line of attendees to greet in the castle entrance hall. It had been over an hour of plastering on a fake smile and mindless pleasantries. Lachie's jaw ached and his eyes watered.

He'd much rather be enjoying the peace and quiet of his study about now.

Your plan will be completed soon. This is the last time you'll have to endure this, just grin and bear it.

"... just fabulous, but of course you *must* meet my daughter one of these days..."

Nodding and murmuring something about *being charmed and honoured* Lachie stiffly kissed the extended hand of the willowy Queen of the Sprites before she floated away into the ballroom.

The other aspect he detested of these evenings. As Guardian of the Realm he might as well put a target on his forehead for a never ending series of propositions. Some acted coy, some tried negotiation tactics, while others simply attempted to drag him off to a dark corner. It didn't help his cause that in the past he would have gladly disappeared into dark corners to escape from his living hell. That reputation still hung expectantly in every attempted flirtation and innuendo that came his way.

You only have yourself to blame.

But these balls were not only about music and gowns. It was secretly his way of gathering intelligence. Lips loosened with good food and wine often revealed secrets. His team were highly trained and knew exactly how to work the crowd. Their task was to move among the guests throughout the night, gathering hints and whispers that might aid them in their fight against the House of Elharean.

After he shook the hand of the last guest in line the tension drained from him like a rope as it turned slack. He stretched his neck to one side with relief. He could disappear for at least an hour, maybe two, before returning for another foray into the crowd to mingle and be seen.

"Need a break, Niall. I'll not be long—" His voice died in his throat as he turned to where his brother had been standing during the formalities. Instead he was met with the source of his stunned silence. Gliding quietly down the grand staircase was a vision that made the entire room around him disappear. The air sucked out of his lungs. He might as well have been enchanted into another realm.

Belle's curves were wrapped in a glimmering emerald gown hugging her every movement as she descended the staircase towards him. A dress that bared the smooth skin of her shoulders, fitted tight against her waist, her bosom, before falling to the floor in a mesmerising sweep of fabric. She was holding up one hem and Lachie could see a glimpse of porcelain skin where her perfect legs moved as though floating effortlessly. Her dark hair was piled high, exposing the long curve of her neck. Those grey eyes knocked the breath from his lungs as they sparkled beneath her jewelled mask.

His every dream and disaster rolled into one... and she had no idea.

Protect.

Trying to swallow right now was an impossibility. His mouth felt like a parched desert. Lachie attempted to move across the vast expanse—since when had the entrance hall become so damn large—to where she had nearly reached the base of the staircase. As her feet touched the final stone step, her eyes flicked up and locked with his. They widened with the slightest of movements and her plump lips parted.

Fuck. She was perfection.

Just as he shifted to close the space between them the cloying scent of heavy perfume filled the air. A set of scarlet talons gripped his forearm.

"Lachlan. How kind of you to wait... especially for me." The familiar voice at his ear dripped with sex and manipulation. Fiery red hair cascaded around bare shoulders. A flash of a blood red gown to match the nails now sunk into his jacket sleeve. The perfume felt like it would choke him. Luciana, the head of the Gravelaan Coven residing in the non-magical world swung herself into his line of sight still clutching tight to his arm.

"I missed you so very badly the other night." Tracing a long sharpened fingernail up his jacket sleeve. "It's ungentlemanly to leave a witch hanging like that."

"Not ever professed to be a gentleman, Luciana." His voice bit out through gritted teeth. The witch dealt in secrets and she would ensure to always get paid her dues. He'd blown off their meeting the other night and Lachie had no illusions that compensation would be extracted one way or another.

With each attempt to swerve around her, those talons dug deeper. Luciana positioned herself firmly attached to his arm and pressed close to his side. It was clear the extraction of her repayment would begin right now. Appearance could be everything in the supernatural world, and right now Luciana only had one illusion she wished to cast. To walk into the ballroom as if they were a couple.

"So generous of you to personally choose *me* out of everyone here to escort into the ball." The purring of her voice was laced with just a hint of retribution. She drew out the word generous with every syllable meant to sound like desires being fulfilled.

Lachie clenched his jaw. All he wanted was to be rid of Luciana's clutches.

His eyes scanned desperately for the sight of glittering emerald and dark hair among the crowd as they entered the ballroom. *Where was she?* This ballroom was filled with far too many supernaturals who were here to progress their own self interests. A witch with Belle's kind of power would be a temptation that lured in the predators disguised in suits and silks. She wasn't prepared for this. He should have done more to teach her to defend herself. Lachie's heart began pounding in his chest.

Luciana soaked up every ounce of attention she received as they made their way into the crowd. Whispers and raised eyebrows behind opulent masks. Glances at where she pressed as much of her body against his with a sultry smile.

"Dance with me, Lachlan." Her voice rasped against his ear as she made sure to rub all over his arm, like an animal trying to mark its territory.

"Perhaps not." She hissed in a breath at his rebuttal. "Don't want to monopolise your attention, Luciana. Enjoy the evening." He pried her fingers from his arm and thrust a goblet of wine into her hand. Making his hasty escape he spied the towering figure of Rowan standing alone off to the side of the room. The usual menacing glower etched into his features. He looked even more deadly than normal which meant everyone was giving him a wide berth.

Perfect.

Passing close to the musicians he saw Niall swing around the dance floor with a glamorous blonde witch. Nearby Fehrn and Lia swayed intimately together.

Just when he had neared the relative safety of Rowan's company, he saw her. The curve of her neck. The rise and fall of her shoulders as she moved with the music. The shimmer of her dress as it caressed her perfect skin. The male hand grasping her lower back. Lachie's eyes flashed a sudden storm and the clench in his jaw pulsed harder. Instinct raged within him to rip the man from her.

Murderous thoughts ran untamed and wild through his mind. Before he could make a move to implement part one of his spontaneous plot he felt a drink thrust into his hand. His direct line of sight to Belle taken up by an impish smile.

"Doesn't Belle look incredible tonight?" Brigid said over the top of her wine. "I would say this ball is the most magnificent we've had in a hundred years, no?" Waving her hand she took in the grandness of the room that had been completely transformed for the Spring Equinox. "Not thinking of spoiling Belle's chance to celebrate her hard work are you, brother?" Brigid quirked her lips as she followed Lachie's intense stare to the location of the man's hands holding Belle.

"He's putting his hands all over her." He drained his glass.

Brigid stepped into him as he went to move past her. A solemn look fell across her delicate features.

"Brother. I can't break my vow to intervene, but I see what good intention lies in your heart. All I beg of you is to think this through before you give her cause to turn against you."

Lachie glared down at his sister. He hated to admit that she might be right. But the protector in him was riding on a knife edge and didn't care to listen to reason. Side stepping Brigid, he stalked towards where Belle was laughing hollowly at something the man had just said. Fingers were pressing into her back and Lachie could sense the tension in Belle's shoulders as she fought against his attempt to pull them closer together.

"I believe you're done here." Lachie clamped his hand on the man's shoulder with a heavy thump. A warning and a threat all in one. The young male shifter whirled around with nostrils flaring at the interruption. Upon seeing Lachie he shrank backwards three steps. His palms held up in silent apology.

"Thank you for keeping Annabelle company." Lachie ground out with an icy tone as he moved deftly between them, grasping a tight hold of Belle. Looking down sternly with jaw set, he was met with her grey eyes equally filled with ice.

"For the Guardian of the Realm, you sure know how to act like a pompous ass."

She had every right to be angry with him, but he was beyond caring. Despite the daggers she was shooting him with her eyes, he had felt her body relax as soon as he had taken hold of her. The air surrounding them immediately pulsed, magic intertwining and thrumming with intensity. Belle's lips were parted as though caught mid sentence and Lachie felt himself unable to take his eyes off their softness. A haze of emotion swept through him as he imagined what it would be like to close his mouth over hers. To taste her.

For the second time that evening it felt as though he had been drawn into another place, with the rest of the room seeming to vanish around them.

"If you're just going to glare at me all night, I'd much rather leave." Belle swallowed under his intense stare. A soft whisper barely audible above the music playing. Lachie felt his body respond to the sound of her voice.

"Won't have you being pawed by everyone in the room." His fingers splayed across her lower back in what he knew was a possessive gesture.

Hypocrite.

He let out a satisfied rumble to feel her hips sink closer to his in response. She held his stare with equal intensity, but the ice had transformed into something more potent between them.

"And what of it? I should be able to enjoy this evening as any other being here."

Lachie knew he walked a narrow tightrope right now. The fine line beneath him shrunk with every step he took forward. She had every reason to walk away from him right now and spend her evening with whoever she chose. If only she knew the truth of his plan. Soon she'd never have to see him again.

"Just looking out for you." He swallowed, breaking eye contact to cast a glance around them. "These supernaturals might look well dressed but there are more hidden agendas here than tiaras. You're too innocent for your own good."

"Is that what you believe?" He felt her stiffen and pull her hand from his. Narrowing her eyes she snatched up a goblet of wine from a nearby server and turned towards the doors leading to the outdoor terrace. Anger radiated from her smooth skin.

Fuck. Lachie jabbed his fingers through his hair and quickly looked around to see if anyone had noticed her abrupt departure. The floor for dancing was crowded and with the drink flowing freely the guests surrounding him were laughing and talking animatedly amongst themselves.

Muttering curses under his breath he followed her outside.

"Wait." He snapped as he strode through the doorway. Belle turned, rounding on him with grey eyes intense with rage.

"You think just because you are Guardian of all this, that you know what is best for me? That I can't be trusted to make my own decisions? Then you have clearly misjudged me." She took a hasty gulp of her wine. "One minute you tell me I'm the most powerful witch for eons. The next you treat me as though I were feeble and pathetic."

"Belle, I—"

"No. You don't own me. You don't get to manipulate me. I've endured too many years of being controlled. This is my life and I intend to do as I please." She breathed heavily as the words lashed forth.

"You. Need. Protection." Lachie clenched his fists. He could feel his heart clenching in his chest and fought the urge to reach out. To touch her skin once more. To feel her softness and warmth that had been all his just moments before.

Crackling blue light pulsed through the dim glow of the terrace.

"I have protection. Lia. Nell. Brigid. *Myself.*"

"Not enough." Lachie moved forward to where she defiantly held her ground, arms folded and swirling her wine.

"Why? Why can't anything ever seem to be good enough for you?" She spat out in frustration.

His hand grasped around hers where she held the crystal goblet. Leaning in so close he could feel the warmth of her body, hear the softness of her breath, and almost touch the flush softly pinkening her cheeks. In the flickering light from inside the castle her eyes seemed to sparkle. He found himself drawn down once again into the vision of her as she ran her tongue across her lips, leaving them wet and tantalising.

"Because this is my role. My essence. What matters to me the most." Without stopping to think he rubbed the pad of his thumb over her fingers inside his grasp and saw her pupils dilate.

"It is my duty to... *protect.*" His thumb reached the inside of her wrist and he felt her pulse tick up with the glide of his touch. "It's why I watch from a distance and why I don't allow myself to get too close. This is not a game."

She was too trusting. Too kind. Too gentle. He knew the real darkness in this world and even though she had suffered her own hardships, she had no idea how close she might have come to experiencing the true meaning of destruction. The thought of her beautiful smile destroyed and sacrificed on the altars of the House of Elharean. He would burn down entire realms if necessary. He *would* tear down their sickening practices and get his revenge for what they did.

He had already failed once in his duty. He wouldn't let it happen again. Not to his mate.

CHAPTER 15

"What do you want from me?"

Belle's breathless voice sounded like nothing she had heard from herself before. All wonton and husky.

Spirits save her, she was on fire for this man. His merest touch and she felt as though she would disintegrate to a million pieces with lust. Her body rode a roller coaster of intense Ampher magic every time she got near to him.

She knew she tempted fate asking that question. Filled with innuendo and suggestion. But her patience wore thin. One way or another she needed to clear whatever this was between the two of them and she was determined to do so tonight.

The more time they had spent together in preparation for the ball had been bliss laced with agony. It turned out life had been far easier when she didn't know what she was missing out on. Now she knew all too well. His scent. His attention to detail. The intimate moments when she caught a hint of a smile cross his features.

Tonight she had glimpsed his magnificence first. When she'd seen him from the top of the stairs—before he'd even noticed her—she'd watched hungrily as he finished the formal greetings. Her eyes had traced every deft movement of his form dressed in a black shirt and jacket. It was only when she'd made it halfway down the staircase that he had finally detected her presence.

The way his eyes had fixated on her. She'd melted into a pool of weak-kneed lust on the spot. Now here she found herself trapped in his web. Unable to flee even if she wanted to. Heat raged through her core. There was no avoiding the fact her pussy wanted everything this man—witch might give her.

"It doesn't matter what I want." His thumb circled her pulse. Belle's heart thudded inside her ears. He must be able to sense what effect he was having on her.

"I lost a chance at that choice long ago." Lachie's aquamarine stare fixated on her mouth. "But tell me, fierceling, what is it that you want? You can't accuse me alone of being hot and cold. Your mouth will say one thing but I see the way your body tells me another."

Stars, she was about to self destruct and he hadn't done more than hold her hand. Heat rushed between her thighs and she clenched them together as a wave of sensuality tore through her.

Biting her bottom lip, she tried to form coherent thought. "You're deflecting."

He quirked a faint smile at the corner of his lips.

Fucking fuck fuck.

This man was sinfully attractive. For the briefest of seconds he moved his mouth towards hers and Belle thought her heart might stop. Was she about to be kissed? Then just as abruptly that dark storm returned to his expression. With a hissing intake of breath he pulled his head back upright, but still held her wrist. Belle could see a war raging inside his mind as he tilted his head to the sky. This was what it all came down to. Lachlan of Nocturne fighting his own inner demons.

Belle wondered if there would ever be a day when there might be a space cleared for something, someone else. For her even.

"We can't do... this." His dark stare clamped back down and he jerked his chin to motion between them. "It's not possible."

Belle steeled herself to not look as crestfallen as her heart suddenly felt. Dumped out in the cold unceremoniously.

"Don't try to paint me as someone good. I'm not." Still he kept hold of her hand enclosed firm in one of his own. With the other he reached out to brush her hair from where it had wisped across her face. She couldn't help but close her eyes at that briefest of touches. Imagining for a second how his hands would feel caressing her body, her breasts, her pussy.

"Fuck, you are perfection."

His hand stilled, cupping the side of her face as she leaned into that intoxicating feeling.

"I know about the other day when Lia had to save you." His voice was soft and remorseful. "I can't bloody sleep for thinking that I should have been there."

Belle reached up to put her hand over his. Holding that searing heat from his palm where it rested against her cheek for fear that any moment this spell would be broken and he'd be gone forever.

"But I'm fine. I've been growing more confident in my magic every day—"

"Not enough to defend yourself."

"Well, then teach me." Belle challenged him softly. "You could spend eternity letting guilt eat you alive or you can train me yourself. Teach me to defend myself. You can't keep me locked in my rooms for the rest of my life."

She didn't know where her confidence had suddenly sprung from. But she sensed that a whisper on the breeze had shifted something between them in that moment. It was like the thread that had kept knotting and tangling them together in disharmony had finally become silken and smooth. Like an infinite loop. Giving and receiving.

"Are you sure you're up for it. My training is not for the faint of heart." His mouth twitched at the corners. Was that another smile? Her heart lurched at the thought of how rare an occasion a smile from Lachlan of Nocturne was. And here she had one all to herself.

"Are you afraid I'll best you?" She breathed.

"Worse."

Belle felt the air thrum with renewed intensity. Her Ampher

magic picked up on a dangerous pulse of power that rippled off Lachie's body.

"Ask me again what I want." He growled low. His grip tightened against her wrist as he pulled her to him. With a gasp she realised her body now pressed against his length. She could feel how tense his muscles had become beneath his shirt and her mind immediately leapt to imagining that expanse of muscle she had dreamt about many nights since her first glimpse from the bathtub.

She parted her lips to speak only to find herself panting and speechless as his thumb ran seductively and slowly along her bottom lip. Every glide traced the contour of her mouth as if to memorise every slope and form.

"Ask me." A command. Gentle yet filled with the eons of power he was able to channel.

Her soul had left her body, she was sure of it. The hunger in his eyes devoured her as he rested the pad of his thumb against her lip, tugging it slightly down. She let out the faintest moan of frustration when his touch disappeared only to suck in a ragged breath as she felt his fingers scorch a trail across the swell of her breasts just at the top of her dress.

"What... do you want from me?" Her words tumbled out in a whisper as her eyes closed in ecstasy and her head tilted back exposing her neck. A silent invitation.

"It's not what I want from you." His fingers slowly traced down the front of her dress and he brushed his thumb across her nipple beneath the fabric. She felt the peaks stiffen under his attention. "What I want ... is you."

Her every sense began to smoulder and crackle as the power surged between them. He lifted her hand where she wore the emerald and gold ring and softly caressed the gem across his lips. His hot mouth grazed the skin either side of the jewel leaving her mind scrambled. What was left of her essence now vacated her body. The pleasure from that minute contact against her skin wracked through her body like a tidal wave.

Then her hand was released. She opened her eyes to find herself standing in the glow of the terrace alone.

He was gone.

In the stillness of the night air music wafted towards her and peals of laughter resonated from within the ballroom. Her pulse raced close to the surface of each place his touch had seared against her skin.

She finally had her answer, clear and unwavering. Lachie desired her.

And she was ready to risk it all in order to have him.

CHAPTER 16

"The attacks are becoming more frequent."

Lachie folded his arms and stared into the distance across the room. The crowded noise of the tavern only a distant hum as he sat with his thoughts.

"You're right. The snatchers never used to cover this much territory." Ceranthe swilled his ale thoughtfully as the two men sat in a secluded booth in the far corner away from prying eyes and ears. They'd met here when needed for the best part of the past two decades. Since Ceranthe had first stepped into his role as Keyholder.

"I've been tracking one pack and they covered five times the distance they ever used to. I'm telling you, something has shifted, Lach." His tawny eyebrows furrowed together.

"Magic or none, you can't go putting yourself in harms way." Lachie knew that Ceranthe had never awakened any potential magic even after all their years working together. While all beings had dormant gifts, there were some who either chose to live without their gift or had ancestors who made a decision long ago to renounce the ways of supernaturals. As far as Lachie was aware Ceranthe had no known family with awakened gifts. Yet he dedicated himself to aiding their cause from within the non-magical realm.

Ultimately it was helpful to have someone with their ear to the ground who could avoid detection from the House of Elharean. Their followers resided within their castle and sprawling estates mostly in the non-magical world where their control and influence could easily take and manipulate power. The kind that could be pledged knowingly by those loyal to the Elhareans, and also stripped unknowingly from those beings who didn't know of their true nature.

"You know me, I'm always with my wits about me." Ceranthe tapped the side of his forehead with a chuckle. "Do you think it has something to do with the Seal?" He cast a glance sideways with a hushed tone. Wary of who or what might be listening.

Fehrn had been on a mission two winters ago to seek information on the Seal of Elharean. What he had uncovered went far deeper than they had ever imagined. They knew there was a great talisman or source of dark magic possessed by the House of Elharean, but the whispers and stories of its true purpose had been lost over millennia. It was during that same mission Fehrn had rescued his mate Lia.

Both had barely escaped with their lives. Not only that, but they had rescued other supernaturals such as Nell from torture and imprisonment by the House of Elharean. It was during their capture they had discovered that the Seal of Elharean wasn't a mystical object, but a portal into other realms and dimensions fuelled by harvesting the magic and life force of supernaturals. One piece in the House of Elharean's dark agenda to enslave and posses the magic of millions across time and space. Beyond that discovery, no one knew anything more about the use of the Seal.

But that was all he needed. That was why Lachie needed to set his plan in motion now after all this time. It had taken him over a hundred years to finally track down the Seal of Elharean. He would make sure it would be destroyed once and for all.

His vengeance would be complete.

"Ceranthe, I have something to ask of you. Not that you don't already risk your life enough for our cause."

"Anything Lach, you name it."

"Annabelle—the Ampher witch—she had another close call with a pack. They came straight for her. Right on the border."

"Ach, is she alright?" Ceranthe gripped tight to the handle of his tankard.

"Lia was there. She disposed of them. Incinerated the lot. But I can't help—" Lachie trailed off with a frown. He was still at a loss to put into words his level of concern. He was duty bound to protect all under his care as Guardian. But when it came to the witch with long silken hair, grey eyes, and perfect lips he couldn't keep pretending that this instinct to *protect* wasn't from something much more mystical. Deny it all he wanted, but she might just be fated to him. And yet he was going to have to destroy that bond to save them all.

"But you're concerned should young Belle be without some adequate defence... on the occasion there be a next time?" Ceranthe studied his ale as though in meditation.

"If you can see to running the packs off that get too close. For now that will give us more time."

"Lach, consider it done." He thumped the table with a fist and nodded sternly. "You need to give her this." Ceranthe reached under his worn scarf wrapped against his shirt collar and pulled out a familiar gold chain and key.

Lachie's scowl deepened. "Not happening."

Keyholders. These were the select few beings—some with, and some without magic—given an enchanted key. It allowed them to portal in and out of the realm as a means to reach safety should they ever need it. Their bravery in the face of the House of Elharean's constant threat couldn't be overstated.

"This will guarantee her safety. No matter where she is." The ornate gold key held in the palm of his hand flashed in the tavern candle light. "I want her to have it."

"But without it you won't have your own protection." Lachie clenched his fists. Ceranthe was invaluable in his service to the realm. Risking his life without possessing magic and choosing to reside in the non-magical world to help them with their missions. The key was one of only a handful ever made granting an immediate portal into safety within their realm. All someone needed to do was grasp hold of it, recite the incantation, and they would be instantly transported.

Ceranthe bravely volunteered over and over for grave and dangerous duties in their missions to rescue newly awakened supernaturals from the House of Elharean. This key was Lachie's only way to ensure Ceranthe himself remained safe. Without any magic to defend himself against snatchers and dark entities this gave him the ability to escape if there was ever the need.

"I insist. If this girl is everything you all say she is, then it would be my honour to help protect her in any way I can. I might not have magic but I have my heart and it gives freely."

Lachie studied the gold engraving carefully. With an exhale and a shake of his head he pushed the man's palm closed around it.

"No. You keep it. We can't lose you, old friend."

His plan was now more urgent than ever.

CHAPTER 17

"I don't believe we've met."

Belle started, taken aback. A wash of intoxicating perfume and a sultry smile from the being standing before her felt oppressive. There was something overwhelming that carried through the short distance between where Belle stood and the witch who had appeared suddenly.

Reluctantly, she had agreed to assist with delivering potions as part of Nell's regular rounds to share supplies with supernaturals residing outside of the realm. Belle's nerves had been on edge since their last run in with the snatchers, but the promise of stopping for new art supplies from a local vampire-owned artist studio had lured her along for the journey.

Standing in the dim light of a sumptuously decorated and foreboding parlour, fingers clutched around her satchel of parchment and paints, she felt about two feet tall.

Nell had assured Belle along each stop of their safety. The Gravelaan Coven had long been allies against the House of Elharean. Lachie trusted these witches, and that should have been guarantee enough for Belle.

But something still crawled across her skin. Nell seemed so certain of their welcome here, she had left Belle where she stood in the parlour with a promise to be back in a couple of minutes. A short witch with a gentle smile had led Nell away through the passageway in a spark of bright chatter.

Stars, Belle regretted not joining them.

Before her stood the witch—or rather seductress—who had arrived at the Spring Equinox ball and started pawing Lachie immediately. Belle had fled into the crowd that night rather than stick around to see any evidence of what kind of relationship the two had to one another.

Real witches didn't dabble in pretty pictures. They clearly had more important business than planning silly balls and painting.

This witch was powerful, indeed. Her physique dripped with sex appeal. Flaming red hair billowed around her shoulders in perfectly formed waves. Her deep burgundy top sat off both shoulders and clung to every inch of her. Fixing Belle with a haughty stare, she twirled her long manicured fingernails through the incense smoke that wove through the room.

"Luciana. And you're standing in my coven." She pursed her lips while narrowed eyes flicked over Belle from head to toe. Silent judgement hung in the air with the subtle arch of one perfect eyebrow.

"Finally, I get the chance to see what all the fuss has been about." She stalked towards Belle. "The first Ampher in two hundred years? Must say, I'm more than a little underwhelmed."

Belle felt tingles as her cheeks burned. Yet she couldn't seem to find any words. Nell was occupied in the back delivering the last of the potions. It was just Belle here facing down this witch. Alone.

"Can't imagine why Lachlan of Nocturne needed to spend so much time with the likes of you." The words spat out with venom.

The air billowed, hanging heavy with her perfume. Belle's lungs started to burn from the enclosed space in the darkened parlour.

Her hands gripped tighter around the leather satchel slung across her shoulder. Where in the Stars was Nell and what was taking so long? Belle wanted to get out of here as quickly as she could. Yet her feet remained rooted in place transfixed under Luciana's disdain.

"I know for certain Lachlan's appetites wouldn't be satisfied by such a pathetic creature." Luciana leaned her hip against the front of her gold filigreed desk. Each long talon tapped against the wood as she smirked. Mocking her.

Belle felt her stomach turn. She hadn't wanted to think of Lachie with other women. Jealousy grabbed at her insides and started to twist. Was this witch one of his lovers? Were they currently involved? Her eyes widened. Was this who Lachie had been dressed to meet the other evening when she had interrupted him leaving his study? Bile rose in her throat. They had seemed familiar enough when she grabbed hold of him at the ball. The flare of a bitter spark mingled with the thoughts of this witch tangled with Lachie.

"Too meek and mild to even speak?" Luciana tutted to herself. "You probably have deluded little girl fantasies of fairy-tale romance hiding away in your pretty castle. Do you think the gentleman Guardian will sweep you off your feet while you scribble away drawing love hearts on that parchment of yours?" She gestured at Belle's satchel with a mocking flick of her red talons.

Her cheeks flamed hotter. Why couldn't she say anything to defend herself against this witch? Her knuckles whitened from their tight grip around the leather strap of the bag.

"No. I do-don't." She croaked. Heart racing. She knew how pathetic she sounded.

"The dark prince doesn't trifle with your sort. There's no tenderness or emotions. He only fucks. He doesn't have sex. He doesn't cuddle and kiss like you delicate little flowers are wanting. There's no attachment. He'll only take a witch who can match him because when he fucks you it will have you screaming his name and begging for more." She studied Belle acidly with a haughty laugh. "I bet you're still waiting for him to peck you on the cheek and whisper sweet nothings in your ear. Quite pathetic."

Belle's heart thudded harder. She was frozen still. It felt like her insides suffocated while her blood pounded in her ears at the imagery Luciana described. Lachie, the dark prince of desire. It aroused her, yet that sensation was met with indescribable pain. Every fragment of air in the room felt like taking gulps from a poisoned chalice forced against her lips.

Luciana pushed off the desk, stalked towards her, and began to circle where Belle stood rigid and unmoving. She could feel Luciana's power running through her veins, her Ampher magic absorbing and expanding its frequency, but it was different to the ways she had experienced it before. This time it felt toxic and immobilising.

Panic started to seep into her consciousness. She hadn't trained for this. She didn't know how to shield herself against this witch. Belle realised she must be amplifying everything Luciana conjured with her magic. The effect became a neurotoxin to her.

"I'll bet he hasn't even told you why he keeps you locked away in that castle." Luciana slid a pointed blood red nail along Belle's cheek. Indents bore into her skin with force as she reached her chin. The witches green eyes glowed eerily as they studied her features in the dim light.

"He'll claim it's something to do with protecting you... the precious little Ampher... when that's no different to what the House of Elharean would do with you. Keep you locked up for their own agenda. He's using you. They'll all just use you."

With a rush of an invisible force Belle fell to her knees. The toxins inside her hurtled through her energy field, consuming her. She clutched at her throat with a voiceless cry.

Luciana crouched down and grasped Belle's chin, tilting it

to face her with a sharp jerk that had her gurgling incoherent sounds.

"No wonder they haven't taught you how to protect yourself from the magic of others. Now you know just a taste of what it's like to truly be an Ampher. When you can't shield yourself from magic you can't handle, you'll end up burning alive."

A roar rushed through Belle's ears. She dropped forward on her hands and knees. Fingers sinking into the carpet to grab at anything that might tether her racing mind. She sucked in deep lungfuls of air, gasping and coughing. Luciana was gone, along with her poisonous enchantment.

The door to her left swung open. Footsteps thudded dimly. A basket dropped as though in slow motion. She felt gentle hands rubbing her back. An echoing distant voice sounded far, far away. Nell's wide eyes swum into her vision. Sounds rushed back all at once like a steam train thundering down a long tunnel.

"Belle... Belle! ... Can you hear me? Can you speak?"

Belle hacked a cough in between gulps of breath. The sweet nectar of fresh air rushed through her. The healing sensation of Nell's aura wove around her and cradled her body.

"I was only gone two minutes! What happened?"

Belle surely must have misheard. She felt as though she had been trapped in Luciana's enchantment for an hour, maybe more.

"Luciana." She croaked out.

A sharp intake of breath.

"Her enchantment. I'm sorry Belle, I didn't think. She can manipulate elements into toxins only she can tolerate." Nell flushed a wave of healing magic through Belle as she spoke. "She can also manipulate time. While it might have been two minutes for me outside this room on the inside it could have felt like hours for you."

Belle gritted her teeth. "Let's just go. She caught me by surprise was all." Collecting up her leather satchel she felt her neck gingerly to see if there was any physical sign of being choked. Nothing. Just the wounds of embarrassment.

"There won't be a second time."

CHAPTER 18

"I need to learn how to portal."

Lachie was met with crossed arms and a glare from Belle that could melt the sun itself. Her Ampher pulsed from across the forest clearing like the tail of a predator as it whipped a warning.

"No. Too dangerous. You need to learn to defend yourself." He planted his hands on his hips and held her stare.

Spirits, this witch could easily send him to his knees. But he was resolved to hold his ground. They had been locked in this battle of wills for the better part of the past hour. Patience was something Lachie prided himself in. Yet Belle pushed him to his own limit.

He took a deep breath in, then exhaled long and slow through his nose. Belle cocked an eyebrow at him.

How was he supposed to explain to her? To even begin to

convey the immense risk in what she was asking of him. He had to convince her somehow that her Ampher could be her greatest weapon, rather than the ability to simply disappear.

Just like she disappeared.

At that thought something dark tugged at his chest. There was no way he could go through losing her. Not while there was still breath left in his body and no matter the temptation that tugged inside his chest to stay. It was impossible. There was no way he could alter his course now. His plan had more urgency than ever before to ensure nothing like that fateful night could happen again. Not to anyone—especially not to Belle.

"Portaling..." He stopped to clear his throat. "...is a use of magic that can endanger the user without adequate measures taken. The soul can splinter into fragments the likes of which not even the ancestors could bestow healing upon."

Why did he sound like a fucking textbook right now?

"So, what are you saying? You'd rather I just let witches like your friend Luciana poison me to death?" Belle's eyes flashed. Hurt lingered in the flicker of a shadow trailing across her face.

"No." He whipped back.

He'd taken it into his own hands immediately to see to Luciana after the stunt she pulled. Safe to say that witch would be grateful her coven still existed after he paid them a visit. He would quite happily cast them all out into the wilderness. Good luck finding any new alliances against the House of Elharean without the Guardian on their side.

"And she's no *friend* of mine." Lachie ground out.

A strange expression crossed Belle's features. She opened and then closed her mouth. His eyes flickered to her lips for a momentary beat.

Could that possibly be jealousy in her eyes? His heart thudded in his chest with an awkward bounce.

Since the night of the ball he'd replayed their moment together. When he'd admitted the way he desired her. The way her pulse had raced beneath his touch. How soft her skin had felt. And the way her scent had clung to him with sweet temptation throughout that night.

The fucking feel of her mouth against my thumb.

More than once his hand had wrapped around his cock at the thought of those lips. The soft curves of her body pressed up against him. Imagining breaching the chasm between them to lose himself in her.

Shit. He needed to get control of his train of thought before his cock got any harder.

"Then help me." Belle's tone softened. "You promised to teach me to defend myself. Please, Lachie."

His knees weakened at the sound of his name on her perfect fucking lips. Her plea wound its way into the furthest recesses of his heart.

What he'd prefer is that she didn't need any of it. That she would be safe no matter what. That the steps he put in place to ensure her safety would be enough. But he knew the reality was more complex than that. Belle had been right when she'd pointed out he couldn't keep her locked away forever.

She needed to live her life. To find love. Even happiness. She deserved all of it and so much more.

The least he could do was train her. Teach her all that he could. And hope that the day would never come for her to need to use it. Even if he couldn't be here to safeguard her future happiness.

"You'll have to learn physical combat alongside the lessons in harnessing your magic from Brigid." His teeth gritted together.

"Ok. So teach me." She bit back.

Lachie continued while he paced the forest clearing, pretending to ignore her interruption.

"When it comes to your magic and understanding how to control your Ampher powers, there is a great deal you can do to defend yourself... or attack if you so wish." He folded his arms across his chest as the dirt kicked up where he tracked back and forth on the same spot. "Supernatural beings are difficult to kill. You might wound, injure, or debilitate your opponent through spells and enchantments, but that is only one part to protecting yourself. The physical act of combat is just as important if you really want to be prepared for whatever the House of Elharean might send your way. To kill a supernatural being you have to decapitate them, which is why those of us here train with weaponry."

"Great. I'm ready." Belle propped her hands on her hips as her eyes tracked his movements.

"It isn't some game. Brigid can teach you to master your connection to Source. As a powerful witch you can learn to wield the elements to your will. My sister has her methods, I have mine. When you're here training for battle I expect you to not hold back. It involves total dedication. Commitment. Do you think you can handle that?" Lachie's scowl deepened. The thought of seeing Belle drenched in sweat and in close combat every day sent a jolt through him.

The real question here wasn't if Belle could handle the rigours of physical training—he knew how strong she had been in the face of adversity. But could he handle what lay ahead? To be so close to her every day? To feel her pulse jack hammer beneath her skin? Drown in her scent?

Fuck. Fuck. Fuck.

Boundaries. That's what he needed to stamp firmly in place. With a sharp cough he cleared his throat.

"I said some things the night of the ball. I apologise. You deserve the space to train and learn physical combat without distraction." Lachie's teeth gritted harder as each word ground out in painful succession. "Your safety is the priority. My priority... as Guardian." He quickly clarified. Spirits, his words bumbled out like a foal unsteady on its legs.

"We're both adults, Lachie." Belle's face flashed with frustration. "I'm here ready to learn, aren't I?"

Her look of defiance needled him. Did she honestly not experience a rage of turmoil inside the same as he suffered from? Was there not a constant yearning to be close enough to touch like he felt? The incessant voice inside his head to *protect.* To safeguard his mate.

With a lurch forward he braced one arm across her chest

and pinned her arm to one side. Belle let out a yell of protest at the sudden attack. It was a rotten move, he'd used the distraction of their conversation to cover his intentions. But he needed to prove this point. Perhaps more to himself than to her.

His mouth rested against her ear as her back pressed into his chest. There was no way she could escape his hold right now, and the thought of that sent his cock hardening in his trousers.

"Lesson one. Always expect a teaching moment. You left your back unguarded." Lachie's breath gusted against loose wisps of her long braid.

"Not exactly fair. I wasn't ready." The tension in her voice echoed how her body fought against his hold.

"Lesson two. Use your magic first. Then fight. You need to weaken your opponent before you try to gain the upper-hand." His eyes traced a flitter of goosebumps over her neck and collarbone. Her body fitted so perfectly into his arms. Her luscious curves moulded against him like only the Goddesses could have foreseen.

A faint pulse of magic pushed at his grip. Nowhere near strong enough to free herself, but Belle tested her newly honed gifts. A growl of frustration left her throat. Good thing she couldn't see the twitch at the corner of his lips where a smile danced.

"That's the idea. But you'll need to strengthen that ability. Right now, it's like a tap on the wrist." Nothing wrong with giving her some positive reinforcement, even if she had a lot still to learn.

Belle's body drained of tension beneath his grip. Her shoulders limp. *Shit.* Maybe he'd pushed her too far, too fast today?

Lachie saw the treeline spin in a whirl above him. His legs snapped out from under him and his head whipped back against the leaf litter and dirt with a heavy thud. Belle sat astride his chest with a glint of blue flame in her usually grey eyes. A smirk plastered across her face. Her forearm pressed to his throat.

"Like that?" She smiled sweetly. Plump lips flushed a darker shade and her cheeks tinged pink at the satisfaction of her success.

Lachie inhaled to catch his breath where it had been punched from his lungs. Clever witch. She'd absorbed his power as he'd held onto her then returned it double-fold against him with her Ampher. The blue flame of his magic sparked in her eyes a moment longer before they returned to normal.

"I can't wait to see you do that to Niall." He couldn't help but let out a laugh. "But yes, something like that."

Belle's face hovered close above his. The smooth skin of her forearm still pressed up against his throat as he swallowed heavily. He realised his hands now rested against her hips where his fingers flexed into those soft curves. Almost as though their bodies knew on instinct to fit together in this way. Drawn again and again to wind up in an intimate embrace. He felt the soft brush of her curls against his neck where her braid slid forward.

So fucking close.

Their lips hung suspended on a mere breath between them. Only the slightest motion and he'd taste their sweetness. To claim his mate and break his vow.

Grey eyes searched his as her body softened further. An unspoken question lingered there in Belle's wide stare. Magic seethed and pulsed in the air surrounding them in the clearing. Her Ampher intermingled with his power in a spiral as she let down her guards with every passing second their bodies pressed flush with one another.

He wouldn't cross that line. Even if she hated him for this rejection. Maybe it would be easier that way, instead of the torment of wanting what he couldn't have.

Lachie pushed at her waist to lift her off him and surged to his feet. Belle stumbled to stand up and brushed her hair out of her face, now flushed with embarrassment rather than the arousal of their proximity.

"Lesson three." Lachie's voice scratched out, gruff and tinged with regret. "Weaponry."

Spirits, the idea of her being hurt due to his actions wounded him like a blade sunk between his shoulders. There was at least something he could do to keep her mind occupied on matters other than how close they had just come... how close he had been to pinning her beneath him.

Although handing her a lethal weapon right now might be a decision he came to regret.

He reached down to where his blade holster sat on the ground near his feet and withdrew both blades. With a fluid motion he flipped one around so that he held the sharp end pointed at himself and extended the handle towards Belle, gesturing for her to take it.

Lachie knew he definitely shouldn't take as much satisfaction as he did in the awe that crossed her face when she watched his slick motion. He knew these blades like extensions of his own body.

Dirty show off.

"So, Belle. Have you ever stabbed someone?"

CHAPTER 19

"He never—I repeat—never comes to these things."

Brigid raised herself up onto her elbows and Belle's eye followed to where she saw Lachie approach his brothers. His tall frame silhouetted against the crackling sparks of the bonfire. It was the night of the Summer Solstice celebration at a cavernous swimming hole not far from the castle. The group gathered in a large circle around a blazing fire. The still night air danced around them filled with enough warmth that it could have been mid-afternoon.

Today felt like a dream. The perfect antidote to weeks upon weeks of training. Belle felt more relaxed than she could ever remember being. Swimming in crystal clear waters inside the enormous natural rock formation. A cavern that could easily fit the entire castle within its interior. Laughing with her new found friends. Watching the moon rise lazy and full upon purple skies.

Pale light streamed through the giant opening formed within the rock. Belle's skin tingled and still glowed with warmth from hours basking in the sun. But beneath that sultry heat flecked across her skin lay something more. The awareness of his presence. It did something to her. Whenever he came near her body sensed him before she saw him.

"I can't imagine who could possibly have inspired my darling brother to join us this evening." Brigid sank back with a cheeky smile into the assortment of cushions where she lay on the grass. She looked like an elfin queen in a matching gold high waisted bathing suit and short halter top with legs crossed in the air.

"If you're in a wagering mood, Fehrn and I know who to place our bets on." Lia giggled as Fehrn pinched her hip then dragged her onto his lap in a possessive hold. Pure adoration burned in his amber eyes.

"Look, he is helping me with my training. That's all." Belle leant back on her hands where she sat beside Brigid on the grass. Sun, water, decadent food, and Fae wine had lulled her into a boneless puddle. Yet her muscles ached with a satisfying tension after the past two months of intensive training. Every twinge felt like a badge of honour from the Goddesses themselves.

To his credit, Lachie had been true to his word and taught her how to defend herself. He had committed to daily sessions helping her master energetic shielding techniques. She had also begun physical combat training alongside Lia and the other elite group of spies and warriors. A mixture of learning to fight with weapons while also using her Ampher magic.

"Well let's just say, I don't see Lachie with his arms wrapped around Niall every two seconds to *demonstrate* a technique." Lia snorted. "And I hear the way you think about him, Belle."

Shit. Belle's thighs clenched together. Yes, she often had thoughts of Lachie's hard body pressed against her. There was no denying how close he stayed to her during training. Every session seemed to bring a new torture of his hands on her body to shift her stance, or adjust her line of sight. Worst of all were the days he looked and *didn't* touch her. His eyes might as well have stripped her naked the way his gaze devoured her body.

And Spirits save her, she'd played his game every chance she got. Purposefully asking for his assistance when she didn't actually need it. A subtle arch of her back against his chest. A brush of her hand over his as he passed her a sword.

But there had been no other moments since the day of their almost kiss. When she had first thrown him to the ground with her Ampher magic. There had been nothing to stop Lachie from devouring her—she'd seen in his eyes the desire as she straddled his torso—yet he'd been the one to break the spell between them. To set her at a distance. Even if he'd been unable to resist the pull to be close ever since. Physically close, yes. But there may as well be a wall a mile high separating them.

"He'll never admit it you know." Brigid wriggled back in the cushions. Her voice interrupted Belle's thoughts. "Lachie's positively allergic to talking about his feelings. Breaks out in a ghastly case of emotional repression."

Fehrn spluttered with a gravelled laugh.

"And don't even get me started on Rowan." Brigid continued. "I swear he'd go into anaphylactic shock if he had to connect with anything on the emotional spectrum. Dallying with swords and breaking bones are his preferred love language."

Lia collapsed in a heap of uncontrolled giggles, her face pressed into Fehrn's chest.

Belle's heart squeezed at the sight of her friends' happiness in their mate-hood.

"Seriously, your progress has been amazing." Nell smiled sweetly with a little hiccup as she poured herself wine, ignoring the others. "The way your Ampher is able to mimic and amplify the fighting techniques and gifts of others. I've never seen anyone learn as quickly as you who has never had any experience before."

"But I need to get stronger. I can't hold it for long stretches of time yet." Belle worried her bottom lip. Her eyes drifted back towards the figure across the other side of the bonfire. His tanned skin glinted golden in the reflection of the firelight.

"It will come." Lia reassured her.

"How do you manage it? You're tiny compared to everyone else." Belle mused. Only giving half her attention to Lia, while her eyes flicked back to the set of broad shoulders she wanted to run her fingers—tongue, definitely tongue—across.

"My greatest weapon is my telepathy. I guess it's almost as if I can hear them predict in their mind where the next move is going to come from. Either that or they signal their next strike in advance with subtle thoughts." She shrugged. "I might not have the muscle or the height, but it gives me my edge. I don't try to match them blow for blow. It's more like a dance where I can see the choreography before they even know it themselves. Plus if it comes down to it I can always send a fireball up their ass."

"Wouldn't get to that point. I'd have ripped their throats out first." Fehrn growled dozily.

Belle was proud of herself. It had been weeks of intense effort on her part. After the run in with Luciana she had thrown herself into being the perfect student. Seeing Lachie shirtless and sweat drenched up close on a daily basis was a near constant test of her ability to focus under pressure. Especially since his confession on the night of the Spring Equinox ball and that near-kiss moment between them. Belle's cheeks flushed in the darkness at the memories imprinted in her mind's eye. Firm hands brushing across her skin. His thumb pulling down her lip.

Fuck. Lia's telepathy didn't need to be privy to these fantasies.

Belle jumped to her feet.

"Speaking of all that training I'm going to go give my muscles another soak in the hot spring." With a wave over her shoulder she picked her way along the wide path of smooth rock.

"Remind me to give you another healing potion tomorrow." Nell raised her wine skyward in a salute.

"Enjoy your... solitude." Brigid's voice lilted through the air after her.

What was that supposed to mean?

The moonlight glow throughout the cavern made it easy to see the steaming water. A delicious invitation from one of the small rock pools up ahead. A spot secluded and well away from the group was exactly what she craved right now. Belle sat on the edge and slid in. Her eyes closed in ecstasy as the warmth flooded through her limbs.

He'll only take a witch who can match him because when he fucks you it will have you screaming his name and begging for more.

She couldn't shake those words. Belle felt a warmth coil low through her core and her thighs clenched together just thinking about it. Nothing wrong with having continual fantasies of Lachie, right? Belle had found her hands wandering and masturbating to thoughts of him on more than one night while alone in her bed. Indulging in wild imaginings of what his hands... and mouth might do to her.

But other than subtly ogling him during their training sessions there wasn't any chance of that happening. Lachie had been the perfect Guardian and teacher. Beyond those touches and *looks* these past weeks, there had been no hint of the emotion he had shown towards her the night of the ball.

Stick to wanton daydreams.

Heat spread between her legs as she remembered the brush of his thumb across her breast that night. Her nipples hardened instantly inside the light fabric of her bathing suit. Belle couldn't believe how aroused she was just from a memory.

Then she stilled. That familiar sensation rippling through her. The signature of magic she could always feel before she could see its owner.

He had followed her.

CHAPTER 20

"Don't go lurking in the bushes. I know you're there, Lachie."

Belle hoped the false sound of playful confidence would hide her shaky breaths. *Fuck. What was he doing here?* She already felt like an explosion waiting to happen.

"Won't have you disappearing off in the dark unprotected."

Belle shivered at the sound of his voice coming from the long shadows of the moonlight. Gruff. Raspy. Raw.

"I'm in a giant cavern surrounded by rock with the realm's finest positioned at the only entrance." Did she sound calm? "I think I'll be fine to soak in the hot springs for a while." Butterflies were damn well beating at her chest.

"Not taking chances." Lachie's statuesque form shifted into the stream of silver light and Belle hitched in a breath. He was gorgeous on any given day, but right now he had a hunger in his eyes that was intensely surveying her. His gaze raked over her where she sat submerged to her shoulders in the water. Fierce and unyielding.

Maybe she had enjoyed one too many sips of Fae wine, but there was no subtlety in the way he devoured her with that look.

Spirits, this was one of her midnight fantasies come to life right now. Her neck flushed hotter. She hoped the steam rising from the water might disguise the very obvious physical response her body was having right now.

He leaned casually against a tree. Muscled arms folded. Truly a supernatural Adonis.

"If you insist on staying... at least get in the water. It's a little less intimidating." *Fuck. Fuck. Fuck. Was she out of her mind? What depraved recess of her subconscious did those words tumble from?*

A languid grin tugged at the corner of his mouth.

"Intimidating?" He tapped a forefinger against his corded forearm. The only sign he weighed up some internal battle of choices.

"Fuck it." He muttered to himself and proceeded to reach behind his head, pulling his black cotton shirt off in one smooth motion.

Belle gripped harder to the rock ledge she perched on. A hasty swallow. She'd seen him shirtless countless times in these past months. This time just about melted her mind entirely. When he straightened up she hastily flicked her eyes away. Not wanting to give a hint she'd been blatantly staring at his muscled abdominals. That sinful V extending down from his hips.

What was she getting herself into?

She heard his boots drop to the ground one by one. Followed by the quiet thud of material as he dropped his trousers. With the sound of each item of clothing removed her thighs squeezed tighter together. Soft footsteps sounded closer, sending her heart rate into a frenzy. Then the gentle roll of water lapped over her as his large frame eased into the hot spring.

Prickles of power danced along her bare skin below the water at his proximity. Everything turned up in intensity in the space of a single breath. The heat of the water. The warmth winding its way between her thighs. The flush down her chest.

She flexed her fingers against the smoothed rock. Cautiously stealing a glance in his direction. Aquamarine eyes pierced her very soul from where he sat directly across from her. She might be swallowed whole by that intensity this evening.

Willingly.

This was her moment. Belle knew it. She was no stranger to sex—mere boys leaving her unsatisfied and unimpressed the times she had given in to the need for some kind of connection. But here was a man her body and soul responded to in a way she had never experienced before.

Belle felt compelled to investigate this power between them. Right now, before she lost her nerve completely. He'd followed her here knowing she was alone. While Lachie might try and lie to himself, there was no fooling anyone when his actions continued to be at odds with his words.

You need to weaken your opponent before you try to gain the upper-hand. Lachie's own words from that first training session replayed through her mind. Maybe the wine had addled her brain, but there might never be another opportunity like this again to test the Guardian.

"I feel your power before I ever see you." Belle breathed. "Is it the same for you?"

Turquoise flashed with gold. A tick in Lachie's jaw.

"I think you do. And that's what scares you the most about getting close to me."

"Already told you, fierceling. Don't go trying to paint me as something good." That rumbled gravel tone had her pussy clenching in response. A heady warning laced with a hint of invitation.

Something deep and primal tugged within. Belle slowly shifted forward. There was only two feet between them where they sat opposite each other. She could see the dark outline of his legs spread wide under the water. Muscular shoulders leaned back against the pool's edge. He was splayed out looking every inch the dark prince caressed by shadows of the night. And she was happily going to go into that darkness to explore his depths.

He didn't flinch as she moved to close the distance. His eyes fixed on hers unwavering.

Swallowing hard she placed her hands gently against each of his arms. The pads of her fingers flexed against the curve of his biceps. After the past two months she was now intimately familiar with Lachie's body. The way his muscles dipped and swept along his tanned skin. She'd traced his tattoos along his chest and forearms with her eyes, memorising their contour against his flesh.

Now she was prepared to explore him for herself. Enough of his maddening proximity during training. She'd been careful. Too careful. Now was her moment to do the *wrong* thing for a change.

Belle's fingertips brushed across those sinful flexes of his muscled shoulders. His smooth skin felt molten against her touch. That aqua gaze burned white hot as she manoeuvred her legs so that she straddled his lap.

She gasped when she felt him long and hard pressed up against her stomach. He was completely naked. So, so naked. And very much aroused. Lachie hissed in a breath.

"Careful not to start something you can't handle, little witch." That husky whiskey tone. The corded muscles in his arms flexed as he kept his hands against the rock ledge.

"You started it first." Belle hardly recognised her own voice. Her body lost entirely. Drowning in the sensation of being pressed so close to him. Wrapped in his scent of cedar and leather.

Golden orbs of light formed in the air to surround them. Rising as though from within the steam. Like fireflies content to float lazy and at their leisure on the night air.

Belle moved her hands to his chest. Power surged from within him up into her palms.

"What do you want from me, fierceling?" She shivered at the way his words growled out. Repeating her own question from the night of the ball. The vibration of his voice against her body ran to her core. She couldn't help but let out a soft moan at the sensation. As her teeth dragged over her bottom lip she watched his eyes drop. Pure greed bled through his stare where he fixated on that small movement.

"You." Belle's voice was barely a whisper.

"Fuck, you'll be the death of me." Lachie groaned as his hands finally moved. A possessive grip curved around her. Moulded to her flesh. Sinking his strong fingers into her hip and her upper thigh.

Heat raced low in her stomach. Blood pounded with deafening intensity in her ears. Her pulse wild and without rhythm.

For all she knew he'd reject her, but she didn't care. She had to taste him. Had to know how it felt to be wrapped up in him just for this brief moment. Leaning forward she slanted her mouth over his. A soft open mouthed kiss. Firm lips met hers and for the smallest of moments she thought he froze. Heart pounding, she felt his chest rise and fall with the ragged edge to his breath.

Belle ran her tongue gently along his lips. He tasted of honeyed wine and the promise of endless pleasure. She lapped with soft, exploring strokes at that addictive taste. Before suddenly being pressed hard against his mouth. Deepening his kiss. A hand grasped at her hair at the nape of her neck. Demanding. Seeking. Yearning to be closer.

"Need you to tell me if you want me to stop, fierceling." A deep gravely command against her mouth.

"Never."

She felt his tug arch her back, baring her neck. Dragging her rock hard nipples up against his chest. She breathed out a moan at the heady sensation. Lights pulsed around her skin. Shameless need raced through her veins. She clenched her fingers against his chest, digging her nails in.

Lachie groaned and deepened his kiss. Their tongues tangled and explored one another. His giant hand on her hip gripped her tighter. Belle ground her body against his, completely overtaken by the pleasure coursing through her.

"Touch me. Please." Belle panted. Pressing her forehead against his. She needed this. Needed more of him.

Flashing gold flickered across his eyes.

"Take these off." The command rumbled low and firm. Fingers dug into her hip and her pussy drowned in a wave of molten heat.

Her breath a little unsteady, she eased herself back to stand in the water. Caged in by his legs. His muscled body took over every spare inch of space. Darkened eyes pierced her with a look that shot straight to intensify the ache in her core. Shimmying down the high waisted bathing suit bottoms, she slipped out of them. The warmth of the water slid across her drenched sex.

"And the rest." His gaze seared across her covered breasts. They felt full and heavy under his stare. Belle shivered with anticipation. Here she was, stripping naked for Lachlan of

Nocturne—the fucking Guardian of the Realm—and her clit throbbed with every passing second. She reached up behind her neck to loosen the tie and let the wet material fall away.

Her nipples floated just at the waters surface and that slight lapping sensation over the sensitive buds sent spirals of pleasure to her clit.

Even though most of her body was underwater she felt like Lachie seared every inch of her flesh. Long hair floated around her shoulders as she tentatively moved back towards his muscled body. He scrubbed a hand over his mouth.

"You want to be touched?" Sex dripped from his tone. Belle nodded in response. Mouth suddenly dry. "Use your words." The rough edge to his voice did all sorts of wicked things between her thighs.

"Please."

Belle shifted herself back to straddle his lap. Once again her breath hitched at the long, hard length pressed into the swell of her stomach. She didn't need to see it to know... Lachie's cock was as impressive and big as the rest of his body.

"Spread those knees for me."

Her lips parted as a wave of desire flooded her aura. Apparently his commands had a line straight to her pussy. She sunk her knees wider across his lap. Bared for him. The sensation of the water against her swollen sex was dizzying. She was already on edge and he'd only kissed her.

"Look at that perfect mouth." Lachie reached up and tugged a thumb across her bottom lip. A soft whimper tumbled out in response. His strong fingers grasped the side of her neck.

She threaded her fingers through his hair. Her swollen breasts pressed together and begged for his attention. Her hips slowly ground against his.

He tortured her. And the flash of desire in his eyes told her just how much he savoured every second.

"So fucking beautiful." His hand dragged down the column of her throat. The other kneaded her upper thigh. Inching ever closer to where she needed him to be. Every slow dip nearer to her pussy teased her into an inferno.

He cupped her breast possessively. With a groan he dipped his head. The hot wetness of his mouth closed over her nipple. A bolt of electrical charge seared her skin. Belle's head dropped back in ecstasy as he flicked his tongue over the sensitive bud. The other hand pinched at her breast between powerful fingers.

"Oh, Lachie—" She let out a cry.

His hand moved up her thigh to press against her core. With a rumble of satisfaction his fingers stroked her pussy. The evidence of how soaked she was slick beneath his touch.

Oh fuck.

"So wet. For me." Lachie flicked his tongue across her nipple. Fingers stroked languid circles around her clit. Belle moaned louder at the sensation. The pooled heat building and building.

Her breath caught as he slid one finger inside. Followed by another.

"So hot and tight." Lachie's groan against her nipple had her clench with pleasure around his fingers. She was so aroused and beyond caring. Let him feel what effect he had on her. Desire spiraled higher as he slid in and out of her slickness. Pumping with just the right pace. Firm strokes against that perfect spot.

"Don't stop." Belle bucked her hips to ride his fingers. Meeting his mouth with hers. Heated breaths intermingled. She dragged her teeth over his lip. His thumb circled harder against her clit. Everything inside her being coiled tighter.

"Yes. Fuck. Ohhh." Her hands tangled in his hair.

"Who does this belong to." Lachie's command spiralled her pleasure higher.

"You. Only you." A whimper left her throat. She would gladly trade eternity for this one moment. This touch that drove her wild with pleasure. To be his for ever more.

"Good girl." His voice rasped against her. Whiskey. Power. His teeth dragged across her nipple.

Belle moaned as her core spasmed and her orgasm tore through her. Wave after wave rolled in a starburst behind her eyelids. The floating golden orbs shattered into fragments of light as she came undone.

She fell forward, boneless and unable to do anything but catch her breath. Her damp forehead leant against his. Lachie's touch now soft and sensual as he gently stroked her down from her climax. His chest rising and falling in time with hers. The still night air filled with the sound of their breaths intertwining.

His lips caressed hers with a feather light touch before claiming her mouth in a hot languid kiss. Time seemed to hang leisurely and satiated between them. A low rumble came from Lachie's chest as he shifted his hands to run across her hips. He drew back and pressed his forehead against her shoulder.

The tension between obligation to the realm and his own passion radiated off his skin. Yet he gripped her tight against him. As though she might slip through his fingers if he didn't hold onto her with enough care.

"Belle. I—We—This." He turned to lick up the side of her neck. Slow and sensual. "I can't be what you want. What you deserve."

Belle pulled her head back. Studying his face. Shadowed by the moonlight she could see the hunger in his eyes contrasted his words. The push and pull wrenching him apart inside that she couldn't seem to touch. His own inner battlefield that clearly tore him between duty and desire.

They'd been here before. Too many times. Each time she inched the crack open under his shell, he pulled away. A futile attempt to protect her, but from what she didn't know. Herself perhaps? Or from him?

The boldness of earlier still danced down her spine. Only time would tell if her strategy might achieve the desired outcome. Whether he'd realise there could be sanctuary in allowing someone—her—to get close.

"You're right." Belle heard the words fall out of her mouth. Entirely unexpected. She must be completely out of her mind. Brain clearly scattered into a million pin bursts of light from her mind-bending orgasm.

His eyes narrowed. Hands stilled on her thighs. The faintest hint of his grip pressed in to her skin.

"What?"

"You're right." She reached forward and pushed his tousled dark hair from his forehead. The familiar touch of a lover.

"Obviously you have other priorities. I'm just a distraction." He thought to fool everyone with his stern facade and brooding exterior. Belle knew the truth. She had tasted it in his magic running through her.

She had studied this witch at close quarters over their past weeks training together. She knew his words often belied his actions. She could sense the turmoil where it floated just beneath the surface. Never did she think herself daring enough to tempt this kind of fate. If he thought to put her at a distance she'd play his game, for now. Even though everything inside howled at her. Insisted she beg him to choose differently in this moment.

Instead, shrugging her shoulders she eased off his lap. *Keep your cool. You can do this, Belle.* She leant forward and whispered against his ear.

"Thank you for the... Guardian experience."

His eyes flashed. Intense glittering beauty amongst the storm brewing.

With a slosh of water she pushed herself out of the rock pool. Belle picked up her bathing suit, making sure to take her time bending over. Smug satisfaction thrummed through her veins at the sight of him dragging his hand over his mouth in stunned silence. His eyes locked on her naked body. Hungry and filled with deep longing.

"I'm assuming you can take care of *that* yourself." She waved her hand in the direction of his jutting erection before sashaying away into the night.

CHAPTER 21

"Spirits save us. Not this again."

Niall rolled his eyes. He kicked the door closed behind him with a boot before proceeding to throw himself at the couch.

Lachie glowered at his brother from where he sat hunched over parchment cluttering his desk.

"Get. Out." A death glare towards the blonde hair and tanned frame currently sprawling his long limbs across the upholstery. Boots crossed over one armrest. Arm crooked beneath his head at the other end. The crunch of teeth against crisp fruit interrupted the heavy silence.

"It's been a week of this, no? You can't hide in here and threaten to murder everyone who dares cross your path." More loud chomping. A partial mouthful muffled Niall's words.

"Don't think I'm blind to the cause of this tantrum. It's rather unbecoming, your majesty."

"Niall. I swear to the Stars—"

"Pain and banishment. I know. I know." Niall waved a hand in the air. "Not got anything more original for me today?"

"Careful not to push me, princess. You'll be in for a hiding." Lachie snarled.

"Look, even Rowan is asking me what's chafing your leathers. If that black hearted hermit is concerned then you can't blame me for poking my nose in here."

Lachie ignored the rest of the stream of chatter coming from the couch. He had plenty of reasons to be on the war path. Since watching long dark hair slip away into the night a week ago. Those bloody words on repeat inside his mind. *"You're right."*

His present mood couldn't possibly be anything to do with constant thoughts of her. Nothing at all to do with the rippling pleasure as she came apart on his fingers. Not at all to do with the taste of her lips. Feeling how their magic surged and intertwined as she moaned into his mouth.

Fuck. He'd replayed that image of her arched back and perfect breasts bathed in moonlight over and over. His hand wrapped around his cock every night while thinking of her body pressed against his.

It was like the air he never knew he needed to breathe, until it was taken away from him.

She had avoided him expertly since the Summer Solstice. Not meeting him at their usual times for training. Acting like nothing had happened between them. As though she hadn't shattered his entire reason for existing.

What was the point of vengeance and self sacrifice when you suddenly had something—someone—you found yourself prepared to live for? Someone you felt utterly compelled to protect.

It was infuriating how Brigid smirked with that damn knowing look every time she saw him pass by the courtyard. Fehrn was off-realm with Lia meeting with the Fae Dominion. He'd tried to take his frustrations out on Niall and Rowan during their sparring sessions. But nothing worked. Instead he'd resorted to spending most of his days holed up in his study.

"—leaving to travel with Nell to the mountains... taking her healing potions and such... wants to check on the vampiress Melinkya's recovery." Niall—annoyingly still talking—drifted into his awareness.

"Fine." He grunted.

"With Fehrn and Lia away, that'll just leave Rowan here with you."

Lachie vaguely registered the words. But his mind was still firmly preoccupied. Grey eyes dilated with pleasure pierced his vision. With a growl in his throat he thrust up out of his chair. Everything felt too stuffy in here. Closed in and tightening around his throat. His senses urged him to move.

"Trust you'll do what's necessary. Travel safe, princess." With long strides he marched to the exit. Propped behind the door frame stood a carefully wrapped package. He grabbed it with one fist. With the other he flung the door open and surged into the cool stone corridor. On a deep inhale he pinched the bridge of his nose. His head pounded relentlessly, his thoughts muddled.

Without thinking his feet started to move. Loud determined strides echoed against the pale flagstones. He could have easily portaled. But with the chaotic state of his head, surely a walk would help calm him? Surging through the castle he found himself headed straight towards the private suites at the far end of the east wing. He took the spiralled stairs two at a time before coming to an abrupt stop in front of the heavy wooden door. The thunder of his pulse raced below his skin. He raised a clammy palm for a second as though to hammer on the wooden surface. Then with a grunt to himself he simply burst through instead.

Bright ethereal light filled the room taking him by surprise. Lachie shielded his eyes for a second to adjust after the dim atmosphere of the castle halls.

When his sight adjusted, he saw her. A golden light that glowed and shimmered like sunlight glinted off the ocean. Belle filled the room with her magic as it radiated from her pale skin. It was as though the clouds had parted and scattered a prism of sunlight filled with joy across the room.

She perched on a large cushion as she sketched. Parchments of her artworks lay strewn like fallen autumn leaves to cover the carpeted floor in front of her. All in various states of completion. Some lavish in their detail and finishing. Others loosely sketched, full of expression and emotive abstract compositions. A series of simple black designs contrasted against the creamy texture of the page.

She snapped her head up at the sudden intrusion. The luminescence crackled with an electrical surge before turning to bolts of blue that shot tingles through his body.

“You can’t just burst in here. I’m busy.” Her grey eyes sparked with an intensity at his presence.

“Don’t care. You’ve missed half a dozen training sessions this week.” *Not that he was counting.* “Remember you asked *me* to teach you how to protect yourself. Not the other way around.”

Belle pressed the heels of her palms against her brow with an audible exhale. “Ughhhh. Can’t you see I’m busy.” She swung onto her knees and reached out to gather up her artworks.

Lachie’s eyes clung to where her robe gaped open as she leant forward on her hands. His fist gripped tighter around the package he carried.

“It’s my duty. You’ll not keep avoiding this.” He ground out.

“I’ll do as I please. Besides, I’ve been working with Brigid every day.” Another stretch forward lifted the silken robe higher on her upper thigh.

His mouth set in a firm line.

“Well, you’re late for today’s session.” With a thud he slammed the package on the floor yet made sure to lean it against the armchair closest to him.

Belle looked up with a start. Mouth open.

Fuck, that mouth. His jaw clenched tight at the sight of her on hands and knees gazing up at him. A flare in her eyes at his impatient commands.

Good. She needed to find out that this wasn't some kind of game. It could very well mean life or death for a witch.

Her Ampher pulsed with a crackle sent through the air as it intermingled with his own magic.

The words flew out of Lachie's mouth before his brain could catch up. Before logic or reason could have any say in the situation between them.

"My study. Now. You have exactly two minutes."

CHAPTER 22

It's been six minutes. Lachie glared at the clock on the mantel above the fireplace. His fists clenched tight. White edges to his knuckles. Blood whooshed in his ears as he paced back and forth across his study.

"Bloody well go back and drag her here." He argued to himself. "Don't have time for this kind of nonsense." His every muscle was tight and coiled. Ready to unleash. Shoulders set as though ready to take a blow in combat.

What if she doesn't come?

He leaned over his desk, hands gripped so tight against the edge of the wood he heard a faint crack. Squeezing his eyes shut he barely held himself still despite the urge to storm back to Belle's suite.

Suddenly a wave of her scent washed through his senses. Jasmine and rose. Spinning round abruptly, Belle stood on the other side of the room with hands on her luscious hips. A penetrating stare pinned him in place. Her eyes narrowed and lips pursed.

"You got me an easel." A statement rather than a question. She stared at him unblinking for a long moment. Then a slow smile spread across her delicate features.

"Careful Lachie, anyone might think you've been missing me this past week." Her voice was light and teasing. Little did she know he'd had the damn thing commissioned a month ago. Only every time he worked up the courage to give it to her, he'd stalled.

No more fucking stalling now.

Lachie launched himself at her. The tension snapped inside him. With two strides he crossed the room and grabbed her by the back of her neck.

"You are not to ever fucking do that again."

Belle's eyes glowed bright as her pupils dilated.

"I—" She breathed out. Pushed backwards ever so slightly by his intensity.

"Never hide from me again. You're not to leave me like that." His chest heaved in a rapid rise and and fall. Heart hammering. Power surged into his palms as his fingers flexed below her nape. His grip unrelenting.

"And why is that exactly? What am I to you?" Belle's fists balled against his chest. Holding him at elbows length. Her expression was unreadable but he couldn't keep fighting it. Fuck whatever the consequences may be. He might lose her but he'd never been one to back down from a challenge.

His eyes darkened.

"You are mine."

He saw the slightest flare in her nostrils. A single pulse of golden light rippled out around the darkened room.

"You made it quite clear the other night you weren't interested in anything between us."

He let loose a growl. "Never said I wasn't interested."

"Well, it seemed otherwise from where I was sitting." Her mouth quirked. His cock pressed against his trouser seam at the memory of her straddled naked across his lap.

"And you're deflecting." She added. "Why did you get me an easel?"

He dropped his forehead heavy against hers. "Your art shines out of you. It radiates through the air when you are in your joy. I wanted you to have something that might bring you that, even if I'm not the one to do so."

"Lachie—" Belle breathed. But he cut her off before she could continue. Not wanting to risk hearing her turn away from him again.

"You're better off without me." He flexed his strong fingers. Contrasted against the softness of her neck. The plumpness of her lips drew his eye to where they glistened. Flushed pink and wet.

He felt her palms flatten against his shirt. A softening of her body beneath his grip. Her Ampher radiated in a slow spiral to encircle them where they stood pressed against each other.

"No. I'm not better off without you." She whispered. Her

voice laced with silken tones. With that soft admission, Lachie wanted to consume every aspect of her being.

"I lied when I told you I agreed. That's why I had to keep my distance." Her fingers pressed into his chest and he felt his heart clench. Heat radiated between them as she slid her hands up and circled around the back of his neck.

Swallowing hard, he searched her face for any lingering sign that she might change her mind. That she might drop away, leaving him holding nothing but an empty void. If only she knew what he had been planning all these years. If only he could explain to her how torn he was on the inside. The guilt of failing the oath he had sworn and abided by for so long.

"I might not know everything about your past. But I'm willing to accept whatever yours might be. As long as you are prepared to accept my imperfections too." Her eyelids dropped heavy as her breathing shallowed. Her face tilted at an angle to reach his height. The sensual line of her back curved to meet his gaze, pressing her breasts against him.

His cock jerked at the feel of her body. Just as with every training session over the past weeks he couldn't stop from touching her. Addicted to that intoxicating ripple of magic shimmering across her skin like a prism scattering rainbow light.

"You're mine, my fierceling. No one else will touch you." His voice came heavy and possessive. The antithesis to her brightness in the room. He knew in that moment there was no way he could relinquish her. He'd burn down every world to guarantee her safety.

Belle's eyes widened at his gravel tone. She bit her lip. Her teeth raked slow and sensual across their plump fullness. In that split second something finally gave way inside him. The last tether that held his restraint. With a groan he crushed his mouth against hers, angling over her lips and tasting that sweetness he craved.

Hard. Relentless. Commanding.

Their tongues tangled, desperately seeking to get closer. His hands ran across her curves, digging in fervently, pressing her hard against his length. Wanting—needing—her to feel every inch of his desire. Soft moans against his mouth had him nearly losing control already.

Panting breaths came from her mouth as she pulled back. Her eyes slid down below his waist with a hunger for more.

If she was hungry, then he'd been ravenous for another taste of her perfection.

Her hands slid under his shirt to tug it upwards. He reluctantly let her go for a second to drag the material over his head before his mouth sought out her skin once more. Lips trailed a wet caress across her shoulder. Then his mouth fastened over the hollow where her shoulder and neck met. Belle arched to give him more access. His desire sparked at the invitation and submission to his hold on her.

Her fingers worked at the waistband of his trousers. Intent on freeing his erection. He grabbed hold of her hands, stilling them. The sound of frustration in her throat had his cock jerk in response.

He wasn't going to rush this moment. Not when he'd dreamt of having her here like this for so long.

With a fluid motion he reached around behind her thighs, lifting her around him, before he dropped her onto the chair closest to the fire. Belle sat flushed and panting with arousal. Her perfect form sprawled across the seat. With a slow prowl he backed away. She was all his most erotic fantasies made flesh. His greedy stare consumed her where she sat as though on a throne. Her nipples hard against the thin material of her robe. The slit hung wide open between her ample thighs with just a hint of her pussy visible. Endless porcelain skin he would claim.

"But—" Her voice rasped with arousal. Frustration evident in her flushed cheeks.

"Be a good girl and take it off." Lachie's eyes darkened.

Her Ampher ran a shiver across her skin. Golden light glinted and merged with the flickers from the firelight. But she did as he asked. Belle pulled at the sash to her robe and allowed the material to float down her shoulders, pooling around her waist.

Lachie scrubbed a hand over his mouth. The sight of her sitting there bare before him was nectar sent straight from the Stars. His eyes raked over every inch of flesh. Her sex glistened with wetness between the V of her thighs as her arousal grew stronger under his relentless scrutiny.

"Show me. Show me what you've been doing at night. How you like your pussy to be taken care of."

Belle gasped. Crimson flushed down her neck and across

her chest. His eye followed that path down to her breasts. Soft, full, and begging for him to suck those tight budded nipples into his mouth. *Mine. Need to protect. Claim.* His magic roared fiercely inside his chest.

Grey eyes fixed on his. She ran her tongue gently across her bottom lip. It took everything he had to restrain himself from taking her right then and there. Tentatively she dragged one hand over her breast. Squeezing. Rolling her thumb across her nipple. Her other hand dropped low to slide along her soft thigh. Then higher between her legs.

Her eyes widened at the sensation, but her gaze didn't leave his. Mouth dropping open, she began to roll her hips. Pleasure flooded across Belle's smooth skin. Her finger moved in slow circles around her clit. Her breaths shallowed and a whimper broke the silence above the crackle of the fire.

"Please, Lachie. I need you."

His cock strained painfully against his trousers yet he wouldn't allow himself to do anything but fuck her with his eyes and senses.

"Who is it you think about, my fierceling? When you touch yourself."

A soft gasp caught in her throat.

"Y—You. Only you."

A satisfied groan filled his chest. "You thinking of how good it felt when I made you come all over my hand, hmm? How you want me to lick that sweet little spot? To come on my tongue?"

Belle's eyelids dropped closed at the picture he painted

with his words. Her finger moved faster in response. His lips ticked up at the corners.

"What do you imagine inside that pretty head of yours then?"

A flutter of her eyelids. Neck arched backwards. Golden orbs of light floated around the room. She was getting close, but Lachie had other plans for her orgasms tonight.

"Tell me." He shifted towards her with both hands leaning against the armrests to cage her in with his body. Not touching her—not yet—but so close he could hear her slick wetness beneath her fingers. *Fuck.* Her soft panted breaths and tiny moans of pleasure engulfed him. He glanced at the tattooed sigil now revealed on her bare hip. He definitely didn't notice *that* their night together on the Solstice. She must have had the enchantment done recently.

Thank the fucking Stars for magical contraception. Witches had the gift of magic and spells to safeguard themselves as they desired during sex. Many chose to do so in tattoo form such as evidenced on Belle's hip. So, she had been thinking of him—and where this thing between them might lead—since that night.

He slid one knee between her thighs. The weight of him pinned her fingers still. Her gaze flew up to meet his. "Not asking you twice."

She let out a frustrated breath at the loss of friction. Lachie kept his eyes pinned on hers. He needed to hear her say it out loud. Belle's voice panted in soft whispers, like hearing her own thoughts spoken for the first time set her body aflame.

"How you're so big and hard. How you fuck me from behind." She rolled her hips against his knee. "How your body cages me in." His cock jerked at the sight of her spread out below him. "Your fingers working me here." With her free hand she circled his wrist. Moving his fingers from where they gripped the armrest, down towards her pussy. Belle bit her bottom lip and levelled him with a hooded gaze.

Fuck. She edged at his control not to sink into her right that moment. But he wasn't going to take her—his mate—for the first time anywhere but the bedroom. She deserved perfection and he'd be sure to deliver that and so much more.

"The only way you'll be coming tonight is on my mouth or on my cock."

Lachie took her mouth in a hard, unrelenting kiss. With a groan he scooped her off the chair. Her soft curves pressed against his bare chest. The heat radiated off Belle's skin as she wrapped her legs around his waist and circled his neck. Her fingers tugged at his hair as she kissed him back fiercely. Possessively.

His thighs hit the side of the bed and he barely had a chance to set her down before he felt her reaching for his cock. *Fuck.* His body hummed for her. Lost in her sweetness.

"Get on your hands and knees." He commanded. Belle flushed pink with arousal. Her delicate hands rested against his waistband. Trust glimmered in those grey eyes followed by slight smile at his tone.

My mate likes that.

She twisted round, throwing a sultry gaze back at him over

her shoulder. He drowned in her essence as she arched her back. Obeying. Inviting. Quickly ridding himself of his clothes, he moved forward to spread his hands over the luscious curves of her thighs in front of him.

He'd do anything to give her the pleasure she deserved. While his words might be commanding her right now, his entire being was ready to serve her. His treasure. A damn queen lying in his bed of thorns.

"There can't be anything more perfect than you." He licked his tongue over her inner thigh. Tasting her juices. Inhaling her scent. Staying just out of reach of where she silently begged him to move to next.

He ran a teasing finger across her slickness. She responded with a whimper. Pushing back at him.

"Please. Ohh—" Her breathy voice was cut off with a muffled moan. Her head dropped to the pillows when Lachie pressed his tongue against her core. He worked his way across her clit, devouring her. Licking slowly. Savouring the honeyed taste of her wetness.

"Fuck, you taste so good." He groaned against her wetness. His tongue flicking, then teasing. When a fresh flood of arousal came in response to his words, he pressed a finger inside her. Belle's hips pushed back against him. Asking for more. Her cries of pleasure intensifying.

"Yes, Lachie. Just like that." Her panting voice drove him wild.

"You're dripping. Such a good girl." Fastening his mouth

over her clit he sucked down. He applied just the pressure he knew would make her fall apart.

"Fuck. I'm so close. I'm—" Belle pleaded. Desperate for release.

A satisfied smirk spread across Lachie's mouth as he drew back. He pressed his thumb over that sensitive nub and curled his fingers inside her. Exactly the movement to have her tumble over the edge.

"Come for me." Part command. Part request. The spiralling desire for his queen's pleasure flooded his brain.

And she did. Her back arched with a moan. Her core clenched around him. The sight of her shattering beneath his touch was perfection. Shards of gold light flashed to fill the room.

Belle was still coming down off her first orgasm when he flipped her onto her back. His hips sunk against hers, positioned with his hard and throbbing cock at her entrance. Something grabbed unexpectedly at his chest seeing her satiated and riding her wave of pleasure beneath him. He'd imagined this moment for so long. Wanted to claim her. Explore her.

He slid his length against her slickness. Running his cock over her juices. Positioned right where he wanted to be.

"Yes. Lachie. Please." Belle grasped at his back. Her voice threaded with need and desire.

With a groan he surged forward.

"Fuck, you're so tight and wet. Just for me."

He sank deeper inside her. Then slid slowly out, before

gently pushing back a little further. Letting her adjust to his size. Feeling her pussy hot and wet around him.

Her breasts arched upwards. Fingers dug into his shoulders. “More, Lachie. That feels… so good.”

Everything pulsed through his senses at once. His magic raced across his heated skin then roved across her like a wild creature. The pulse of light caressed every curve. It was like they consumed each other. With mouths, touch, and power.

“Ohhhh yes.” Her hands grabbed at his back. Urging him deeper.

“So greedy for more?” Her eyes flashed in response at his husky tone. “Do you want to be fucked, my fierceling? Do you want me to take you hard? Have you come on my cock?”

Her moan came loud and urgent. A flood of wetness. Nails dug into his flesh.

With that he hitched her leg higher. Spreading her wide to him. He slammed into her. Over and over. The darkness pulsed with electric blue and gold from their sweat slicked bodies. She felt like ecstasy and redemption. His queen dragged him skyward from where he’d lain so long in darkness. Lifting him to a sense of pleasure he thought never possible for his tarnished soul. His hips bucked against hers, responding to her demands for him to go harder. Deeper.

He felt her tighten around him. A clench around his cock that had stars pin pricking behind his eyes.

“Lachie. Fuck, I’m so close.” She panted with a whimper.

He reached down between them and rubbed his thumb over that bundle of nerves. Her head thrown back in a silent scream she exploded beneath him. Walls clamping around his cock.

A groan ripped through his chest as he barrelled into his own orgasm on the heels of hers. With a shout he bucked wildly. Collapsing over her. In awe of her magnificence. Already planning their next round.

Your fated mate.

She wasn't going to be leaving his bed, or his arms. Ever again.

CHAPTER 23

"I was told the dark prince didn't do attachment."

Belle teased as she wriggled herself backwards against his torso. Wrapped tight in his powerful arms. Delicious and possessive energy bundled her back tightly towards Lachie's chest. The dim pre-dawn light hung drowsy in the air.

Lachie held onto her with a fierceness. As though he couldn't bear to risk her slipping from his grasp. A continual touch of her skin. The pads of his fingers stroked gently across the soft swell of her stomach. Fingers laced with hers. Open mouth kisses against her neck. She allowed a quiet smile to spread across her features, recalling how he hadn't let her go for a moment since the night before.

He'd watched her every ecstatic climax. Responded to her

every movement. Absorbed her essence with a reverence that felt all consuming.

The detached mask he so carefully curated for the rest of their world had dropped away piece by piece throughout the night. He had unravelled in more ways than one. Letting her see his heart laid bare.

"You're mine."

A warmth danced across her lips, Belle felt more powerful and in control than ever. Choosing to surrender to his commands. Holding her strength while allowing him to take charge. His sensual whiskey tone flooding her with pleasure over and over. He adored her with his words, his mouth, and his body.

Spirits save her. His body. More specifically his cock. Long, hard, and the perfect thickness. Her clit throbbed at the thought of it filling her once more. How was she already needing him? Belle felt a fresh wave of arousal between her legs.

Neither of them had slept. Too far lost in exploring each other. He'd made good on his promise to only have her coming apart on his mouth and his cock. Again and again. Her thighs clenched involuntarily at the mere thought of him buried inside her.

Lachie was the perfect mixture of raw desire and respect. Hard and shattering in his claim on her, yet tender and sensual in his adoration. Who knew that having Ampher powers would result in endless pools of pleasure. She had the vague soreness and post-orgasmic bliss to prove it, but was ready for more.

He pinched her thigh. A low warning growl sent a wave of tingles through her body. A slow stroke of his magic straight to her clit.

"Did I not show you enough last night to prove otherwise? When it comes to you..."

She arched back into him. Feeling his erection, already hard and demanding against her flesh.

Belle wanted him with every fibre of her being. To be his, as much as she desired Lachie to belong to her. With her. Intertwined forever.

He cupped her sex firmly, his touch a thrill and command all in one. Teeth nipped on her earlobe as he rasped against her ear.

"Know this, my fierceling. You are the essence flowing in every breath I take. The extension of my heart. Where you go, I will always be. There is no realm or magic that could separate me from you."

A sensation grew from the palm of his hand where it firmly cupped her flesh. Soothing yet imbued with an undeniable strength. She felt it wash through her, suddenly relieving all the previous evidence of soreness. His magic healed her in more ways than one.

"I like this side to you much better than that '*this can't happen*' mess you came up with on the Solstice." Belle bit her lip. Now she really was wildly aroused. A flutter of something unfamiliar rose deep inside her.

"Do you need me to repeat myself?" With a swift motion he rolled her beneath his frame. "You. Are. Mine."

"Always." She reached and placed her palm over his heart. Infusing soft Ampher magic through into his chest. Determined to show him her inner most essence. Where no barriers guarded them from straying over the edge and plunging into a chasm of vulnerability.

"And you, Lachlan of Nocturne, are mine." She purred.

Lachie's aquamarine eyes darkened into lust laden pools.

He reached down to slide his cock between her wetness. Belle's back arched in response. Desperate to be closer. Magic skimmed her every nerve ending and drove her wild. The head of his cock pressed at her entrance. The tantalising moment sent a shiver up her spine. Her tongue ran across her bottom lip and the closeness of him filled her once more.

On impulse, Belle grabbed the back of his neck to pull him down in a rough kiss. Their lips crushed together. Her own small way of claiming him in that heartbeat moment. Pushing him to feel how desperately she needed him. Their mouths fused together in a breathless spiral of pleasure. Tongues tangled in a wave of passion and unspoken promises.

Lachie broke away with a wicked smirk and nudged her chin upwards with his nose. Lips brushed against the column of her throat. Teeth nipped softly at her flushed skin.

"Not yet satisfied?" He gripped her hands and shoved them over her head. Her wrists pinned in place. The ache between Belle's thighs intensified. A flood of wetness soaked her at the gravel in his voice. Need surged through her veins. She was beyond ready for him to be inside her.

Not just her body, but her heart and mind. Totally

consumed by the perfection of this witch. His care and attention threaded throughout every moment together.

"Is this sweet pussy of yours needing another good fucking?" Lachie surged forward. Both groaned at the sensation as his cock slid inside her drenched entrance. The solid thickness of him moved in short, slow thrusts.

"Fuck. You take me so perfectly." A strain carried in Lachie's voice as his hips bucked forward.

Only Belle's soft pants and moans filled the air in reply. Her body all consumed with the stretch of her inner muscles. Then the bliss as he drove deep. *So fucking deep.*

"Yes. Harder." Her head fell back on a loud moan.

Lachie's eyes blazed. His jaw tightened as his thrusts snapped forward. Slamming their bodies into the mattress over and over. Every slide of his enormous cock stoked the fire where it raged within. Intense pleasure rippled beneath each unyielding hard pound of his body.

Belle didn't want to be treated gently in that moment. She wanted every inch of him. To be reduced to nothing but pleasure. Raw passion. To see him let go and expose that deepest part of his soul just for her.

After a lifetime of being unwanted. Abandoned. Kept in servitude. Here wrapped in his arms she was exalted into a realm of pleasure. Adored and protected. Given her own power and encouraged to use it. More than that... empowered to wield it.

Belle's head thrashed against the pillow. She tried to twist her wrists free, but his grip held firm. She needed all of him, yet was ready for desperate release. To melt into the white hot light of her climax.

Her mind blazed with the surety that even in the rough moments, she could trust him to take care of her.

"Please—I..." Her words faltered in her throat when Lachie sucked one hardened nipple. A spiral of pleasure sent her wildly close to the edge. With every thick stroke of his cock hitting just the spot to have her vision blanking. Lost in the depths of how good she felt.

His hot wet mouth moved over her other breast. Dragging his teeth across the pebbled bud. With a sudden cry Belle felt the wave crash inside her. Her orgasm rolling through in an all consuming release. Violet light surged from her skin. Gold specks glittered in the darkness filling the air above their bodies.

She was still riding the wave of her orgasm when Lachie pulled out and flipped her over onto her front. Boneless and delirious with pleasure. Face and arms pressed hard into the pillows. Only her knees held her up off the bed.

His powerful arms caged her in. The searing heat of his mouth grazed between her shoulder blades as he thrust forward. Slow, deliberate motions stretching the ecstasy tighter. He drew out to the tip before plunging back in again. His groan echoed around the room.

"I can feel it all. So good. You're fucking perfection."

It was all Belle could do to murmur incoherently into the pillow. Her brain completely scrambled. Her veins pulsing with his magic. A heady fervour lit her on fire along every nerve ending.

Already heat built in her core. His rhythm stoked that dark desire. Soft moans streamed from her mouth mixing with his deep groans. Their breaths panted shorter and faster.

She pushed back at him, wanting more. For him to experience his own release.

"Right there—Ohhhh." She breathed.

She reached down between her legs. Her fingers rubbed needy circles over her clit. So close. The swell of tension had her dancing right on the edge again.

Lachie shifted his weight so that he pressed along her back. Hot skin melded against her own. Covering her completely with his body and addictive friction. Her body throbbed. His power flooded her senses. An electrical charge tensioned for explosive release.

"Good girl." His voice rasped against her ear.

Fuck. He might as well have found her orgasm button with just those two words.

Belle cried out as wave after wave of pleasure ran through her. Her walls rippled around his cock. Lachie shuddered. His groan rumbled across the back of her neck. His orgasm barrelling through him. His hips bucked against her as his hot release filled her over and over, running down her thighs.

Their bliss rolled through the room. Sparks crackled and forked like lightning from their naked bodies.

Her gasps came in ragged breaths. Lachie's chest heaved against her back where he draped over her body. His mouth pressed against her molten skin. Each kiss against her reverently followed the sheen of sweat glistening down her spine.

With a satiated groan Lachie rolled them both so they fell on their side, not yet moving out of her. His palms caressed up and down her body. Adoration covered every curve of her flesh as his touch ran across her skin.

His hand stilled. Fingers brushed with gentle exploration across her stomach where her wounds had been from the night of the attack. Lachie shifted his weight down her body and kissed softly along that spot.

Where once there had been only darkness, he now filled the void with hope. Possibility. Maybe a deeper connection of their two souls. The kind of love her guarded heart yearned for in secret.

She wasn't willing to let herself go there. Not for now. That opened up too much risk.

"I'll hunt them and kill them all for what they did to you. You'll never be harmed again, my fierceling. I'll make sure of it until my last breath." Lachie's lips pressed against each invisible wound.

Belle wriggled around until she faced him. Her Guardian. Her fingers reached up to trace the frown lines where they cragged across his face.

"I know you will, old man." She teased, wanting to keep the air light between them.

A wicked glint crossed his eyes. The smallest of quirks tugged at the corner of his mouth.

"Three hundred years is hardly *old* in this realm." He

dragged her to lie in the crook of his shoulder as he shifted onto his back.

An easy silence fell between them. Belle could hear the steady thud of his heart beneath her head as it rested against his torso. Every beat a steady reassurance for her soul.

"You still have your ring on." Lachie's voice held a tone of both relaxation and reverence. As though he couldn't quite believe it to be real. His fingers twined with hers as he brought it to his lips.

"You said never to take it off. Why?"

He paused for a beat. His thumb brushed across the pulse in her wrist. Belle could practically hear her Guardian's mind at work calculating a careful answer, before he exhaled. The internal battle put down for a temporary truce.

"As long as you wear this ring..." He started, then paused with a heavy swallow.

Was he nervous?

"I can portal directly to you. No matter where you are. Across any realm or dimension." His fingers squeezed a fraction tighter against her hand. As though braced for her to flee at his admission.

"It binds me to you."

CHAPTER 24

It binds me to you.

Belle felt a lazy grin spread across her face as she recalled Lachie's words. The way they had melted her insides. Spirits, she was in deep with the way that witch undid her.

She lifted her chin to the warm glow of sunlight as she stepped outside. The air here in the courtyard vibrated with the pulse of magic. The castle felt comforting. Inviting. It felt... like home.

"Oh, so you *are* alive then?" A loud voice cut across her thoughts.

Brigid's impish grin lit up from where she sat sprawled in her recliner. Positioned in her favourite sun drenched spot to oversee the other witches harnessing their craft. She sat draped in a gold robe with a silver coloured fan in one hand, looking every inch the elfin queen as usual. The courtyard contained its regular hive of magic swirling through the air. Small groups of supernaturals bunched together with various elements soaring through the space.

Belle scurried across the gravel, narrowly avoiding a surge of water from a cluster of young witches. A series of mortified expressions plastered across their faces as they watched the swirling liquid veer wildly out of control.

“Could you keep it down?” Belle hissed as she threw herself onto the pile of luxurious cushions scattered beside where the Enchantress sat.

“I’m just relieved my brother has finally permitted you to leave his lair.” With a giggle Brigid cocked a knowing eyebrow. “I was beginning to think you might be held hostage in his bed until the Autumn Equinox at this rate.”

“Brigid!” Belle’s cheeks flushed with heat as she let out a protest.

The problem with having a Seer around was that Belle could never tell just how detailed the witch’s sight was. Spirits, how much would be evident about her time with Lachie?

Her thighs clamped together at the rush of images.

“Is this sweet pussy of yours needing another good fucking?”

The grip of his fingers against her skin. His lips branding hers. Those commanding growls that turned her insides to puddles of pleasure. Tingles ran through her skin at the thought. She had convinced him they both needed daylight, fresh air, and proper food. Lachie had argued they could enjoy all of that from his rooms, but eventually relented after dragging her into the bath with him that morning.

Stars, her entire being was consumed.

She didn't dare think about the state of her heart. Surely if she stopped to look she would find it had vacated the premises. Gladly given over to his possession.

"Rusakia! You have to hold your line of sight! Your water flurries are going to flood the entrance hall." Brigid's shout cut through Belle's daydream. With a snap the fan whipped closed and Brigid pointed the end at the young witch who had nearly soaked Belle moments before.

"Draya, you show her what we practiced last week please." She turned and fixed her gaze back on Belle. "Phew, is it just me or did it suddenly get rather steamy out here." With a flourish she flipped her fan back open and gave an exaggerated flutter across her chest.

"This is so embarrassing." Belle buried her face in her hands. Certain that every inch of her skin must be crimson.

"You understand that I've seen this coming for a long time, no?"

"You've... what?"

"Well, more precisely, I've seen different variations of this moment. There's always different ways the same result pans out in the bigger scheme." Brigid uncrossed then recrossed her legs with a distant look on her face. "Of course it isn't a precise thing, I see the possibilities but rarely a decisive outcome."

Great. A kaleidoscope of all the ways Belle could have

wound up falling into Lachie's arms. She shifted her weight, tugging on a tasseled edge to one of the purple velvet cushions.

"How do you live with it? Surely holding all that must be heavy on you?" Belle sensed there were a multitude of depths to this. More than Brigid was prepared to let on.

"Ah, my Seer's privilege from the Goddesses. Know all. See all. Let go of all." She paused to watch a pillar of flame erupt from the far corner of the courtyard. "My vow of non-intervention to the deities gives me trust. What is meant to be will be, no?"

There was a wistful tone to Brigid's voice. Her usual brightness had an edge to it that felt like grasping at the last rays of sunlight. A sense of inevitability that accompanies the darkness one must transcend before the coming dawn.

A crackle of electricity whipped along the outer wall to the courtyard. Starbursts exploded from each branched fork. A short witch with brown skin and curly pink hair let out an excited squeal as she stared at her hands in awe.

"Epherenie! That was magnificent!" Brigid dropped her fan and clapped her hands together. "Next we'll work on extending your range."

Others ran over to where the witch stood beaming, quickly surrounding her with hugs. Belle felt her heart squeeze at the sight. Her Ampher soaked up the buoyant celebrations from across the courtyard like inhaling a rainbow. All wondrous hues and textures of excitement shimmered through her aura. She closed her eyes as the sun caressed her face. Her body humming with relaxation.

"Is Nell in the herbarium?" Belle wondered out loud, eyes still closed.

"Not exactly..."

Belle's eyes popped open.

"She needed to travel to the mountains. It was all rather sudden, and seeing as you were a little preoccupied..." Brigid's elf-like features gave an exaggerated wink.

Letting out a groan Belle dropped her head back. "So Nell knows everything I'm guessing?"

"Couldn't leave them in the dark now could I?"

"THEM?"

"Lia..."

Shit.

"And of course Fehrn, since they have headed off-realm..." Brigid continued and ticked off her fingers as she spoke.

Fuck.

"And then Niall is travelling with Nell, so he was right there."

Spirits. No.

"So then everyone knows? Where we've been? And... what we've been doing?!" Belle squeaked.

"Rowan eventually came looking for Lachie when he didn't show up for sparring, so I gave him the good news too." Brigid's eyes danced with mischief.

Belle flopped face first into the cushions. Rainbow aura or not, this wasn't exactly how she intended to share the progression in their... situation. Surely there must be some kind of protocol around the Guardian of the Realm's attachments—

romantic or otherwise—but Lachie hadn't indicated what that might be.

"Would you rather Rowan had interrupted you both? He was on his usual grumpy war path straight for Lachie's rooms when I headed him off."

"NO!" Belle clutched at Brigid's arm. "Thank you. I am grateful."

Ancestors. Open a pit right here and let the ground swallow me up.

"Here, sip on this." Brigid waved her fan and a steaming tea set on a gilded tray appeared beside Belle. "You're looking a little peaky. I've charged it with something to take the edge off."

With a relieved sigh Belle scooped up the cup and saucer, cradling it to her lips. The liquid seeped down her throat, trailing a thread of sweet nectar. Her shoulders softened. Ease flooded her chest undoing the knots formed while they had been talking.

"You're not the first supernatural power couple to walk these castle corridors and you won't be the last." Brigid coyly hid her face behind her fan, wiggling her eyebrows over the top of the black silk.

Another sip drained the last of the tea. Belle set the saucer back down on the tray only to watch it vanish before her eyes. She massaged her temples and let out a long exhale.

Everything is ok. You've survived much worse than this.

"How did I possibly manage to miss the fact that everyone has vacated the castle?" Belle mused out loud.

"I'd say it had something to do with my brother..."

"I knew Lia and Fehrn were due to travel, but Nell?" Belle pointedly ignored her interjection.

"Something about healing qualities and the mountains."

"You know why she's gone, don't you?"

"Of course. I know all."

There was something off in Brigid's mannerisms now as she spoke. A tension where her fingers gripped the edge of her fan. But Belle couldn't quite put her finger on it.

"Now Lia and Fehrn might be some time. They're tracking the source of disturbances in the Fae Dominion. Their royals sent a request for urgent assistance."

A sense of unease rushed into Belle's chest. Surely this was what had needed Lachie's attention today. But no doubt he should have been present sooner. Guilt clawed at her throat. Would he see her as being a distraction still, despite everything that had passed between them?

"Niall will make his way to join them in the Fae Dominion once he's delivered Nell safely. Rowan is on his way there with Lachie now." Brigid narrowed her eyes, studying the courtyard in a way that appeared to see the unseen.

"What happened?" A prickling sensation ran up the back of Belle's neck.

"The Fae King. His entire lineage has been assassinated."

CHAPTER 25

"Can't I come with you?"

Belle fluttered her eyelashes from where she lay tangled in the bedsheets. A freshly washed Lachie tugged his black shirt over his damp chest. The sight of his muscled chest, tousled hair, and half dressed state scorched a line straight to her clit.

Nevermind the three orgasms already this morning and the hazy glow of waking up with Lachie's tongue between her thighs.

Obviously her brain had vacated, leaving behind a body that was enthralled by his touch.

And Belle couldn't be happier.

Lachie's lips twitched at the corner as he raked his gaze across her disheveled state.

"I think you'd best be getting some well earned rest." His eyes sparked with mischief.

"But—"

The side of the bed dipped under his powerful frame. He leaned over her, resting his weight on both hands. His dark stare caused her breath to stall in her throat. Where his eyes fixed on hers she could see they glistened with intensity.

"But nothing, my fierceling. Trust me. I desire nothing more than to crawl back into this bed and keep taking care of that needy pussy of yours."

Molten heat clenched between her thighs.

Oh. Fuck. The way those words undo me.

"And yet, I have to go meet with Niall and the new line of succession in the Fae Dominion. Since the assassination there is a new lineage the crown has passed to." He nuzzled her neck and drew in a deep inhale. "I also want to pay my respects. The Fae King was a good man. His family too."

"But I—" Belle struggled to sit up while clutching the sheet to her chest.

"No." The command in his voice was unmistakable. Gentle, yet with firm resolve. "I can do my duty much better knowing you are safe right here."

She opened her mouth to protest before snapping it shut. He was right. Though she was loathed to admit it.

"Can you trust me that it is safest for you *not* to travel to a Dominion in turmoil and now potentially infiltrated with unknown numbers of loyalists to the House of Elharean?" His voice was stern but there was a teasing glint in his eyes.

"Fine." She huffed out a breath.

He let out a chuckle at the sight of her reluctant concession.

"Now, let me have one last look at what I'll be missing all day." With a slow glide of his hand the sheet slid across Belle's breasts, over the soft curve of her stomach, and stopped just below her hips. The material trailed a blaze of sensation in its wake. Aquamarine pools of desire coated every inch of her flesh in adoration. She felt so exposed. Fully naked under his stare while his muscled frame stood tensed and fully clothed. The contrast of their two forms a heady mixture to take in.

Something lurched in her chest at the smile dancing along the corners of his lips. An ease that softened around his eyes.

Dangerous territory, Belle. Best not to think too long about that.

Before she could take another shaky breath Lachie slanted his mouth over hers. A searing promise of devotion. Long, languid strokes of his tongue melted Belle under his attentions.

A vague recognition stole into her mind of his fingertips brushing over her hip. Without breaking their kiss his thumb traced short strokes across her skin. Tingles shot everywhere through her body like a shimmer of gold dust. Was that from the kiss? His touch? His magic? Belle didn't know and didn't care.

He pulled back with a satisfied rumble. Lips parted as though words were ready to pour forward. Yet they didn't come. The air between them hung heavy with unspoken emotion.

One hand wrapped around hers. A brief second of contact as his finger slid over her ring. A light smirk flicked across his features. Then swirling mist enclosed his figure. The weight on the bed where Lachie had been only a moment before vanished.

She was alone.

Spirits. That's one heck of a way to avoid vocalising your feelings. Just portal to another realm.

Belle flopped her head back against the pillow. Her days still felt tinged with aimlessness here in the castle. Besides training to harness her magic and her art, she had expanses of time at her disposal. With no upcoming ball to organise or herbarium tasks without Nell around, it left her adrift. Becalmed in the midst of a vast ocean of magical possibility.

The lure of hot water and steam proved irresistible. Even in the face of the gnawing uncertainty about her future. With a huffed out breath, Belle swung her legs over the side of the bed. She flicked her wrist and heard the sweet sound of water cascading from the bathroom. Steam and the scents of sandalwood, citrus, and lavender enveloped her as she opened the door.

Fuck I love magic.

Belle's smile stretched wide as she walked under the waterfall of warm water. A magical infusion of healing and soothing potions through each droplet. A cloud of steam gathered above her head and below her feet. The source of the water and where it magically disappeared into. She ran her fingers through her long hair, massaging her scalp with the liquid potion. Her eyes dropped closed at the memory of how Lachie had pressed her against that exact spot on the stone wall yesterday. His slow, rhythmic thrusts in and out of her beneath the waterfall.

Shit.

A wave of intense pleasure coiled low inside her stomach. Her clit throbbed.

What was that?

Her body usually reacted to little daydream moments of Lachie, but this felt far more intense. Belle shook her head. It was nothing. Time to dress and pour her energy into some artwork. Even if she had no words to express what was happening in her life right now, drawing always helped.

A wave of her hand cleared the air, the water disappearing before her eyes. Magic hummed across her damp skin like a dewy afterglow. The glide of her favourite silk robe hugged her curves as she tied the waist in a bow. She had barely returned to her own rooms of late. The privacy of Lachie's suite was far more preferable. Especially since he'd kept his promise to have her screaming his name every night. She never imaged herself so... vocal in bed.

A flame crawled up her neck and scalded her cheeks. Her breasts felt heavy. Nipples hardened into tight buds. Her pussy as slick and wet as if Lachie was settled between her thighs.

Fuck. What is happening?

The ache of keen arousal spread through her. She was barely on her own for an hour and was already a tinderbox waiting for a match to strike alight.

This was going to be a long day.

Parchment, brushes, and her portfolio lay on the window seat. Belle settled back against the cushions with her legs tucked under her. A quick tap of her finger in mid air conjured her favourite tea and she reached eagerly for the cup. She surveyed the drawings and sketches fanned out over the velvet seat.

Belle's fingers flexed around the ceramic, the warmth of the tea gently stroked her skin. Her mind drifted once again to the rapid unfolding of events since the news from the Fae Dominion. Lachie took everything in his stride with calm and considered thought. He truly had a gift as Guardian. The soft patience she had witnessed as he answered the many questions of the Fae who chose to live here in the Soterian Realm.

He was a study in duality. A fierce warrior when required. At other times a compassionate leader who grounded the energy of those around him despite any storm raging outside. Her heart squeezed at just how generous this witch could be.

And her thighs squeezed at the thought of just how generous Lachie could be in bed too.

Belle's lips parted on a soft moan. Her head dropped back. Eyelids hooded with pleasure.

Fuck me that feels so good.

Her pussy clenched as the sensation filled her. A pulse of friction hit just the right spot inside. It was as if— no it couldn't be possible? Another moan escaped her throat.

It was like Lachie's fingers pushed into her. As if... his hand was right there fucking her.

Stars. What in the magical orgasm enchantments is this?

With a jolt, her eyes flew open. The cup clattered onto its saucer. With shaky fingers she clawed at the edge of her robe to bunch the material up. Staring back at her from her hip was the blue glow of a star shaped sigil.

That smirk on his face just before he portaled. The brush strokes of his thumb on her hip. It all swam into focus.

She was going to kill him.

CHAPTER 26

The swirl of mist billowed beneath his boots as Lachie stepped into his study. A burnt orange glow swept across the room as the sun hung low and heavy on the horizon framed by the massive windows. He peeled off his jacket and glanced around. Belle's drawings lay sprawled across the cushions below the window, bathed in the light of the setting sun.

"YOU."

Lachie turned towards the sound of Belle's voice. Harsh and accusatory.

"I. Am. Not. Amused." She ground out.

He fought back a laugh with a cough into his fist. His little witch stood flushed and breathless in the doorway to the bathroom. Her cheeks stained pink. Eyes wild.

"Fuck. You." Belle's hands balled into fists at her sides.

Stars, his cock jerked at the vision before him. He'd spent the day trying to imagine what would await him upon his return. This was infinitely more erotic than he could have dreamed.

"How was your day?" His words slid out like silk. Happy to play innocent awhile longer and draw out this game. With a casual shrug he dropped into one of the armchairs beside the fireplace.

"Don't even— You can't possibly—" Belle tripped over her words.

"Something wrong?" He cocked an eyebrow and his lips twitched. Part of him wanted to launch at her, pin her to the bed, and lose himself in her body. To make her come undone over and over. The other part enjoyed seeing just how far he could tease his beauty while she stood before him.

Her plump lips parted in silent protest. Electricity crackled through the ether between them.

"Did you have a stimulating day?"

"Not funny."

"Anything in particular occupy your mind?" He couldn't help himself. The bait dangled in front of him and he gladly swiped at it like a hawk.

"My hip. The sigil. Your magic?" Her voice dropped low and breathy. She gripped the back of the chair in front of her.

Lachie felt heat pulse low in his stomach. Fuck. He needed to hold tight to his chain. This witch undid him at every turn. He needed her to feel just a taste of how it felt for him, lost in her depths day after day. The constant pull inside his chest to be near her. An insistent and all consuming desire to protect what was his.

Your mate.

“What was on your mind today, my fierceling?” Lachie’s voice came out low as he eased to his feet and prowled towards her.

Belle whimpered. Her head dropped backwards with heavy lidded eyes.

“You have to use your words.” It took all his strength to keep from reaching out to touch her. To tug at the silk tie at her waist and see just how soaking she would be. He could see her body held tense.

“I can’t... I tried... please...” Soft, muffled noises of frustration came from her throat.

“Tell me. Who were you thinking about today?” He hovered over her ear. Close enough to feel the heat scorch between their bodies. Still yet to touch her.

“You. It got worse. Every time.” Belle’s hands fisted her silk robe at her thighs. The fabric inched higher under his stare.

“And what did you do? Did you touch yourself thinking of me? Did you try ease that ache, my little beauty?”

Belle nodded. Eyes squeezed closed.

“I did. But I couldn’t—nothing helped—I don’t know why.”

“Ahh. Do you need something?”

Another soft moan was Belle’s only reply. She bit her bottom lip. Lachie’s cock strained against his trousers at the sight. His pleasure and pain intermingled in a frenzy inside his chest.

Fuck. Fuck. Breathe. She needs you to go slow.

"Belle." His voice now dark edged.

Goosebumps skittered across her arms in response as she stood wrapped in his magic. Desire flooding through her aura. Gold orbs formed and spiralled slow about the room. A mirror of the pressure wound tight in his own muscles.

"Lachie. I—" Her voice died in her throat.

His resolve snapped. The chain shattered at the plea of his name on her lips. He moved back across the study to the couch and dropped onto his back. With a quick shove of a pillow behind his head he laid down. Eyes fixed on his prize.

"Up here. On your knees." He commanded.

Belle's eyes popped open. Crimson rushed down her neck to disappear below the join of her robe. She scrambled forward to straddle just above his hips. At the touch of her palms against his chest and thighs pressed to his sides a surge of power raced through his veins. Her eyes widened at the sensation as it coursed through her own body.

"Oh fuck." She sobbed.

"Just the start." He ground out. His erection pulsed against the curves of her backside. What he wouldn't do for this witch.

"Please…"

"If you pull this silk up, am I going to find you dripping for me, little fierceling?"

Belle bit her lip. Hard.

"Show me." His hands gripped her thighs. Fingers dug into that soft, smooth flesh.

Her eyes flashed. Pupils blown and fully dilated. With a

slow, unsteady breath she reached for the split in the silk. A small tug pulled the robe apart to splay across her hips. Lachie let out a groan at the sight. Her pussy, swollen and pink, glistening wet in the firelight.

"Lachie." She breathed. Luscious hips rocked slightly against his body. Desperate for friction.

He reached one hand for the curve at the top of her thigh and brushed the pad of his thumb over the glowing sigil. It vanished as he unbound the spell he cast that morning. Her fingers gripped his shirt in fistfuls. A choked sound escaped her throat followed by a shudder rippling through her entire body.

"Look at that pretty pussy of yours. Needy for attention. So fucking wet. You're soaking me, my fierceling." Lachie murmured. A slide of his hands higher up her thighs. His thumbs parted her as his eyes locked on her clit. Hungry to give her exactly the pleasure she craved.

To give her everything. Pleasure. Love. Unending. Forever.

"Please. Please. Please. Just fuck me." Belle begged as she trembled under his touch.

A guttural sound burst from Lachie's throat. He hooked behind her thighs and dragged her up to his mouth.

A surprised cry turned into a babble of incoherent words. Her fingers curled tight in his hair. His tongue flicked up and down against her clit, her taste pure nectar to his senses. She ground her hips against his mouth. The hours and hours of pressure ready to combust. To shatter into a million pin pricks of light on the night air.

With a moan Belle came apart against his tongue. Her

orgasm barrelled into him. Rapid and demanding. Their magic intertwined like an ouroboros chasing its tail. Nothing to separate between where one began and the other ended. Lachie lapped at the flood of wetness as she shuddered above him. Her body collapsed across the edge of the couch with soft keens of pleasure.

He continued to run his tongue over her. Massaging her down from that first release. His fingers flexing against her thighs to ensure his grip held her pressed firm against his mouth. A rumble of possessive desire surged through his veins.

He'd wring every ounce of pleasure from his little witch. Show her the care and attention she deserved. No, commanded. The ruler of his heart, soul, and mind. He would gladly lay down everything to worship the very air she breathed.

Careful to avoid the over sensitised nub, he worked his tongue back and forth. Pressure alternating with gentle strokes. A slow build of pleasure. Adoration infused with each tease and temptation.

"I need... I need you, Lachie." Belle panted, her voice hoarse and laced with a wild urgency.

A spark of pride flared.

My name looks good on my mate's lips.

Lachie moved his mouth over her hip. Lips brushed hot against her soft, perfect skin. A frustrated whine let loose from Belle's throat.

"Hmm, I don't even have to touch you do I? I could make you come through magic alone, my fierceling. But where's the fun in that? I'm selfish when it comes to you, little witch. I want to feel every ripple. Each tiny flicker of pleasure across your skin. I crave every grip of your pussy around my fingers and my cock when I talk to you like this."

Belle's mouth hung open. The look in her eyes pure sex.

"You're going to take everything I give you. You've been needy for my touch only a day. I've been needing you for an entire lifetime." Lachie rumbled. His breath hot against her thigh.

"Then hurry up." Her fingers tugged at his hair with a sharp pull.

He nipped the skin of her hip. Impatience looked divine scrawled across every inch of her creamy flesh.

Belle thumped the heel of her hand against the cushion.

"Lachie, please. I can't take it. Stop teasing me and fuck me."

"Not before I savour you."

Devour you. My mate.

Lachie's mind raced. His breath an unsteady and unfamiliar pattern. This had started as a flirtatious idea this morning. But his heart no longer belonged to him. It resided outside his body. Cradled in her hands to do with as she pleased. Nothing in the sigil placed false emotions inside of Belle, this lust and desire was already there. His spell only amplified what already existed and held it tensioned until his command allowed for release.

And that knowledge sent an aching spiral barelling through him. The unyielding need to touch, taste, and consume her body rode him. The drive to protect what was his. A fierce contract between their souls roared for attention like a meeting of waves at the shoreline. Never separate. Always connected. An ebb and flow of magic that swirled and danced around their bodies.

He'd always kept his true self in check. Hidden away behind the mask of duty. Never hoping to have something precious that was his and only his.

But now that old version of him had crumbled. He didn't want to ever go back to that lonely existence.

"Please."

The beg fell from Belle's throat. Raw and sultry. A softness in her plea that undid him completely.

His mouth fastened over her clit. A fresh flood of wetness soaked his tongue. Mist swirled around them and enclosed the small cry from Belle. An erotic echo pressed into the vapour. Their bodies fell through the portal onto Lachie's bed. He'd never normally use magic for such a short distance, but rational thought had long since scurried from his mind.

Ridding himself of his clothes, he pulled at her silk robe. The material hung bunched around Belle's waist. Her chest rose and fell in anticipation. Cheeks flushed and lips plump with arousal. Rosy budded nipples begged for his attention. His cock jerked at the sight of the vision spread across the sheets before him.

Dark pleasure pulsed through his core. With a yank he grasped her hips and flipped Belle onto all fours.

"Remember, little fierceling..." His fingers tugged her hair until his mouth brushed her ear. The head of his cock slid against her entrance. Her thighs soaked from her juices. His fist tightened around her silken mane. Eyes hooded at the sensation of her slickness coating him.

"You begged for this."

Lachie thrust forward with a single powerful motion. His cock slammed inside her tight, wet heat. Hours of arousal had her pussy so drenched he slid in easily. A groan erupted from his chest. Her walls fluttered around him.

"Fuck." Another, deeper growl.

"Yes. Yes." Belle's breath came in shallow pants.

Her neck arched a sensual curve along her spine. He withdrew enough to catch his breath. A soft keen muffled against the pillow. She pushed back against him.

"Good girl."

Lachie slammed forward again. His hips found a rhythm of pleasure and carnal devotion. Moan after moan filled the room.

"Your pussy is so fucking wet. So perfect for me. Taking me so beautifully."

His goddess cried out. Another clench around his cock. Adding more fuel to his desire to worship and give everything to her.

Again and again he thrust into her. Lost in her. Drowned. Her moans and small cries stoked the flame burning between their bodies higher. Golden light pulsed through the darkness. Their magic manifested in an intuitive, visceral form.

"Oh—OH." Belle's hands fisted the sheets. Her body tensed. Another climax about to crash through her.

"You'll come all over my cock, little witch. Give me what I want like the good girl you are." He reached around to stroke her clit. Hips pounding against her.

"Fuck!" Belle shattered under his touch. Her walls squeezed tight against his cock. Body shaking under his grip on her hips.

Lachie pulled out and turned her over before pressing back inside. Her body glowed with pleasure and molten desire beneath him. He slowed his pace, but kept up that rhythm he knew would have her body on edge again within moments. He couldn't fucking get enough of this. Of her.

His mate.

Soon Belle let out soft whimpers of pleasure. Another ripple of her pussy as it clenched around him. He angled deep, hitting the spot that would undo her beneath him. Grinding his hips harder.

And then she fell apart. Her moans filling the room. Lachie let out a curse as his movements shifted to rough thrusts. Heat and pressure seared down his spine, building and building until his release burst through him. His every sense blinded. All sound drowned out.

He slumped forward over her. Their heartbeats thundered and their pulses skittered against one another. His fingers ran along her curves. Hot skin and sweat slick between their bodies. He pressed his lips across her temple.

Time seemed to evaporate like the stars greeting the dawn. It was still there, present, but unfathomable. Her fingers trailed lazy strokes along the muscles of his back following the length of his spine.

A yawn crept from Belle's lips. She nuzzled into his shoulder with a tender, feather light kiss.

"Better?" The words rumbled against her softness beneath him. Still inside her. Neither of them able to move.

"Mmm. But I'm still going to kill you."

CHAPTER 27

"I'm nervous as fuck."

Belle chewed her lip and shot a glance at Brigid. The enchantress threaded her arm through the crook of Belle's elbow.

The great hall was a commotion of noise. Supernaturals from the Soterian Realm and beyond had gathered together for the Annual Nightfall Eclipse. They streamed across the castle grounds carrying lanterns or illuminating magic above their palms. According to Brigid this was a time when the change of fates and amplification of powers could be most potent. A little bit of chaos welcomed in to charge each individuals magical gifts and if the Goddesses decreed, perhaps bestow new magical attributes.

Expect the unexpected.

"You know there's nothing you have to do, no?" Brigid squeezed her arm with a laugh.

"But I feel like I'm on parade. Everyone keeps looking at me."

Belle heard the whispers. Or more accurately, could feel them as the snaked line headed towards the forest. Yet her magical shielding proved successful in the throng of the crowd. No accidental Ampher usage would be happening tonight.

"That's because you're the first Ampher..."

"In two hundred years. Yeah, yeah. Still doesn't make it any less intimidating."

"Well, if it helps we could give them something else to talk about. I'm sure my brother will be around here somewhere." Brigid trailed off as she mockingly scanned the crowd.

"Don't you even think about it!" Belle whispered loudly through gritted teeth. She knew Lachie wasn't nearby. He wasn't attending the Nightfall at all. He had left earlier to meet with Niall in the Fae Dominion. There was no doubt Brigid's gift as a Seer was perfectly aware of that too.

Nevertheless she certainly didn't feel ready to announce her and Lachie's relationship to hundreds of supernaturals. She'd had barely enough time to come to terms with those closest to them in the castle knowing about... what to even call what they had between them? Their bond?

Relationship felt like a paltry, pale shade of a word. What connected her and Lachie represented something so much more. Something soul deep and seeped in ancient magic. A contract across time and space.

You're mine.

The way Lachie rasped those words to her at night when they lay in bed. His arms holding her tight against his chest. As if he feared she would vanish beneath his fingers.

Those words connected to something primal within her magic. It didn't feel possessive or controlling. Being with him felt empowering. She felt cherished. Adored. Celebrated for being exactly herself. As if on her own she was powerful and being together only added to those gifts.

Every moment with Lachie erased those awful memories of what might have been. Of the night when her life as she had always known it ended. One way or another, the old Annabelle was meant to die that night. Whether at the hands of the snatchers or the shadowy figure of her nightmares. Every soft kiss and whisper against her hair from Lachie filled that darkness. Replacing those memories with hope and comfort.

Perhaps even love. The kind that commands every fibre of a being. Love that traverses lifetimes. Love that endures even the greatest challenges.

"Brigid of Nocturne. May Nightfall blessings shower upon you from the Goddesses." The syrupy tones cut across Belle's thoughts. Heavy perfume wound its way through her senses. There was no mistaking the witch whose voice carried across the night air.

Luciana.

Crimson fingernails pulled at the hood of her golden cloak, folding it down to reveal long red curls. Of course they fell perfectly in place. Belle couldn't help but take in the full ensemble Luciana wore for the eclipse. No doubt planned meticulously to draw attention. A skin tight gold dress clung to every curve and accentuated her voluptuous form beneath the long cape. She radiated power, sex, and opulence.

"Luce, don't you look pulse-stopping as always." Brigid purred. Trust the elfin Enchantress to be lured in by an outfit of full gold. Belle's eyes rolled in her head. So much for solidarity in agreeing to loathe this witch for eternity.

"And of course, Nightfall blessings to you too... Ampher." A pair of narrowed eyes flickered up and down Belle in assessment. Or more likely judgement.

"It's Belle, actually." She squared her shoulders.

"Ahh. Look at you. Finally learning to shield yourself." Luciana gave a wry laugh. "Would hate to see harm come to Lachie's little pet on a night like tonight."

Her Ampher rippled at the edges of her aura. The witch pressed against Belle's magical shield with her own power. A test of the boundary between them. This time the poisonous magic was repelled and held back from entering Belle's system.

"Luce." Brigid's voice remained bright, but held a sternness that wasn't there before. "You'll recall our little conversation recently, no?"

Belle shot a look at Brigid. Eyes slightly widened in silent question.

"Of course. Just congratulating the lovely Belle on her achievements is all." The sickly sweet words grated. And since when had Brigid been having private meetings with Luciana?

"Anytime you need, our coven is at your service." With a

wink, the gold cloak and flaming red hair spun in place and the witch slipped into the darkness.

A quick glance confirmed the gathered crowd had moved deeper into the forest. Twinkling lantern lights scattered in the distance pin pricked the darkness through the trees.

"Shall we?" The grin and sparkle danced in Brigid's eyes. No hint of what had just transpired left in her demeanour. They might as well have been lazing beside their favourite swimming hole in the sunshine.

"You go on without me. I think I'd rather head back to my suite." Belle's fingers ran over her hair to tuck it behind her ear. The last thing she felt like doing right now was being surrounded by supernaturals.

"Are you sure? I can walk you back?"

"No, I'll be fine. Go on. Promise to tell me all about it over breakfast tomorrow?" Belle wondered what the chances were that Brigid had already seen this entire conversation play out in her mind's eye.

Despite the care and attention her friends lavished upon her, Belle still felt an unease surrounded by this many other supernaturals. Almost as though she had learned to be in this new and unfamiliar world, but not yet be fully part of it herself. An outsider looking in. The small doses she had experienced so far were more than enough. But she needed more time. Tonight's gathering felt like a bridge too far. Having the knowledge that she could retreat into her solitude back at the castle was a welcome reprieve.

"Deal." Brigid pecked a kiss against her cheek. A flicker of something tugged at her features for the briefest second, then it was gone.

"Nightfall blessings bestowed by the Goddesses come no matter where you are or what you do. The whole meet in the forest thing is just an added bit of fun. Sleep well." Brigid disappeared towards the forest, her lantern swinging playfully in the darkness.

"Count me out on receiving any extra blessings, thanks. I've got more than enough to try manage at this rate." Belle muttered under her breath.

Turning, she made her way back to the castle. Windows glowed warm and inviting as she hastened inside. She turned towards her own suite as she climbed the grand staircase. It had been days since she was last back there. Yet even now it felt strange to think she had ever been content staying apart from Lachie.

Even so, her recent visits had only been to collect a few more things for her art. She hadn't spent any time here for... she had lost track of how long. A pang of guilt nipped at her insides. Was it wrong to fall so fast and so hard into the welcoming embrace of Lachie? Should she be trying to set some distance between the two of them?

Her head pounded at the thought. Now wasn't the moment to be trying to make decisions about boundaries in their relationship. She felt wild and unsettled. Too strung out from the encounter with Luciana. No, she wouldn't be in the right frame of mind to sketch tonight. She had books to collect from her rooms.

A good book and a soak in the bath would calm her frayed nerves.

The flame from her lantern filled the room with a soft golden hue as she pushed the door open. The books lay just where she had left them on the window seat. She crossed the room, scooping the stack up.

As she bent down blood drained from her face at the sight before her. Belle's legs buckled and the lantern clattered to floor.

A tunnel of darkness enveloped her as she sank down. Numb.

CHAPTER 28

Another chilling wave swept through Belle's body. Legs pulled tight to her chest. Back wedged against the wall. Her eyes scrunched closed. A numb sensation had long permeated her bones. One that threatened to extinguish any residual spark that lingered.

The room pooled inky black around her ankles. Her lantern long since burnt out. Her shaking hands unable to focus any trace of magic to relight the wick.

A perfect metaphor for the crumpled state she found herself in. Hope and possibility snuffed out with one swift change in the wind. The fates had sent her the foul, insidious taste of the unexpected indeed.

The scent of cedar wood and a cool dampness brushed at her skin. Despite the gloomy thrall of her rooms, the now familiar billows of mist pressed up against her.

Warm hands enclosed her face. Lachie's forehead pressed to hers.

"Are you alright?" His voice cracked. Softness underscored with a fierce demand for her response.

Belle squeezed her eyelids tighter. Not yet willing to open them and allow the vulnerable contents of her soul to be witnessed. This wasn't his battle. She couldn't bring herself to allow the hurt to spill over into Lachie. He was too honourable. Too generous. She knew he would offer to take it away, yet it clawed at her insides to hold it in. Not to burden him with the raw pain gripping like a vice around her throat.

A gentle thumb stroke brushed against her tear stained cheek.

"My fierceling. Look at me." He murmured. Soft and coaxing.

Lachie gripped her chin, but she refused to give in to the comfort in his touch. Her mouth twisted. The dam holding emotions captive threatened to burst. Hot tears stung her closed eyelids. Sobs threatened to cascade forth in brutal torrents.

"Belle." The Guardian edged to the forefront in his tone.

With hesitant blinks she opened her eyes. The puffed and swollen skin felt leaden. Belle's cheek turned to face the spot on the floor beside his boots where he kneeled before her. One look in his direction and it would break her resolve.

He doesn't need to bear this.

I can protect him from this.

My pain is my own burden to carry.

Her eyes made out the faint shape of the books spilled across the floor. The pale, nauseating glow of a sheet of parchment stared back at her where it had dropped from her hands.

Strong fingers still grasped her chin and guided her face forward. Lachie tilted her chin upwards ever so softly. Beneath the tender action stalked a trembling rage. She could feel the weight of it thrumming through his veins.

Unable to resist the magnetic pull of him, her eyes rose to meet his. Aquamarine flames glinted in the dark. A thousand questions raced intense, unyielding, and unspoken.

"Who. Did. This. To. You?" Words came through gritted teeth.

The barbed wire encasing her throat strangled taught. Hot wet tears spilled over in rivulets down her cheeks. Her shoulders shook. The wall she had held up crumbled under Lachie's touch.

The room tilted as she found herself dragged into his lap. Her body enclosed by his. Lips brushed her temple and hands soothed across her back. Belle buried her face into his neck, her body convulsing with each sob that tore from her chest.

His magic wove through her aura. Allowing her to express every fear and thorn of despair in heavy succession. Yet as each jabbed through her she felt the lightening of the burden. Her Guardian didn't try to prevent her from experiencing the emotion but allowed them to surface, carefully replacing each layer with something to sooth and support. Again and again.

Silence enveloped them as they sat together in the darkness. The sound of hearts beating and soft breaths the two anchors Belle clung to in the endless stretch of this moment between them. Her fingers dug into the soft cotton of his shirt. His scent eased through her senses. Lachie's mere presence was the anchor she didn't realise she needed.

He welcomed her emotion.

Calm. Grounded. Centred.

The new sensations formed as a balm to sooth the open wounds of her heart.

No longer adrift in the chaos of the tempest inside her own mind.

"Tell me who I need to dispose of." The deep tone resonated from Lachie's chest pressing against her own.

Belle dragged a hand across her wet cheeks.

"I—I don't know. It was just here. Someone had been in my rooms. They left it..."

She gestured towards the folded parchment fallen to the floor beside the scattered books. Despite the shroud of darkness inside the room she could still feel it. She didn't need to see it to know its poisonous signature. To know exactly where it lay on the floor folded inside the note.

Belle could sense it.

The blood red feather.

Her aunt's calling card.

"It shouldn't be possible." She sniffed. How to explain this to Lachie without her Guardian losing control.

Lachie braced her weight with one arm and reached for the parchment with his free hand. His grip tight against her shoulder, she couldn't help but let a quiet sob escape as she heard the brush of his fingers against the note. Then mist encased them where they sat on the floor in the darkness.

In a mere second Belle felt the warmth and familiar scents of Lachie's study surround them. Relief flooded her veins like a silvery cord spreading the length of her arms and legs.

"Care to elaborate, my fierceling?" Lachie didn't shift her from his lap, but sat them both against the back of the couch. A silken soft blanket appeared around her shoulders.

Even still, the sight of the heavy cream parchment in his hand caused her back to stiffen. Goosebumps flecked her skin at seeing it once more in the light.

"My aunt. The red feather was her calling card. Someone must have played a joke." Belle was just as unconvinced by her own lie as she knew Lachie to be.

"Belle. This holds more meaning to you than a prank or a joke, and we both know it." His voice held a rigidity. The kind usually reserved for giving orders during his sparring sessions.

"It's nothing." Her voice came out hoarse with the throb of rawness in her throat.

With an exasperated grunt, Lachie pulled her chin to face his.

"What I saw in there was not a reaction to *nothing*. Tell me or Spirits save me, I will tear this castle apart looking for the being who did this to you."

"I don't know!" Belle let out a frustrated sob. Her eyes avoided his. "Honestly."

"Then explain what this is."

She took an unsteady breath. Her eyes drawn to where she

could feel his gaze focused upon her. The aquamarine depths of his penetrating stare stalled her heart in her throat. Thousands of promises swirled within, each laced with a furious need to understand how to fix whatever this was. The pulse of his aura and magic ticked as though on edge. Like the flick of a cat's tail when contemplating their next strike.

Belle gulped.

"It's a warning."

Her fingers fiddled with the edge of the blanket before she continued.

"It means they know exactly how to find me."

CHAPTER 29

"It must have been someone with connections to the non-magical world. To my aunt... and... him..."

Belle's voice croaked, raw and scratchy from crying.

Lachie's jaw clenched so tight he was sure his molars had ground into dust.

When he had portaled to her from the Fae Dominion earlier that night he had pictured finding his little witch curled on the couch. Skin warm from the glow of the fireplace. He had planned on scooping her up and carrying her straight to his bedroom.

Instead, his connection through the emerald ring she wore had landed him in the chilled darkness of her suite. Those soft sobs clenched tight coils around his heart the second he stepped through the portal.

Red mist had descended across his line of vision. He had been prepared to destroy any and all beings involved in causing her pain. Still was now.

Her voice drew him back from the edge. Pulled his attention to where he was needed.

"The night you saved me. That's... It's who I was running from. Who I had been running from."

With a shaky inhale she shifted back to search his face. Lachie's hands stilled against her back. His shoulders tensed. The satisfaction he had taken in knowing heads rolled that night. He would gladly resurrect those ghouls and mete out savage retribution over and over for their part in her suffering.

Anything to protect my mate.

"Give me the word and I will end them."

Belle shook her head feebly.

"She's already gone. The week before... she... shit, Lachie, I don't know what happened that night. But I woke up covered in blood. My aunt's body and some others I didn't know. All dead on the floor. I think... I think I killed them." Her lip quivered. "I ran. But I knew others were after me."

"Who has access to your rooms?" He barely recognised his own voice. Nothing would stop him from setting out right now to end this.

Lachie's mind already knew the futility of his own questions. There were hundreds of supernaturals in and around the castle for the eclipse. Nightfall celebrations regularly drew in the supernatural diaspora from across many realms. Whoever planned this had known this would be the perfect night to conceal their movements through the castle.

Easy to move around unnoticed. Even easier to gain access to Belle's rooms if they had known she wouldn't be there.

This was a threat intended to be discovered much later. If they had wanted to deliver their message straight away they could have slipped the note under the door to his study. It was no secret where the Guardian of the Realm resided within the castle.

No. Whoever did this had planned ahead. They knew exactly where to find Belle's private chambers. Had stood in her rooms. Touched her possessions. Lingered in what should have been her sanctuary.

He had made a promise she would be safe here.

The sickening thought turned his stomach. A chill swept a trail of pin pricks up the back of his neck. This was as much of a taunt towards him as it was a threat against his little witch. The unspoken menace crashed a cacophony against his eardrums:

"We know how to get to her and you did nothing to stop us."

Belle's voice interrupted his thoughts.

"It sounds insane. But I can't help thinking... I had another run in with Luciana tonight." Her features strained at the mention of the witch.

"What did she do to you?" His entire body tensed.

I didn't plan on dismembering a witch tonight. But here we are.

"No! No. I was with Brigid. We just had—it was tense,

that's all." Belle's palms flattened against his chest. "I don't know why but she seems to have me in her sights."

"Leave it with me." His voice dropped low.

"But... she would never admit it."

"I'll be the judge of what information I can and can't extract from another supernatural."

"If Luciana is somehow involved with... them. Do you think she might have used her powers the night the snatchers attacked me?"

Lachie's jaw set rigid. The fixation the snatchers had on Belle was unnatural. He doubted Luciana had ties with the House of Elharean. But he couldn't be certain. Assumption never led to a desirable outcome. The Gravelaan Coven had always been allied to the Soterian Realm. But a long shadow of doubt now cast itself across the entire community knowing their castle had been infiltrated tonight.

"There's something else. Something I haven't told you... about my Aunt." The crack in Belle's voice reached deep inside his chest and wrenched at his insides.

"She was the one who tried to... who sold me." Silent tears ran rivulets down her cheeks. "My own Aunt sold me into what would have been an abusive marriage."

Lachie's stomach went into free fall. That was why she was running the night he found her. This was her secret pain. Her nightmare she had been so desperate to escape.

"A name." His words turned to ash in his mouth.

"I knew him as the Marquis." Belle's lips trembled as fat tears gathered across her eyelashes.

Everything inside Lachie turned to stone.

Morçaeus. Or as he styled himself in the non-magical world the Marquis de Morçaeus. Depraved, ruthless, and notorious. A powerful sorcerer within the highest echelons of the House of Elharean. Known throughout the realms for purchasing and marrying young witches, only for them to disappear soon after. Never to be seen again.

It all made sense. The snatchers and their obsession with Belle. How she had been attacked that night. Her fear of the ghosts chasing her. Even if she hadn't been awakened to her magic and knew nothing of the supernatural world. The prospect of enslavement and abuse was unbearable to think of. The fact she came so close to being lost to him forever slid up his spine with a shudder.

Morçaeus was a ruthless hunter and obsessed with procuring rare magic. He must have somehow known of Belle's magic before she awakened to it. An Ampher residing in the non-magical world was like a delicate rose surrounded by a volcano. At any moment she could have been annihilated by the likes of that monster.

Perhaps the Goddesses had intervened to ensure her safety. To make sure he had been in that exact location that night. All along he had thought it seemed like chance his mate had come into his life. But now? His heart daren't grasp at the hope fluttering within the darkest recesses he had shut away long ago.

In that moment Lachie swore to himself he would do everything to protect her. She would never have to fear that kind of menace again. Even if it took the last breath in his body he would stay by her side. This changed everything.

Belle shuddered a breath where she clutched against his chest.

"Lachie. It's a warning. It means he's coming for me."

CHAPTER 30

"I don't give a fuck if she is going to be crowned almighty Queen of all realms and given a glowing unicorn to ride in a parade. This is not working out."

Niall paced across the silken carpet. Irritation cloaked his frame. He appeared intent to tread a line into the immaculate flooring. The opulent state room within the palace of the Fae Dominion had been their meeting point of choice in recent weeks. Much too visible a location and far more ostentatious than Lachie would have preferred to gather in. But with Niall's duty now to act as private guard to the soon to be crowned Queen, their meetings were required to be in close proximity to her quarters. At all times.

All efforts to trace the killer had so far failed. The Fae Dominion closed ranks on their royal lineage in fear. The throne passing into a new line of succession had come about as a shock after the slaughter of the entire royal family. They simply couldn't risk another assassination.

Lachie hadn't seen Niall so on edge in recent memory. The precious blonde princess must have to actually work for a change. Clearly his customary tactic of charm and wit had not resulted in the desired effect on the soon-to-be Queen.

Brilliant. About time someone put him in his place.

"We've found no trace of where the House of Elharean are hiding within the Fae borders, Lachie." Fehrn ignored Niall's complaints as he leaned across the gold edged table. His hulking form wild and out of place against the intricate carvings, gilded flourishes, and mirrored luxury of the Fae court.

"But they are most certainly still here." Lia interjected to finish her mate's statement. "I've heard enough with my telepathy to know they are present and pose an active threat. It's just … their trace seems to go cold almost as quick as we catch a hint of a possible location." Lia frowned. Her shoulder leaned against Fehrn's hip where she sat in one of the ornate gold chairs. The heavy set gold seats looked more like individual thrones surrounding the table large enough to seat twenty beings.

Lavish and ostentatious power. That was the message their court desired to portray to any supernaturals who entered the palace walls. The nature of which only those descended from the ancient Fae could possess. The overwhelm of silver intertwined with gold seemed to cover just about every surface and every piece of furniture.

It gave Lachie a headache. He was forever conjuring an

enchantment to ensure not a speck of dirt from his boots remained after his visits.

"So in other words, you're saying my work here is far from over?" Niall shot Lachie a look from across the table where he stood. Eyebrows raised in silent question. Or more like demand.

"You're the best for the mission that we've got. Not only can you sense any malicious intent within others here inside the palace. Your magic will give enough warning if there is a potential threat from within. No doubt you can help ease the new Queen through this process with your... influence. I imagine this has been incredibly traumatic for her." He levelled his brother with a stern look. As an empath witch Niall could influence another beings emotions to ease distress, provide calm, and elicit a wide range of emotional states. Ranging from bliss to euphoria.

A shadow flicked across Niall's face. His mouth opened then closed. Opened then closed again, before it set in a firm line.

Lachie shot Lia a look. He allowed the smallest crack in his own shield around his mind. Just enough for a single string of a thought to float through the ether between them.

Anything you can read on him? His silent question enough to be detected by Lia's telepathy.

She averted her eyes down towards the table and shook her head with the smallest of gestures. Without needing to say a word she confirmed what he suspected. Niall had shielded his own thoughts from their resident telepath.

Concerns that would have to wait for another day.

Lachie had his own witch—his mate—to worry about. And the matter of the threat from Morçaeus.

"Rowan, I trust you have the palace security detail handled? Weapons and technique training?" Lachie turned to where his brother's broad shoulders stood silent in front of the large window overlooking the forest. A far cry from his comfort zone on the battlefield or being tucked away in his isolated cottage fortress. He couldn't look more out of place with his scowl and black demeanour in amongst the delicate finery of the Fae. But there was no one Lachie would trust more than his brother with ensuring the palace guards were ready for any upcoming threats from the House of Elharean.

The assassination had thrown all realms into disarray. Where peace had once held firm within borders, now there lay a trail of chaos and fear. Even if there was no evidence of the House of Elharean's presence, the suspicion of one realm under attack had led to paranoia across all. Precisely the turmoil the House of Elharean chose to instigate and thrive on. The toxic fuel they harvested as the source of their dark power.

Without a way to ensure the Fae Dominion could be safeguarded, they would have to defend themselves from the threats that lay within their own borders. A challenge the likes of which these supernatural beings had never faced before.

"Yes. Leave it with me, Lach." Rowan's gaze remained fixed on the forest. His back turned to the room. Ever a witch of few words. And even fewer emotions.

Of course Lachie didn't have to promise the service of his

most skilled warrior on an extended stay here in the Fae Dominion. But Rowan knew his role here involved more than correcting fighting technique and weapons skill training. Intel gathered and time spent listening to the words unspoken gave the greatest strategic advantage in this kind of situation.

It was just as likely the assassination had been orchestrated from within the Fae Court itself. Rowan's usefulness lay in the time he would spend embedded here within the ranks of the Fae. To secure access to any secret agendas that may have gone undetected.

Being Guardian of the Soterian Realm meant that Lachie was one of the most well known faces amongst supernaturals. Hardly conducive to covert operations. Rowan however possessed enough of a *fuck everyone* attitude to typically keep a low profile.

"Go, Lachie. We know you've got other places to be." Lia gave him a knowing smile. "How is she doing?"

Since the night Belle had found the warning in her rooms he found it harder and harder to leave her for any extended length of time. The overriding urge to guard her day and night gave way to logic when it came to leaving the realm. He would rather not risk bringing her here.

"As well as can be expected."

"Have you any news on Morçaeus?" Fehrn's growl came low and rigid at the mention of the House of Elharean sorcerer. "I'd be more than happy to dispatch his head for you, Lach. For all of us."

He had tasked Ceranthe with investigating more into the

death of Belle's aunt. The red feather provided a clue that might unravel this tangled thread. As far as Belle was aware her aunt had possessed no magical abilities. Yet she had links to Morçaeus in her attempt to sell Belle into his clutches. A shudder flecked his skin at the thought. But there was something else that sat uneasy within his being. There were no coincidences, and there seemed to be too many interwoven pieces to this situation he was determined to resolve. To protect Belle. Whether that was from the ghosts of her past or her present.

He would hunt the beast Morçaeus himself. No matter what desolate realm that required him to travel to.

"I'm handling it. Need you here. I'll return tomorrow and you can brief me then." He chewed over his words. Then with a resigned huff he simply nodded and allowed himself to dissolve into the mist as he portaled from the room. Following that incessant tug on his heart like a rhythmic beating of a drum.

Straight to her.

Portaling to the magic of Belle's ring held a different nuance to it. A unique kind of surety that held him steadfast. Like waking up from a dream and being able to sense her warmth right there beside him. His magic bound in that ring linked them in a way that continued to amplify the whispers. Those reminders from the fates telling him she was his mate.

When he used his magic to portal anywhere else there was always an anticipation. Muscle memory that prepared for whatever might await him on the other side of that threshold. He never knew what he might be portaling towards. But with this—with her—it felt comforting. After three hundred years of facing down unknowns this tethered him.

Within a second his feet touched solid ground. Mist parted as he stepped forward. The familiar scent of jasmine and roses flooded his senses. Warmth enveloped him in the still darkness where he found himself stood beside the bed.

Their bed.

Funny how he didn't think of it as his own anymore.

The faint glow from the fire burned low and he could see her long hair fanned out across the pillows. Belle's chest shifted ever so slightly beneath the covers with soft breaths as she slept.

He rubbed at his chest absentmindedly.

Lachie was tired. Exhausted and bone weary from his single minded focus on vengeance. Trying so desperately to atone for his mistake had drained his own life force. For so long he had tortured himself. Denied any opportunity for others to get close to him. That fear of losing someone again had ruled his existence with an iron fist. He had believed himself unworthy of the right to get close to another.

And now...

He was done. Enough running from his own demons. Time to face those shadows and take a chance at exploring what it meant to live life. To do so because someone made it worth living. No more trying to avoid life in retribution for what was long lost.

A confession of the dark secrets he had for so long kept from her and his brothers.

Brigid knew. Of course she knew. No doubt that was why she had vanished in recent days. It was often the case, the Goddesses spiriting his sister away during times like these. Perhaps they sensed how close Brigid might actually come one day to let them into the insights of her brilliant mind. The Seer often gave him a hug that lasted too long. Or an unusual look when she thought he didn't see. But she had her vows to the Goddesses to keep. Time and time again she had proved she wouldn't intervene. But her heart overflowed with love and he knew deep down it must wear upon her soul to carry the burdens she shouldered.

Belle deserved the truth.

To know of his plan.

And that it had now all changed.

He needed her to know how being with her—knowing her—had changed his mind.

She had shown him a glimpse of life and all its possibilities.

He refused to go back to the bleak existence he had lived before.

He'd tell Belle everything.

Soon.

CHAPTER 31

"Alright you grumpy fucker. There must be something here I can use to get you back."

Belle muttered to herself as she glared at Lachie's desk with her arms crossed.

He had come to bed long after she had fallen asleep last night. Then slipped away again before she fully woke with whispered promises to return to her side... soon.

She still hadn't exacted her revenge for the stunt he pulled binding her with the sigil. It was much better to keep herself occupied with plotting a way to get her Guardian back, rather than let her mind drift to the warning she had found inside her rooms. The feather with its crimson taunt that Lachie had taken with his promise to investigate. A bloody reminder of memories she would rather leave behind in her past.

In these quiet moments when he was off-realm Belle had

been secretly looking for a soft spot in her Guardian's flawless armour.

Apparently he had none.

She had pressed as many supernaturals as she dared in the banquet hall. Encouraging them to divulge any little morsel of information she might be able to leverage. To her irritation there came only glowing reports of Lachie's dedication to safeguarding the realm. The younger trainees simply looked terrified if she mentioned his name in their presence.

At least he had successfully kept his reputation as the fearsome dark prince intact.

Although her elevated status within the castle as someone close—important even—to the Guardian of the Realm would take some getting used to. The constant awareness of wide eyes and hushed whispers behind her. She knew nothing was meant in a negative manner, but it couldn't be more of a contrast to her former life.

The invisible one. The enslaved one. The ignored one.

Just as she found her feet in this new world, time and time again something came along to disrupt the peace she had acquired. Her fingers tried to grip tight to the fragments of calm within this seemingly endless storm. Lachie had become her anchor in a world of shifting sand.

She didn't want to ever let him go.

Belle puffed a breath to shift the lock of loose hair fallen across her eye. Her search through the bookcases of Lachie's study this morning had also proved fruitless. The shelves overflowed with more magical tomes, histories, and grimoires than she could hope to read in one lifetime. But it was all so... Guardian like.

And wasn't that the exact dichotomy of Lachie himself? The cool, calm, level-headed exterior of the dutiful leader presented to the outside world. Yet, Belle knew the depths of emotion and nuance inside her witch. The dry humour and the playfulness that she alone bore witness to.

Despite her enjoyment keeping those secret sides to Lachie all to herself, she wished others could experience those parts he locked away so firmly. Was it selfish to privately enjoy having him open up only to her? Probably. Did she fall endlessly for him in the soft moments when it was just the two of them? Absolutely.

But that didn't mean he would escape her retribution. No matter how many orgasms he had given her since that day. She still wanted the satisfaction of getting one back. His perfect-guardian-lordship would get a taste of his own magic one way or another.

She uncrossed her arms and leaned both hands on the edge of the wood. Parchment, portfolios, and bookmarked pages swam in front of her eyes. Nothing to see here.

With a step back she surveyed the front of the desk. Three sets of drawers ran down either side. Intricate metalwork in various elemental patterns formed the handle upon each. The different designs worn into a brassy sheen from hundreds, if not thousands of years of usage. A deep imbued signature of Lachie's magic hummed from the surface of the wood like his scent that lingered on his pillow.

Belle crouched at eye level and braced one hand against the lip of the desk surface. With the other hand she reached forward to try the top most handle. It refused to budge. Locked. She chewed her bottom lip, then tugged on each of the others in turn.

All remained resolute. Sealed by magic.

Her stomach gave a little flutter of relief. She didn't actually want to betray Lachie's trust by rummaging through his most intimate possessions. In a way there was a sense of relief that she couldn't in fact open those drawers.

She crouched and ran both hands across the metalwork detailing on the front of the drawer at eye level. Wisps of smoke to represent air within the elements. On the others there were depictions of flora for earth, flames, and rolling seas for water. A lightness and delicate forging of the metal only an artisan with a talent for this kind of magic could conjure. Belle flattened her palm against the design work to run across the grooves.

A light snick reverberated through her fingertips. The emerald ring on Belle's forefinger pulsed with magic like a rapid heartbeat and suddenly the drawer beneath her palm popped open of its own accord. Belle shot back with a start and fell on her rear. Eyes wide she scanned the study.

"Hello?" Her voice wavered a little.

Silence met her confusion. Her words hung in the air.

The ring.

Belle stared down at her hand, turning it over to look at the underside of the band where the gold had touched the desk itself. Of course. The ring Lachie was so adamant she never take off. His magical conduit to ensure he could portal to wherever she would be. There must be traces of his magic encoded within the ring that could act to unbind the spell on the desk drawers.

Now what? She had been relieved when they didn't open. Now the drawer, protruding from where it had previously sat flush with the rest of the wood, taunted her. Was this some kind of morality test from the Spirits? Or was this a sign that what she sought lay within that exact drawer.

With a shift forward onto her knees Belle reached for the handle. The sensation of magic thrummed through the ring softly. No need to open any others she reasoned to herself. Just look inside this one. After all, there aren't any coincidences in life.

A cautious finger snagged the metal and pulled forward. The wooden casing slid forward featherlight and on a smooth glide. Inside lay folded sheets of parchment stacked one on top of the other. Letters written but unsealed and undelivered. Belle peered down, not yet willing to touch what lay before her. She could see indentations of writing where the nib had pressed through. Maybe four, or five folded sheets sat neatly one on top of the other.

Belle licked her lips. Her throat felt like she had swallowed sand.

She glanced over her shoulder. The study remained quiet and still. Was this about to cross an unforgivable line in their relationship? Or had Lachie made sure her ring could open this particular drawer? Curiosity now clawed to the forefront.

If this was private then surely he would have ensured her ring had no ability to break this particular spell?

Blood whooshed in her ears as her fingers clasped around the stack of letters. She sat back on the floor and unfolded the top most paper. The heavy texture felt cool beneath her thumb and forefinger as she held it open. The strong creases kept the letter folded in thirds and she had to prise it apart.

A frown creased her forehead. She turned the letter over. The indents in the back were clearly visible, yet on the surface where she expected to see the inky scrawl of Lachie's handwriting across the page was... blank.

Belle refolded the letter with care, the firmness of the parchment quickly sprang back into place as though untouched. She moved to the second letter in the pile, opening it only to find the same blank page.

Maybe this was for the best? Did she really want to be reading Lachie's—or whoever wrote these letters—private correspondence?

She blew out a long, whistled breath.

What if... No. Surely not?

Belle ran the emerald gemstone of her ring across the surface of the page. If the desk's spell was connected to her ring, then perhaps the same would be true for the enchantment on these letters. Like a flicker of a candle being lit for the first time, words began to appear on the page as her ring moved across the parchment. The contents revealed in slow motion.

The familiar looping scrawl of Lachie's handwriting spread as the ink materialised.

She hitched in a breath.

"It's for Niall." She said aloud to herself with a loud exhale. Some of the tension in her chest dissipated with relief.

Not letters to a secret lover then.

A warm smile stretched across her face at the familiar traces of ink. The way Lachie's essence reflected in his mannerisms set down on the page. Every weighted stroke and emphasis so true to his personality. Much like an artist can be recognised from the way they apply their medium to a canvas. She ran her thumb gently over his signature at the bottom of the page. As her eyes drifted back up and across the opening lines something vice like gripped her throat. Icy cold tendrils wound their way through her chest. The words blurred together as she registered what this letter contained.

As she realised what this letter was.

No. No. No. No. No. No. No.

She snatched at the other papers. Her hand shook as she held the ring to reveal the text. One by one the names revealed themselves.

Brigid.

Rowan.

Fehrn.

All contained the same sickening message.

Numbness extended down each of her arms. Her skin became clammy as the chill descended further and hit the pit of her stomach. Static filled her ears as the last letter fell from her fingers. How long had Lachie kept this ugly secret locked away in that drawer? How long had he been intent to deceive them all?

The final page trembled as she lifted it and forced the ring against the paper with a rough shove. A letter addressed to her would confirm he had chosen this path after their meeting. If her name appeared on that page it would prove he had lied to her from the very beginning.

Rage burned in her throat as the letters slowly formed beneath her fingertips.

"Belle. I'm sorry."

Feeble words written only once at the top of the page. Then crossed out. The message—lie—left uncompleted. The remaining parchment blank. But the intention had been there to share the same letter as he had written for the others.

Her fists crumpled the paper. A scream threatened to rip from her throat, but none came. Just agonising pain. Hurt so potent she was only dimly aware of the swirling mist and footsteps moving across the room towards her.

The arrival of a liar.

CHAPTER 32

"Belle?"

Lachie's voice echoed in the distance. The roar of blood pounded relentless inside her ears and drowned out any other words he might have said in that moment. She felt submerged. Pinned down by the weight of her pain.

The touch of his hand against her shoulder brought the room into focus with a sickening spin. Her lungs burned as though starved of oxygen. Like she had emerged from the darkest depths of the ocean and now burst into the light. The pit of her stomach seethed and unsteady hands gripped the crumpled paper.

She scrambled to move across the room. Her rage needed to put distance between them. Two halves battled for supremacy inside her. One ready to fight. The other wanted nothing more than to flee. There wasn't enough air in the space as the walls seemed to cave inwards. Her vision spotted at the edges.

Belle reached for the back of the armchair beside the study fireplace to steady herself. A shield of sorts to safeguard her soul currently breaking into a million shards. Her body turned to face him.

The liar.

Lachie remained rooted to the spot where he stood behind the desk. His eyes trained on the papers where they lay scattered on the floor.

The very spot where the carpet had been ripped out from underneath her entire existence only moments before.

"What. Is. This?" Belle's words lurched from her throat. Hoarse and razor sharp.

Her eyes bored into his skull, willing him to turn and fully face her. Every agonised thud of her heart tore it into smaller tattered fragments.

"I—I can—please just let me explain." A catch in his voice. His face twisted into ripples of agony. Knuckles white edged where his hands balled into fists.

"Belle. I'm sorry?" Her shriek pierced the room as she read his scratched out words aloud. "You were too much of a coward to even write anything to me. Let alone *say* anything." She hurled the crumpled paper across the room to hit Lachie in the chest. Belle's hands shook uncontrollably where they gripped the back of the chair. Books on the shelves began to rattle as her magic spiralled on a crest of emotion.

"Those letters. I never should have written them." Lachie's voice came soft and measured.

"What? So you could just disappear without telling us instead?" Belle's breath jolted out harsh and stilted. "So that was your plan. All this time? To sacrifice yourself? You honestly think that's what your sister would have wanted? For you to take down the House of Elharean single handedly? *To leave me?*"

"Belle—"

"NO. You don't get to do that. You don't get to lie to me anymore." Her hair floated wild around her shoulders. "What were you going to do? March in there alone and start swinging your blades? Take down one or two of their most powerful sorcerers? You might be the most powerful witch this realm has, but what good would that do in the face of an entire dynasty?" Her voice pitched into a yell. "It would be suicide and you knew that. You always knew that."

The papers on Lachie's desk hung suspended in the air several inches above the woodwork. A number of books tumbled from their shelves while the rest continued to rattle incessantly. Belle knew she needed to reign in her magic. The fury and despair that flooded through her veins tapped into chaos. A darkness deep within.

Years upon years of hurt and suffering bubbled to the surface. The full force of her scarred heart bore down on the ether between them.

And in that moment, she didn't care if the entire room might explode.

She wanted so desperately to make it go away. To rewind time and go back to the way things were an hour ago.

But the false facade had been incinerated. Only the crumbling ruins remained of what had been fleeting happiness. The lies that now turned to ash on her tongue.

Belle pushed off the back of the armchair with a frustrated cry.

Need air. Need to get out of here.

She spun to head for the door. Her path immediately blocked as he portaled across the room in a blink. Careful not to touch her, Lachie held his palms raised in a gesture of surrender with eyes wide. Beseeching. Begging.

"Please. Belle." His jaw ticked and his voice cracked as her name gusted from his lips.

She shook her head and stepped around him, wincing internally at the pain she detected pulsing through his aura as she passed by. Their swirled energies intertwined in a desperate exchange of unspoken emotion, guilt, and regret. Lachie didn't move to stop her this time.

Belle reached for the door, opened it, then paused. With a shaky hand she pulled off her ring. Tears burned as they fought to surge forward. She only just managed to hold them at bay.

Just one more minute, then you can fall apart. But not here. Not in front of him.

"Don't bother following me. If you ever respected me at all, then you'll let me leave. You'll give me space." She placed the ring on top of the chest of drawers beside the doorway.

With the heat of a thousand sobs crawling up her throat she slammed the door behind her.

Light had long since faded over the horizon. Any trace of that golden orb of warmth had vacated the skies and the moon had yet to show her face. A pale grey gloom of long shadows cast themselves across the forest clearing. It was like the land itself reflected the Guardian's inner world.

Lachie's blades sliced through the air. His body drenched. His muscles screamed enough, but his mind pushed through that threshold. The only way he could stand to bear what had just erupted into chaos around him had been to come here. Alone.

Now he found himself in the dark coated in sweat, dirt, and abject misery. Swinging blades at shadows. A vain attempt to keep himself occupied by pummelling himself into the ground. Over and over. It was the only way he knew right now to prevent himself from following her. She had set her desires for space in no uncertain terms. Yet every fragment of his soul screamed at him to go to her. To fall at her feet. Stars, to somehow search for the words to explain it all. To right the wrongs he had set in motion when he wrote those fucking letters.

It had all been foolish. He knew that now. Belle was right,

his plan had always ended with the inevitability of his own death. He'd run through every scenario for two hundred years, but the missing piece over all those years had been the knowledge of the Seal of Elharean. Once Fehrn and Lia had brought news to him and the location of the infamous Seal—the dark source of power and destruction—it had cemented his decision. Galvanised him into action. Blinded by hatred and desire for retribution, and to atone for his own part to play in his sister's fate at Elharean hands.

Selfish actions. Fuelled by a lifetime of regret.

There had only been one thing on his mind. To act with swift and deadly accuracy. Fehrn knew how to access the House of Elharean castle, he'd done so before. Lachie had every detail he required to infiltrate their sick and twisted world. To destroy the Seal and the portal it activated would take immense power and skilled control of magic. The kind that only Lachie possessed as the Guardian. It had to be him to do so and he would gladly make that sacrifice in the face of protecting countless others.

It wouldn't bring Fiadh back. But it would allow his lineage and parents to rest well in the ancestral plane. He could meet them there with head held high in the knowledge his death had purpose. That he ensured the Seal had been destroyed and the House of Elharean rendered impotent. No longer able to continue their dominance and subjugation of other beings for their own twisted ends. An inevitable domino to set their ultimate destruction and demise in motion. He could entrust his siblings to continue their work and slay the many heads of the beast in ever more powerful blows.

But then everything had changed in an instant. That fateful night. The moment those grey eyes captured his. One singular heartbeat that spanned centuries of hurt and healed his soul in ways he couldn't fathom. He didn't deserve her. Yet the fates had conspired to propel him towards a different destiny. One that meant he would live and breathe for her.

For his love.

Hours had passed since Belle walked out the door. Since her final words to him. The sting of her pain and sense of betrayal lashed at his mind on repeat while he trained.

"If you ever respected me at all..."

Fuck.

If only she knew.

If only he had found the words to explain what she truly meant to him.

Lachie's chest clenched tight at the memory. The reverberating echo as the door had slammed behind her. Like a thunder clap jolting the body long after the initial crack of lightning had vanished.

One glance around the room after she vanished was all it took. Everywhere he looked something reminded him of her. Jasmine and rose lingered in the air along with the resultant chaos of her magic. Books and papers scattered the floor like a stinging slap. Each a callous pointer back onto himself to demonstrate exactly what he had gambled with.

What a fucking idiot. Too much of a coward to open up and tell her the truth. And now you've lost her.

Your mate.

He would have destroyed every last item in that fucking room if it meant her forgiveness. If it meant she didn't walk out that door.

He let out an agonised roar into the night sky. Why didn't he just wake her up the night before? Pour his heart out right then and there. Explain that after two hundred years of single minded focus he realised how asinine he had been. To confess to Belle that she had shown him how to truly live. How to open up and invite joy back in to paint over the bleakness that had encased his heart for so long.

To tell Belle how she had shown him what love could be.

Not some childish emotion of infatuation.

The kind of love that infused deep into the very fabric of his reality. A love that inspired him to be the best version of himself, for her.

He jabbed the fingers of both hands roughly through his hair.

Fuck. Just to tell her he loved her.

If she ever spoke to him again, he'd be sure to tell her—no, show her—the untold depths of how he adored her. In a million different ways. Seeking forgiveness across a million different lifetimes.

Lachie sheathed his blades in their twin holsters across his back and lifted his damp shirt to wipe the grime from his face. He turned towards the wooden cottage that sat dark and empty. Rowan's fortress lay quiet and unoccupied in the gloom of the night air. Offset from the clearing. Hidden amongst the trees with a camouflaged moss covered roof and blackened wood exterior. His brother would have to extend forgiveness later for the intrusion of his privacy. Rowan would be none the wiser from his current post in the palace of the Fae Dominion.

And Lachie couldn't face returning to the castle. Not tonight. With his empty rooms only filled with Belle's pain.

"One night won't hurt the black hearted asshole." He muttered to himself. His stride paused as he reached the pillars either side of the black stone path. Rowan always kept his fortress enchanted to the back teeth to safeguard against intruders—family or otherwise. With him being gone on such a long assignment the magic would be extra potent no doubt.

He raised a palm in the air between the pillars. The thrum of the enchantment rippled under his fingertips. Invisible to the eye, but designed to maim anyone who dared cross the sacred threshold.

"A blood debt? Really Rowan?" Lachie shook his head and pinched the bridge of his nose. "I thought you had moved onto less barbaric forms of protection this past century."

But old habits die hard. Especially for one as familiar with the psyche of supernaturals and dark foes as his brother. No amount of blood wards and debts could keep at bay the demons he held within himself.

Lachie reached over his shoulder to pull out one of his blades. Ironic that he would, of course, need to draw physical blood to complete this day. He already felt like his heart had been ripped from his chest to fall bloodied upon the floor. Why not add a little extra?

As his grip wrapped around the handle, he stilled. His senses pricking with awareness. Rapid footfall came from the direction of the castle. The crunch of leaf litter through the tree line unmistakable on the still night air. He whirled and crouched down. His magic manifested above his palms, ready to strike if necessary.

"Lachie?" The familiar voice of Ceranthe called out.

Shit. Something was wrong. His friend wouldn't have travelled here inside the realm at this time without good cause.

He stood to his full height, blue light flaring above his palm to reveal his location. Eyes narrowed on the quickening approach of the man. Heaviness lined Ceranthe's face.

"Lachie. You have to come. Now." His breath hitched in and out in uneven gasps. He had been on the run. But was he racing from something, or towards it?

"It's your Ampher." He coughed out. Half winded from exertion.

Blood drained from Lachie's face.

"She's left the realm. I—I think she's in trouble."

CHAPTER 33

"Where is she?"

Lachie's voice was feral and raw. An unfamiliar sensation slithered around his stomach like a twisting serpent.

Fear.

She took the ring off.

The throb of his pulse in his forehead intensified. Fuck. He couldn't portal straight to her without it. The serpent's coils wrapped and squeezed tighter in the pit of his stomach.

This couldn't be happening.

Not again.

"Lachie. We need to move. The longer we wait..." Ceranthe chewed his bottom lip. Unwilling to finish his train of thought.

"Tell me where she went." His tone dropped low and demanding.

"Last sighting she was headed for Fisx. The village where—"

"Fuck." Lachie cut him off before he could finish. Almost the exact place Belle had been attacked and nearly killed. The night he saved her.

"The woods just outside the old walls. You know the place?" Ceranthe cocked his crossbow. Ready for whatever might await them as they emerged from portaling.

"Don't worry, old friend. We'll find her." With a nod he stepped in closer to Lachie.

He clasped a hand on Ceranthe's shoulder. Mist swirled and rose below their feet. His mind raced with the effort of blocking a hundred different scenarios of what they might find. All where Belle's body lay mangled and bloody at his feet. Her head severed from her body. The chill of the portal threshold enveloped them as weightlessness took hold.

Before he had time to draw breath he felt the firmness of ground materialising below his feet. The damp, earthen smells of decaying leaf litter hit his nostrils. Something wasn't right. His magic flitted across his skin like goosebumps. Unease crawled up the back of his neck.

As he reached to draw his blades from their holsters a flash of crimson light blinded him. Magic surged up from the ground under his feet in twisted, glowing coils.

A binding hex. Dark magic. The signature of the House of Elharean. In his blind rush he had portaled straight into their grasp.

He lurched to shove Ceranthe out of harms way, only to find he stood alone.

The hex wound its way higher. His lower limbs now stunned immobile. Lachie swung his blades. His magic poured from the swords in a blur of blue flame. Shards of red shattered like glass under each blow, yet for every one he managed to repel more appeared like the head of a blood thirsty hydra.

He felt the coils tighten around his waist. With each swing his reach became less and less. Suffocated under the weight of the dark magic wrapped around his body. The hex's power crippled his magic. His knees buckled under the force of the enchantment as it overwhelmed his senses. With a yell, Lachie found himself pinned to the ground. His hands now manacled behind his back. Both blades clattered from his grip.

His chest strained under the pressure. A crack as one of his ribs gave way beneath the force of the binding. Lachie's vision spotted at the edges.

Belle.

His only thought, as the force of the hex bound tighter, was for her safety. What if she had fallen to the same fate here in these woods? And he hadn't been able to protect her. Despite everything he had done to try and keep her safe, he had still failed.

The hex's dark magic seeped into his throat. Choking him. Air struggled to reach his lungs. A haze drifted across his vision and blurred his sight. His senses vaguely detected movement at the far corners of his awareness. Feet appeared and came to a stop before him. Muffled voices exchanged words he couldn't detect.

A shadowy figure crouched down. Features blurred and twisted in front of his eyes. He struggled to focus beyond the pain of the enchantment's binding. Something cold pushed at his chin lifting it upwards with a shove. The smooth metal jutted against his throat.

Not a blade. A crossbow.

Please. No.

"I have to thank you, old friend. You made this much easier than we expected." Ceranthe's voice drifted through his awareness.

Not this way. Not you.

"To think. This is how we finally meet, Lachlan of Nocturne." A woman's voice came from nearby. "Naughty witch." She tutted. "You've kept something that doesn't belong to you. Now you're going to help us get it back." The voice lilted through the night and penetrated the fog in his mind.

Did he recognise it from somewhere? He couldn't tell. The hex made everything sound echoey and distant.

More figures appeared to mingle with the shadows. Was any of this real? Had his friend been part of the House of Elharean all this time?

Ceranthe's crossbow dug into his windpipe. Lachie's head was forced back further as though being prepared for sacrifice. His unseeing eyes watered with the strangle hold on his neck. Throat laid bare. An invitation for the swift slice of a blade.

"I've been waiting a long time to do this." The voice, once so familiar, now dripped with malice.

The butt of the crossbow crashed against his left temple with a sickening blow.

Inky blackness crept in and took hold as he sank to the ground.

"Now Ceranthe, darling. Let's take the infamous Guardian somewhere more comfortable shall we?" A bitter laugh from the woman. "You can have your fun later. We don't want to be late for him."

Him? Spirits. No.

Lachie's body began to lift into the air. Rigid and helpless against the force of the enchantment. Every part of his body encased in the hex's magic. His mind scrambled with the dark power binding him. As he slipped out of consciousness he clung to the faint thread of magic still connected deep within his heart. The as yet unspoken bond tying him to his mate for eternity.

Run, my fierceling. I'll finish this for both of us.

Belle had lost track of how long she had spent submerged in her bath. The steam and herbal potions scarcely soothed the heaviness within her chest. It sat there ominous and weighty like the descent into a cold abyss. Tears had poured all night and the grey light of dawn only confirmed how puffy eyed and numb she appeared on the outside. What was a pale shade in comparison to the aching hollowness left within her. The feeling of a soul rubbed raw with anguish.

She didn't want magic to conceal the evidence of her sorrow. Let it remind her just how easy it was to fool her open heart.

"Don't go trying to paint me as something good."

She'd replayed every subtle hint. They'd been there right from the beginning. She'd just refused to see the truth. Too eager to believe what they had between them might overcome the hesitations Lachie had clearly had all along.

Belle had needed space alone to think, to process the shock of her discovery. It had all been too much to take in during the heat of the moment. All her past wounds had been gashed open with the contents of those letters.

Abandonment.

Indifference.

Unwantedness.

A line up of memories she long sought to heal and move on from now dragged back to the forefront of her mind.

Her past wasn't Lachie's fault. But it didn't excuse his actions and his choices. It didn't excuse his decision to lie to her and break her heart in the process.

He warned you. Right from day one. And you didn't listen.

Was any of it real? Belle didn't know what to believe.

She scrubbed the heels of her palms against her eye sockets with a frustrated sigh. The look of agony on his face last night was imprinted in her memory. How his eyes had pleaded with her to let him explain. A part of her wanted to stay and hear his explanation. To allow him an opportunity to rectify his actions. But her rage had barrelled in hot and vengeful. That force had swept her in a tornado of pent up emotion let loose after years of torment at the hands of her Aunt.

She wasn't proud of any of it. But Spirits it had felt good for a moment to allow it to be wild and untamed. To succumb to the deep well of pain within that never quite seemed to evaporate. There was always a residue there. A sludge she didn't want to acknowledge. She had let it consume her last night, with all the fury it contained laid bare.

Only for her to collapse in a heap of regret once she reached her suite of rooms. Maybe he deserved her anger and bitterness. But maybe he deserved her compassion too?

At least he had respected her wish for space. The tiniest part of her held onto a flicker of hope he might have ignored that demand. She half expected her door to burst open at any moment throughout the night. But her Guardian never came.

With heavy limbs she pushed up and out of the bath.

Can't hold it against him for listening to me.

She dried herself and lathered on a soothing balm. A potion from Nell. The light moisture absorbed into her skin and tingled with her signature herbalist magic. As she dressed herself she considered the irony that this would of course all happen when everyone she had grown close to had departed the realm. With Lia gone indefinitely to the Fae Dominion, Nell's abrupt departure for the mountains, and Brigid nowhere to be found since the Nightfall ceremony, it only added to the layers of abandonment.

Not their fault. Just my own shitty collection of trauma to resolve.

Her fingers twisted around the empty space where her ring usually sat. The exposed skin felt strange and unsettled her. If he hadn't cared for her—if it had in fact all been a lie—then why would he have insisted on her wearing the ring at all times? What purpose would that have served? If he felt nothing for her then surely a magical bond would have been the last thing he might have thought to maintain.

Belle worried her bottom lip. In the cold light of day she still ached. Her tender heart needed space to work through her feelings. But that hurt was just as much a consequence of missing him as it was being angry with him.

Before she could make sense of it, her feet had carried her to the corridor outside the doorway into Lachie's rooms. As she stood in front of the expanse of wood it brought memories flooding back of the first night she loitered here in this very same spot.

Despite it all, she wanted to fix this. To give him a chance to explain. Her heart might risk being shattered further, but it was better to know right now if he still intended on leaving her. If his plan to sacrifice himself was truly more important than their bond. Something in his reaction last night spoke whispers to her that his intentions had changed.

And besides, she wanted *her ring* back. It was pretty.

With a deep breath she pushed open the door. As she

stepped inside she saw her ring exactly where she had left it on the chest of drawers. Her hand shot out to grab it and she slipped it back onto her finger. Relief at the sight of the gemstone back where it belonged quickly transformed as a chill trickled down her spine.

Something was wrong. Very wrong.

Chaos still lay strewn across the room from her anger the night before. Lachie had made no attempt to clear the mess. His study seethed with unfamiliar traces of enchantments. The lingering trace sizzled in a violent hiss.

Dark magic had been here.

CHAPTER 34

"You really pulled off a marvel, Ceranthe."

The icy tone of a male voice pulled Lachie back into consciousness.

The sharp end of a cane pressed against his shoulder, flipping him onto his back. His entire being still bound immobile and powerless by the hex. Imprisoned within his own mind and without use of his body. Or his magic.

He blinked his eyes, desperate to focus. Where had they brought him? Under the grip of the enchantment his senses were smothered. But he knew he needed to start to piece together whatever details he could. That was the hope he clung to right now.

When backed into a corner, against all impossibility, arm yourself with knowledge. It had always been his preferred weapon. Apparently now he had no choice but to make use of his mind.

Lush carpet cushioned his head. A faint smell of lilies. Cloying perfume wound around the room. The ceiling above him possibly ornate, but hard to focus upon any exact details. Clearly this was no dungeon or cell. Neither was this the infamous castle of the House of Elharean.

Scraps. Mere tattered threads of information. But at least that gave him something to work with.

Why here?

A gaunt face swam across his vision. Straw coloured hair pulled back in a que at the nape of the man's neck. A crisp white tailored robe with a hint of red lining beneath the collar. Beady eyes framed by a sharp pointed jaw and hooked nose.

Morçaeus. Evil incarnate. A foul stench upon the world of magic.

Lachie would see his blades sever the sorcerer's head from his body and his corpse turned to ash before this was over. His plan had always involved destroying their dark lineage. Retribution for the suffering and enslavement the Elharean's had left in their wake. Now he had his opportunity to finish what he started two hundred years ago.

To fulfil his promise. Atonement for being unable to save his sister. Retribution for what this monster thought to do to his mate.

His vengeful train of thought was cut short with another jab from the end of the cane. This time to his sternum.

"I must say. This is quite the surprise." The silver pointed tip pressed forward. The man's weight leaning upon the length with venom as he spoke.

"Here I simply desired you bring me my Ampher, and instead I get the Guardian himself."

Lachie's brain snapped on hearing those words. Urgent need for focus clawed at his insides.

Belle. Is. Mine.

"You were quite the unexpected wrinkle in our plan, turning up that night. Never mind, that's all in the past. Turns out we've got something much more potent to tap into now. Broken hearts and pain always do make for the best kind of magic to harvest." A sharp pointed boot punted into the side of Lachie's ribs. He gasped out a rough lungful of air.

"Have we pleased you, sir?" The woman's voice, the one he had heard in the woods, came closer. The source of the sickly perfume.

"Oh, but of course Fustara. Both you, and Ceranthe have done exceedingly well." The man paused to examine the tip of his polished boot with a frown. As though there might have been some stain left upon it.

"If you please, Fustara." He snapped his fingers and gestured at the woman.

Lachie found himself transported through the air. His body upright. The hex still encased him, but now his arms were stretched above his head. The woman—witch—in command of the hex drew the threads high towards the ceiling. It hung his body as though from a hook. His head lolled to one side.

Searing pain knifed through his temples as the enchantment reinforced its hold on his body.

He forced his eyes to focus. From this new position he could start to make out the room. The female witch was dressed in a heavy set maroon dress, intricately beaded, with a high ruffled collar. Typical fashion of nobility in the non-magical world. As she turned towards the man with the cane beside her, something caught Lachie's eye.

In her hat. A crimson red feather. The same as Belle had found in her room that night.

It couldn't possibly be.

The room spun incessantly. His stomach lurched. This wasn't possible. Belle had found her aunt dead. She didn't know of magic before the attack that night. The threads that he couldn't sew together now began to crystallise. Could Belle's Aunt have been involved with the House of Elharean all this time?

A trail of dread wound up his spine.

Belle couldn't possibly have known. Those ghouls nearly killed her that night. The House of Elharean had hunted her relentlessly. She couldn't have been involved. Could she?

Straining, he lifted his head to scan the room for Ceranthe. That fucking vermin. What he would do to eviscerate that scum when he escaped this hex. The realisation hit as his eyes rested on what once had been a familiar ally. A friend for over thirty years. One who he believed to be human. But now it was so plain to see. In this light, surrounded by the dark magic of the House of Elharean it was obvious Ceranthe had been part of this world for far longer than a human lifetime.

It was rare, but not unheard of, for a witch to willingly allow their power to be drained. The agonising process was more often favoured as a punishment or torture method by the Elharean sorcerers and their loyal followers. Nell had been subjected to the procedure before her rescue by Lia and Fehrn. The process was rumoured to be excruciating. Few witches lived to tell the tale.

Nevermind. Death would be the sweet balm of relief when Lachie was through exacting his own form of savage reprisal upon Ceranthe.

"I've long hoped we might meet one day, Lachlan of Nocturne. The infamous Guardian. I never imagined you'd be the one to deliver me my bride." Morçaeus' gaunt face leered close.

No! Not Belle. Not my mate.

Lachie's neck snapped as his torso strained against the hex's binding. Eyes wide with fury. Fury tensioned to unleash. Bile rose in his throat as realisation sank in.

This monster intended to keep Belle.

"Oh dear, the Guardian seems a little tongue tied." The man tsked. "Fustara, let's do something to help our guest find his voice." A cold, distant menace laced his tone as he waved his cane towards Lachie.

"Of course, your lordship." The witch practically kissed the ground below his feet. She chanted silently under her breath and Lachie felt the binding give a fraction around his throat. He let loose a ragged cough at the release of pressure.

"Now. Tell me, Guardian. Why did you decide to take my bride, hmm?" The man's cane tapped an impatient rhythm against the carpet. "I'll admit, she is rather pretty isn't she? Perhaps you decided you might like a taste of her sweetness yourself?"

Red mist descended across Lachie's vision.

"I vow, the last thing you'll taste is the kiss of my blade." He spat.

There was no way she could be allowed to fall into their clutches. His brain spasmed at the thought of what this beast might do to her.

"Quite the feisty one. I suppose I can see why your pathetic realm filled with sycophants cling to you like leeches."

"You'll never find her." Lachie's jaw clenched tight.

A stifled giggle came from the female witch. Shrill and syrupy. The Marquis smirked and eased himself down into a chair facing the spot where Lachie was strung up. He lazily threw an ankle across his knee. His beady eyes fixed and hungry.

"We don't need to find her. She will find us. And now we have you here, it will only draw her in that much quicker. Making it so much more ... satisfying when the time comes."

"She means nothing to me." His stomach churned at the lie. "You might as well just take me. A scalp you have been after for hundreds of years."

"Don't listen to him, your lordship. He and the girl have

been involved." Ceranthe was still here. Hidden in the shadows like a cowardly poisoned arrow.

"I said. She. Meant. Nothing. A good fuck. That's all." The words sat like poison on his tongue. The muscles in his jaw ticked.

Morçaeus' eyes glittered with malice

Lachie knew he needed to shift their focus. Dangle himself as bait. He could still find a way to take down the House of Elharean from within. He'd always planned to sacrifice himself to destroy the evil of their regime. A noble death he would choose time and time again to protect the ones he loved.

If it meant saving her, he was prepared to let her go.

"Nothing but lies. He's protecting the girl." Ceranthe's shadowed form lingered at the far reach of the room.

"We don't need him, your lordship. See how he dares disrespect you. Let me end him for his insolence." The female witch hissed. Her palms raised towards Lachie.

"Calm yourself, Fustara." The Marquis' cane snapped against the witch's forearm with a loud smack. She winced and shrunk back like a kicked dog. Morçaeus rose now and strode towards Lachie.

"Your feeble lies mean nothing. I have no doubt the girl will come to me. You see, Lachlan of Nocturne, you might have known the girl for a fleeting moment in time." The Marquis' thin lips smirked. A smug, twisted expression. Violent intent bred from immortality gained in the darkest of reaches of the underworld.

"But she's been my bride for two hundred years."

CHAPTER 35

"She's been my bride for two hundred years."

Acid retched in Lachie's throat. His muscles tore under the strain of his binding as he fought against his restraints. His chest heaved with ragged catches of breath.

Yet those nauseating words still hung in the air.

"You took what was mine. I have owned that girl since she was born. I will reclaim my Ampher. And you will watch. Before I let Fustara enjoy disposing of you." Flecks of spit flew from Morçaeus' mouth.

Lachie's vision hazed. Black spots began to crowd the edges of his sight. This couldn't be possible. Not his mate. She was everything good and kind in this world. The fucking ray of sunlight in every room she entered. Nothing made sense. How could she have survived these monsters for so long?

"Perhaps a little demonstration is necessary. To show you

exactly who that girl lives and breathes to serve." Morçaeus lifted his cane. The silver dome engraved with runic elements began to glow with a red smoke. He touched the end to Lachie's temple. Immediate sparks of ice cold agony spread through his head and down his neck. Everything twisted in a sickening whorl. The room around him disappeared, then reappeared in an instant. Only this time it looked different. Older.

A SHORT FIGURE shuffled through the room. A slight limp on her right side.

Lachie blinked at the sight. It was the same room where he had been only moments before, but now the scene had changed. Was he inside a memory perhaps? He looked down and saw his body free to move across the carpet.

The girl appeared young, perhaps in her early teens, but she didn't sense his presence.

He must be inside the sorcerer's enchantment. The more details Lachie took in, the more deeply unsettling the scene became.

The girl was dressed in fine clothing—as if she were nobility—yet carried a bucket of suds and a scrubbing brush. She bent over the tiles of the unlit hearth, on hands and knees, and began to scrub. Her head was bowed in a way that prevented him from seeing her face. Bruises covered the back and side of her neck before they disappeared below her shawl. Her fingernails were raw and bloody as though from attempting to escape a confined space.

A growl formed in his chest at the sight of her injuries. Lachie crossed the room, he still hadn't seen her face, but the ache in the pit of his stomach already told him everything he needed to know.

This was Belle. Much younger. In a different time to when he first found her.

A sudden shriek came from the distance. Belle's shoulders stiffened as though braced for impact. She dropped the brush with a clatter.

Harsh, striking footsteps thundered closer. An older woman burst in holding a beaded shoe in one hand. Her face bright red with anger. Lachie recognised the witch as Fustara.

"Annabelle. This is a disgrace. You call this mending?" The woman roared at the girl where she cowered on the floor. "There are two beads missing. And this heel is scuffed. I should throw you back in the gutter where your parents left you."

The girl wrung her hands in her skirts. Eyes fixed on the floor. Lachie moved to reach for her. To comfort her in the face of this woman's unjust anger, but neither were aware of his presence.

"I'm sorry, Aunt. I tried my best, but... my hands..." She winced and wrapped them tighter in her skirts.

"You'll be truly sorry after I've striped your hide with my cane. You useless child. This is the thanks I get for taking you in all these years?"

Lachie roared a yell and lunged at the woman, but the scene vanished beneath his feet. The witch was her Aunt. She was still alive?

. . .

He tumbled through darkness before the world around him rematerialised.

The same room now lit with candles. Low voices filled the air. Lachie found himself looking straight at Morçaeus. The sorcerer stood in hushed conversation with Fustara. Only this time dressed as the Marquis in tailored silks and with a cravat instead of his House of Elharean robes.

"The girl has no memory of her magic or the times she has been through the process before, your lordship. I have made certain." Fustara spoke hastily. A glint in her eye.

"And her darkest moments? You are certain you have broken the girl sufficiently to commence the harvesting this time?"

"Yes. Yes." Fustara enthused.

"Good. We shall activate her powers. Just as all the times before." Morçaeus nodded.

"All is prepared. I shall ready the hex for tonight." Fustara bent her head in a bow and kissed the ring on the Marquis' finger.

"Sancte Elharean." She murmured.

"You continue to serve the Great House well."

Lachie's hands balled into fists. The evil that lay in this house was like a festering wound. Purposely breaking Belle over and over. Hiding her magic from her, then activating it through trauma. His stomach lurched at the thought of everything his mate had been through.

He would destroy them all.

• • •

A THIRD TIME the room and scene before him twisted. Except this time Lachie was prepared for the tumble into darkness, only to rematerialise in the same place once more.

"YOU BELONG TO THE MARQUIS. These men are here to take you to him. You will obey every command, every wish, and satisfy every desire he has. Do you understand me?"

Fustara yanked Belle's hair back with brutal force. Her back bowed as she scrabbled at Fustara's claws where they gripped her head.

She was older in this scene. This was the Belle he knew and loved. Lachie let out a yell and ran forward to rip the woman off his mate. But found their figures to be ghost-like apparitions. His hands grasped at air as he tried frantically to rescue Belle.

Fustara threw her to bend on hands and knees. Belle let out a sob as she hit the ground. Lachie saw her cheek coated with a greenish purple hue. Evidence of an old bruise spread below her eye socket.

He stabbed his fingers through his hair. This was torture, knowing he could do nothing, and that this had been Belle's life. Her prison.

Men appeared now. They closed in on Belle where she lay prone on the floor. One grabbed her roughly by the arm and jerked her upright. The others moved closer. Menacing.

"Please, no. Don't do this. I'll do anything, Aunt. Please. Don't send me to him."

The sound of Belle begging for her life twisted a dagger in Lachie's chest. He bellowed in frustration.

"Ain't she a pretty thing. Better make sure she can put out for the boss. I'm sure she'll be good for a few turns before we deliver her to the castle." One of the men sneered as he loosened his belt buckle.

No! Lachie hurled a chair at the figures before him, but it passed straight through their shadowy forms. He couldn't bare to watch what inevitably came next.

A thunderous noise erupted. Inhuman and otherworldly. Light pierced every corner of the room in a blinding flash, like an explosion. Lachie shielded his eyes and crouched his body low, desperate to keep Belle in his sights.

The noise broke into a primal scream. Raw pain and fury combusted into a terrifying cacophony. As the glare receded, Lachie squinted and saw bodies strewn across the floor. Blood coated Belle in thick splattered swathes, yet she was on her knees and still moving. Her chest heaved. Stars, she was somehow unharmed. The bodies of the men around her lay mangled. Her Aunt's body twisted on the floor, blood strewn, and still.

Belle let out a loud sob. Her hand shoved against her mouth as if to bite back a scream. Her eyes wide she surveyed the carnage that surrounded her.

Her Ampher power. This was how they had activated it. By pushing Belle to the edge and then forcing her to explode. Manipulated by fear and terror.

THE ROOM DISAPPEARED in a sickening mist of blood. Lachie's mouth gone dry, he registered thin, bony fingers digging into the sides of his chin. Released now from the enchantment, the gaunt visage of Morçaeus glared down at him with venom.

"And just as my Ampher was truly broken and ready to be put to use again, you came along and stole her from me. Ceranthe was due to transport her that night. But you just couldn't resist taking something that didn't belong to you." His voice dripped with a cruel indifference. As though talking about a coat or a pocket watch. An inanimate object to be owned and used.

"Fortunately I've been able to keep track of my Ampher's whereabouts. Ceranthe's... access to your realm has been the most unexpected of happy coincidences."

CHAPTER 36

Something was terribly wrong. Belle reached out tentatively with her Ampher power to investigate. If she could just identify the magical signature left behind in the room...

She jumped in shock as the dark magic snapped at her senses like the sting from a scorpion.

This was both confusing and yet simultaneously had a taste Belle felt she had experienced somewhere before. She rubbed her arms at the chill it left behind in her body.

Ominous and foreboding.

It was like the room itself wanted her to know of its presence.

Closing her eyes, Belle raised her palms outward and chanted the spell to form a protection shield. She needed to focus and the risk of amplifying whatever blackness lingered in the air was too great a risk right now. Her emotions still ran high. The lump in her throat lodged firmly in place. Only now there was a silent pit of dread knotted in her stomach to add to the list of concerns plaguing her mind.

Magic used from a place of fear can be extremely dangerous indeed.

Brigid's words echoed in her ears. Where the fuck was that elf anyway? Belle squeezed her eyes as hot tears threatened to fall once more.

Pull yourself together, Belle.

Surely Brigid—the Seer—knew exactly what had happened between her and Lachie. Knew about his ridiculous plan all this time. Surely that little fairy knew about the letters too.

She would know where her brother was. How to find him even? What use was Belle in this kind of situation when she couldn't portal herself anywhere, was under threat of attack if she dared ride outside the borders of the realm, and had barely gained mastery of her magic?

Pathetic. Useless. That's what she was.

Brigid had likely seen premonitions of this very moment. No doubt laughed it up in her tinkling voice at Belle's expense. And yet conveniently was nowhere to be found. Enchantress and Seer or not, it wasn't fair that someone with so much power wasn't here to fix this mess.

Why would the Goddesses grant Brigid the gift of premonition if it meant a sworn oath not to intervene?

She might be furious with Lachie for lying to her. But despite it all, she missed him. Wanted him to appear in a swirl of smoke and wrap her in his arms. She wanted to breathe in his scent and bury her fingers in his hair. Maybe she'd kick him in the shins for being such a gigantic ass while she was at it, but she just wanted to be close to him.

Belle pressed her fingertips to her temples. A frustrated sigh burst out of her throat. She would have to figure out how to find him herself. Whether she wanted to admit it yet or not, the knot in her stomach grew tighter as every minute passed without her Guardian appearing.

Dark magic in Lachie's rooms.

Chaos still strewn everywhere.

No sign of a struggle.

But no Lachie.

She chewed the inside of her mouth. Her eyes roamed across the room, finally landing on the desk. Belle winced at the sight of the letters laid out in a haphazard pile. They stared back at her with their crisp folded lines and unblemished parchment.

What if he had left to carry out his plan? Nausea swept through her stomach at the thought. A shiver rocketed up her spine.

She wouldn't let him. Couldn't allow him to sacrifice himself. There *must* be another way. A means to make him see reason. To realise his sister's memory was worthy of honour through life, rather than death.

A way to remind him of his pledge... to protect her.

She wasn't a fool. Words in the bedroom often had no bearing on reality and the cold, harsh light of day. But Lachie had vowed to her of his own volition. He had told her he would always be by her side. That no realm or world could separate him from her.

Belle gritted her teeth. Time to collect on that promise. She'd be damned if her Guardian was going to walk away from this. From them.

She was supposedly the most powerful witch across the realms.

It was either now or never for her magic to prove itself. If only she could portal.

Her fingers splayed across the letters. Her palms flattened against the parchment. As her ring touched against the surface she sensed the binding on the lettering unravel. The enchantment revealed itself just as before. Belle remembered how her ring had been the key to unbind the spell on the desk.

Lachie used the ring as a conduit for his own magic. To travel across space and time throughout realms to appear wherever she was... as long as she wore the ring.

It was connected to her magic just as much as it was intertwined with his. She twisted the ring around her finger. He connected to her through the enchantment that bound it. But what about the other way around? Would she be able to reverse the spell? She'd have to tap into all the power she could amplify.

That meant opening herself up to the dark magic lingering in the room.

Did she want to risk this?

With every part of her soul.

Belle brought the ring to her lips and she let out a long exhale.

"Goddesses, please. If I splinter into a million soul shards, at least make it quick."

She dropped her shielding magic and allowed her Ampher to build. The power surged through her veins. Darkness seeped in and wound its way around her aura. Everything began to spiral. The unfamiliar essence felt like a drug. Intoxicating and seductive power. Her hands shook with the pressure of the wave building in a tornado around her body. Belle pressed the ring harder against her lips and thought of her Guardian.

Aquamarine eyes.

The quirk at the corner of his lips.

Strong fingers pressed against her waist.

His laugh rumbling through his chest.

The glide of his thumb over her pulse.

His growling words.

...You're mine.

Her body felt weightless. Mist swirled up around her legs and torso. She swallowed a heavy gulp as her vision of the room clouded over.

Everything descended into a chilled black void and the bottom dropped out of her reality.

CHAPTER 37

Belle's feet touched against a firmness before her eyes could register where she was. The dim light revealed only shadows as the mist cleared. It took a moment to adjust to her surroundings before she stilled.

That cloying scent of perfume. Lillies.

Bile rose in her throat. She doubled over. Unable to contain the retch in her mouth.

The pattern of the carpet registered in her mind.

No no no no no no no.

This couldn't be happening. Not here. Please not back here.

A muffled yell dragged her head up where she met Lachie's wild eyes. She had found him. Still alive. Relief flooded through her only to be replaced in the next second by a plummeting dread at the sight of anguish across his face. Red rope-like bindings of a hex hung him in the air in the corner of the room.

Strung from the ceiling like a gutted pigs carcass. He couldn't speak, but his eyes only conveyed one emotion.

Horror.

With a sob she rushed towards him and saw his features contort in agony. Her chest erupted in searing pain like a hot brand burning against her flesh. Belle clutched her sides. The force of dark magic ricocheted through her like an explosion. It sent her in a crumpled heap to the floor.

"Annabelle. We've been waiting for you. How good of you to return to us." A woman's voice pierced the silence in the room. Familiar and laden with malevolence.

Her Aunt. The impossibility of this moment brought a deafening rush of blood through her ears.

"But—How?" Belle's words scratched her throat. She fought back against the overwhelm of blackness that threatened to consume her vision.

"Oh yes, I'm still very much alive. And your betrothed is very disappointed you chose to attempt an escape." Her words lashed at Belle like a whip.

"I don't understand." She choked out.

"Pitiful child. Always the same. Begging and confused." Her Aunt snapped her fingers and Belle felt her head jerk back in response. Cold eyes bored into her. A face that had so often tormented and abused her throughout her life. "You thought you killed me that night, hmm? Just like all the times before."

Belle's eyes widened. Her heart hammered inside her chest.

"Don't believe everything you see. My hex showed you exactly what I wanted you to see. To have you convinced you had murdered a room full of people. Every time without fail you would flee. That's where the fun really begins." The woman's face morphed into a twisted satisfaction. "I always enjoy the hunt the best."

Nothing made sense. Belle felt the blood drain from her face.

"Fustara, allow me." Words snaked out of the darkness that turned her body rigid with fear. A voice that had haunted her ever since that night.

No. Not him.

Belle turned to Lachie. Her eyes pleading. Her past collided with the present in an intense overwhelm of memories and nightmares. But her Guardian had only one focus in the room. Locked on the source of that fearsome voice. Murderous intent glittering in their depths.

The Marquis.

He had found her.

"Fear is such a powerful emotion. Much more so than any other I have found." The Marquis' voice stalked closer. "Fear has to be nurtured. Allowed to take root. That way it can grow into the most marvellous of creations."

With another snap of her Aunt's fingers, Belle's head was forced away from Lachie to meet the gaunt face of the Marquis. He now reclined in a chair, silver tipped cane resting against his thigh. His thin mouth twisted in a cruel sneer.

"Ampher magic is something so unique. It needs a potent source of emotion to truly reach its potential. And you, my dear, have proved time and time again just how powerful you are when fear has blossomed inside you."

A wordless croak escaped Belle's throat. Her head pounded under the pressure of the dark magic that bound her. The words she heard didn't make sense. It was almost as if… this had happened multiple times before. Panic gripped at her chest with long, sharp talons.

"Ahh, can't you feel how magnificent that is? The pure scent of terror from the girl is thrilling. Is it not, Fustara?" He drew a sharp inhale.

"Most excellent, your lordship." Her Aunt—the ghastly apparition—nodded enthusiastically.

"Enough. Please. What do you want? Who are you?" Belle's voice strained.

"How dare she question you. Allow me to teach her some respect, sire." The woman's voice pitched shrill and dangerous.

The Marquis clicked his tongue.

"No need, Fustara." He turned his attention back to Belle. "She won't remember all the times we've met before, of course. Morçaeus is my name, girl. And I own you. I own every inch of your power. Now I am taking back what is mine." The cane tapped against the floor with an impatient twitch.

A guttural sound burst from Lachie's chest as he fought against the binding of the hex.

"You have been my property—my bride wedded in enslavement—for two hundred years. I purchased you. Sent you to Fustara, where your magic has been harnessed for my usage. Over and over. I experimented with different methods over time, but the most powerful has always been a variation on this scenario. Have you believe this woman was your Aunt. Stoke the fire of your fear until the point your magic explodes. Hunt you down with the help of our Necēris. Harvest the potency of your torment and fear. A simple mind erasure spell was all it took to begin reaping your magic again."

A roar between her ears deafened Belle. She dry heaved onto the carpet. Her soul screamed into the abyss of emotion stretching out before her.

Two hundred years. My entire life. A lie. Tortured for my magic. Abused.

"I must say it has been an unexpected twist this time. Thanks to you, Lachlan of Nocturne. This added element of heartbreak... it has really done something to heighten the potency of her Ampher." Morçaeus waved his hand through the air as if to draw the scent to his nose. Pitch black bled across his eyes. His visage a terrifying sight as he surveyed Belle on the floor at his feet. A viper about to strike with deadly precision.

"And now I shall claim my property."

CHAPTER 38

"Wait!"

Belle raised a palm. A quiet beg for pause. Spit flecked the sides of her mouth as she struggled to draw breath. Her limbs felt numb. The controlling vice of the enchantment around her chest burned through layers of flesh.

She had come here to save her Guardian. If it meant giving these monsters exactly what they wanted, she would gladly offer herself up to know she had guaranteed his safety.

"I'll do whatever you want. Just... please, let him go."

Another muffled roar ripped through darkness of the room. Belle winced under the force of Lachie's wordless rage.

"Release him. You have me. You have what you want. He's no use to you."

A high pitched laugh pierced the room. Her Aunt. No. Not

her Aunt. A vile beast hidden behind a mask of silks and beaded gowns.

"Oh, I don't think so. There's no telling what the witch might do. There's much more fun to be had with him when this is over." Fustara crossed the room and ran her fingers across Lachie's shoulders. His eyes burned white hot with the threat of retribution.

"Don't. Touch. Him." Belle warned. Her voice daggers and fists clenched against the floor. If only she could get free of this binding. She would destroy them all for what they did. For grooming her from day one. For feeding the darkest parts of her with torture and pain.

They had taken her power. Stripped her of her life. Ripped her magic away from her. Again and again. The searing agony in her chest extended like dark tendrils throughout her body.

Belle knew in that moment what she must do.

"I'll do it. I'll give you my power." Her mouth felt numb. She willed Lachie to look at her. Needed to reach into his soul and tell him. To find the way to convey the boundless depths of her love for him.

His eyes met hers across the room. Those aquamarine pools scorched fierce and filled with regret. Belle held his stare. No need for words. Their connection spanned an eternity. The spark of lightning against a touch-paper ignited the air. A never ending spark that stretched between them. A bond that she had daren't dream of experiencing for herself.

"Let us begin." Morçaeus snapped his fingers and stood to position himself in front of Belle.

"Ceranthe." His voice clipped out an order across the room.

A man appeared from the shadows where he had lingered unseen by Belle until now. He moved in closer. Silent and with a hunter's precision. The figure stalked around Belle trailing a red powder in his wake. The substance hissed and glowed as it touched the floor. He completed an unbroken circle. A spell cast to surround the space where she knelt on the ground.

Her Ampher responded immediately. Muscle memory from all the times she had unknowingly been through this ritual before. The ceremonial sacrifice she had been forced to be for two hundred years. A cold, brutal demand wrenched at her insides. The dark magic commanded her subordination without respite. She cried out in pain. It was too much. Her body felt torn apart from the darkness that welled up inside her.

Every ounce of fear trapped in her body began to expand. Swelling with vehemence. Red mist clouded her vision like a swirl of bloody vapour. Belle felt it pour from her throat. A metallic taste coated her tongue. Tiny flecks of the grotesque substance swirled from her palms like a crimson mist, filling the space within the circle. Her eyes rolled back in her head at the intensity of the dark grip upon her. Eons of shadows and terror amplified by her magic pulsated in and around her body.

She hung suspended in mid-air. Mouth open in silent scream as more of the bloody vapour poured forth. The coppery tang consumed her senses. Her Ampher built into a spin within the confines of the circle.

Belle sensed the shift as soon as it began. The whirl of mist began to syphon away from her body. A sudden connection that reached into the poisonous depths of another. Morçaeus.

She felt every molecule as it was ripped from her and began to assimilate within the sorcerer. Every boundary she had learned to put in place crumbled under the dark command to obey.

A vague sound of three voices chanting drifted through her mind. She felt her Ampher connect with three points around the circle. A triad into which her magic drained. The majority of which flowed to the sorcerer. A shackle that locked her in place at the centre.

Their greed sucked harder upon her life force. Relentless. Set on a singular goal. To bend her to their will until she broke.

Belle screamed through the bloody mist.

This was for every time she had been abused. This was for Lachie. His sister. Every Ampher that had come before her over millennia. This was for all that she had lost and now sought to reclaim.

With a pulse of her Ampher, she opened herself fully to their dark essence. Now acting as the syphon towards herself. The triad of connection began to flow towards her. Magic dark and foul filled her. She drained their power as though she were starved of oxygen. Every moment the flow quickened, she became stronger. Potent, liquid life force flew to her as though it sensed the more powerful source and desired to be in its orbit.

She felt their bodies writhe and twist as she continued to harvest every ounce of magic left within them with callous intent. She was insatiable. Drunk on their dark magic. Gluttoned on the feast of suffering she inflicted upon her tormentors. Their cries fell upon her ears like the notes of sweet revenge played out by an orchestra of the underworld.

All thought escaped her. Gone in a crush of bleak, vengeful desire for the darkness. She no longer knew why she was there. Sweet reckoning and power her only thoughts.

Beneath where Belle floated in mid-air the circle began to spiral. A tear through the fabric of time and space formed. The yawning void of the portal below her hung open like the mouth of a savage beast.

A clench of her fists was all it took to pull the three bodies —now withered husks—inwards as she plunged them into the cavernous void. Their remains tore to shreds as she watched the deformed creatures fall into the hellscape on the other side of the portal.

Belle closed her eyes. This was where she belonged. Limp bodied, she let herself fall through the threshold. The molten heat of the unknown realm subsumed everything.

The portal sealed behind her.

CHAPTER 39

Lachie's screams tore his vocal cords. His shoulder dislocated as he fought against the binding of the hex. Every nightmare manifested before his eyes.

How had it been possible for her to find him? He didn't know, but he needed her safely away from this place and the evil that lay inside it. He'd heard every twisted admission of their plan. Their torture. Her manipulation throughout two centuries. All for the sake of power hungry greed to fuel the House of Elharean.

Now there was a greater horror unfolding in front of him.

Belle hung in mid-air. Encased in a swirl of millions of blood soaked droplets. The gruesome substance poured towards her mouth and palms. Morçaeus, Fustara, and Ceranthe had formed three points surrounding Belle as they began to harvest her Ampher.

Then Belle had taken control, with horrific consequences.

She sucked the life force from each of their carcasses with macabre delight. Everything they possessed, their dark magic, power, and life force was drained until nothing remained.

As Fustara weakened, he felt the hex give way. His body hit the floor with a sickening thud. His mind scrambled for a way to save Belle... from herself. She might have successfully destroyed her abusers, but she would be lost to him forever if he didn't act.

The floor below Belle opened into a great cavern. She had wrenched open a portal. Across the threshold a desolate void stared back. This was no realm Lachie had ever encountered before.

He yelled her name, but it was futile. His voice barely a whisper. There hadn't been enough time yet for his throat to heal. There was no way to reach her. No way to break through the enchantment she had surrounded herself with.

In one motion three bodies were tossed into the portal. Lachie watched in silent horror as Belle's body went limp and dropped through the air like a lead weight. Her fragile form tumbled straight into the void below. As she disappeared from view a flash of emerald green caught his vision.

His mate wore her ring.

Lachie lunged at the rapidly closing portal in front of him. His focus only on one thought before he tumbled into nothingness.

To be with her.

His body collided against dust covered ground. Ash coated

the barren landscape. Hazed orange light filtered through the air thick with smoke-like particles. His lungs struggled to breath the heavy sulphur.

Belle's body lay beside him. Unconscious, but still breathing. Her hair tangled and covering her face. Her veins were threaded with black lines that stood out against her pale skin all across her limp form. Lachie dragged her to him and held her across his lap.

With gentle touches he pushed her hair back. Her eyes stared back. Open and unseeing. Blackness had bled fully across the whites of her eyes. Trails of inky darkness threaded their way under her skin and covered her face, neck, everywhere he looked. His fingers traced her lips. Their colour completely drained under the weight of the toxic power she had consumed.

There had to be some way to purge this power before it drowned her. He dropped kisses across her forehead. Belle's skin sizzled and hissed with menace where the evil she imbued claimed it's ghastly hold. Yet the surface felt chilled and pallid beneath his touch.

The sight shattered him.

What he wouldn't do for her. To protect her. Yet all he had done was end up repeating the same pattern over again. In trying to safeguard her, the darkness had only ended up taking her down to its morbid depths. He had failed in the very thing he set out to achieve.

He rocked her body against his chest. Desperate to give

some of his life force. As if by holding her he could try and share some of the burden she now carried within her soul.

The thought of losing his mate. His love. It was too much.

This was all his fault.

Lachie saw it so clearly now. How his own need for vengeance had driven him into the dark. By clinging to that need for retribution he had unwittingly written this script. For two hundred years he had plotted and schemed. For two hundred years Belle had been subject to torture. Their fates had danced a twisted cord threaded together by destiny.

And now he teetered on the brink of losing her.

He didn't know how long he sat clutching her against his chest in that desolate wasteland. Willing her to return to him with every faint flicker of her pulse.

Lachie's fingers stroked across her hair. He held her against his mouth and murmured against her dark locks.

"You're my mate, my fierceling. I'm so sorry I denied it for so long. I should have told you, but I was stubborn. A coward and a complete mess when you came into my life. But you woke something in my soul that first night we met. Something that I now know had been there for three hundred years. A part of me I had never dared to dream I could experience."

His fingers flexed against her. The faintest scent of jasmine and rose still clung to her. A trace of her to cherish with all his might.

"I used to think a mate—to be mated—was a weakness. As though the Spirits laughed in the faces of those who had no choice in their own destiny. But I was so wrong. It is an unimaginable strength. It's what brought me to you."

Lachie squeezed his eyes shut. Hot emotion bubbled raw in his throat. With one hand he cradled her head. The other he moved to thread his fingers through hers. Bringing each one to touch against his lips with a shaky hand. Her emerald ring felt as cold and lifeless as the rest of Belle's body. As though lost amongst a storm raging within the barren wasteland inside her.

His mate. His everything.

That unbreakable bond. It was what saved them. She had used the ring in ways he couldn't even fathom to connect their magic. To achieve such a feat? The strength of her reach across realms to find him—to save him. Lachie couldn't begin to comprehend what that had taken.

Her bravery to even attempt such a thing. Knowing the consequences it might have had for her soul. It destroyed him.

"To be wherever you are is enough for an infinite number of lifetimes. I'd gladly sacrifice everything for our time together. I don't need anything in return. You were brave beyond anything. To be with you is enough. To love you... that is all the sustenance I need."

Wrapping his hand around hers, he moved the ring and pressed it to Belle's lips. The jewel now warmed from the touch against his skin.

"I'm never leaving you. I will stay here in the darkness with you for an eternity. I love you, my fierceling. What I feel for you... it defies the Stars. It refuses to be distilled down into meagre words."

Lachie didn't know how long they lay together. The void of desolate space stretched out around them without bounds or form. It could have been hours. It could have been days. He daren't try to portal while she remained in this state. To transport someone while unconscious was one thing, but this? Magic of this nature was impossible to predict. He didn't know whether Belle's soul resided within her body, or whether she herself had been subsumed by the dark magic now evident in every vein below her skin.

Terror kept him locked in stillness. In an endless embrace.

After all this time, he imagined his death would come from the destruction of the Seal of Elharean. To use his magic as a cataclysm to bring their lineage to dust. Now here he found himself stuck beyond worlds and time.

Awaiting death to come claim him.

CHAPTER 40

Lachie curled his body around Belle. She remained lifeless except for the toxic magic where it seethed through her veins.

Where they lay pressed together he murmured into her ear. Reminded her of every moment they had spent together. Recalled every glance. Every brush against her skin. Shared how deeply he had cared for her, even when his actions were a foolish attempt to distance himself. He told her stories of Fiadh and their childhood. What it was like to grow up alongside his siblings. Memories of their parents and how he one day wanted to take her to meet them in the ancestral plane with the blessing of the Goddesses.

With every word spoken Lachie shared more than three hundreds years of history. He shed layers that had been sealed off from the world and stripped himself down piece by piece. Admissions of guilt, of love, of happiness all intermingled.

Lachie didn't know if she could hear anything he said. There was no sign of awareness. No movement. Only the pulsation of the dark magic where her sweet blood should be.

He'd woven his magic around them—hours, or maybe days ago—to form a nest of magical threads. His power was weakened but fortunately still existed in this realm. The glow of the silken cocoon cushioned their bodies against the desolation of the place they found themselves. If he was to be stuck here for eternity he'd damn well make sure his mate could do so in comfort. Even if Belle was lost to him, he could hold her fragile form tight.

Hope and a desperate desire just to hear her voice once more would have to be enough.

Lachie wrapped his arms tight around her waist. His nose brushed against her neck, the tender spot where her pulse should have ordinarily been. Closing his eyes with pleasure at being close to her, even if his heart shattered at their circumstances. He placed tender kisses down her neck.

"Want to know what I dream of, my fierceling? Our future. How I will spend every day of our long lives putting your happiness first. I dream of sunrises together and long nights under the stars. All of them with you."

He clasped one large palm around hers. The heat of his palm encased her fragile hand with her ring as his fingers wrapped her tight in his grip.

"Of course nothing across any realm can compare to your

beauty. But I want to show you all the wonders of these magical places you've yet to enjoy. There's so much good, Belle. I want to share every moment with you. To make up for all the time I spent just waiting to find you."

Lachie tucked her body tighter in his embrace and trailed kisses across her shoulder. As he glanced down at her skin he blinked. Could it be? Did the veins of black begin to shift and recede below his eyes?

"My fierceling. Fight it. I know you're there. I need you. Come back to me. My beautiful mate."

His thumb caressed the inside of her wrist. A flutter, then a jump of her power raced beneath the pad. He twisted to look at her face. Frantic hope lurched inside his chest.

"That's it. You're so brave. Such a miracle." He crooned.

Lachie stared open mouthed. The black lines tracking through her veins withered as he watched. He twisted to kneel over her body, one hand still held hers tight and the other braced beside her head.

"I'd do anything just to be with you. My mate. I love you endlessly. Please come back to me."

With each agonising second her eyes cleared of the inky darkness. Each visible trace of the poison within her snaked down and down. Weaving in threadlike motions. All gathered towards her hand.

Not her hand. Her ring.

"This would be a terrible choice of location... to admit I'm your mate." Belle's voice croaked hoarse and whisper soft.

Fuck. If he didn't all but fall apart at the sound of her voice.

"You couldn't have told me you love me somewhere... less... apocalyptic." She groaned and struggled to raise her head.

"Belle." Lachie breathed. Still too stunned to speak. His eyes widened as the black ribbons disappeared into the stone.

"Shit! What is that?" She studied the hand with her ring with a glazed look. "Was that... inside me?" Her hand flexed and twisted in front of her face as she watched the last of the black lines trace into the gemstone. Her pallid skin regained the faintest pink as blood returned to replace the poison.

Neither dared to breathe as they took in the enchantment at work. After a long pause Belle shifted her stiffened joints. Her body pliant and relaxed against his as though coming down from an intoxicated high.

"I heard everything. All your words." She whispered. "But the magic, it was so seductive. It dragged me under and under. I can still feel it's claws."

"I thought I'd lost you forever." Lachie's throat hitched with emotion. Raw relief etched his face. His hands shook as he stroked her cheek. Desperate to make sure this moment was real.

"Did I—the others? I killed them." Belle's eyes squeezed shut as memories of the chaos returned.

"Not likely. Weakened. Drained their life force. They'll float along, lost to who knows where for a long time. But no, you didn't kill them." His voice soothed her bubbling emotion.

For a long time they sat rocking together. Until her quiet sobs eased against his chest.

"Did you really mean everything you said? You want a

future with me?" Her soft voice was barely a whisper beneath his embrace.

"Every word. I've loved you from the first moment. I knew even then you were my mate and I'll spend the rest of my days proving it to you... if you'll allow me." With a soft grip he tilted her chin to meet his eyes.

"I love you." Her words caressed his soul as they drifted from her lips.

"You saved me. Us. Belle... I owe you my life. Can you ever forgive—" Lachie's words cut short as Belle's lips touched his. Soft and filled with tenderness.

"Make it up to me later. For now, please tell me you can get us the fuck out of here."

CHAPTER 41

A strong arm draped across Belle's waist with a firm hold. The warmth of the muscled chest pressed against her back was definitely her favourite way to wake up each morning.

Since they had portaled back from whatever desolate plane she had dragged them into, Lachie had rarely gone long without touching her. The smallest of gestures. A kiss on her shoulder while she sketched. The brush of his fingers across her leg when she sat beside him. She understood what it meant to him to know she was still there.

That she wasn't lost to him.

He didn't sleep much. Forever on alert to protect her while she slept. And when he did drowse it was fitful, but the nightmares had slowly eased with every dawn.

That first night he had been in full Guardian mode.

Without a single word he had tended to her. With reverence. Gently. Treated her like she was made of glass. In that moment she felt as though she might well have been. Fragile didn't begin to touch how close she had been to shattering. Lachie had bathed her. Washed every inch of skin with a slow, deliberate, and methodical tenderness. There was nothing in his attentions to try and arouse her. It was as though he wanted to imprint new memories with every caress.

She knew he did it for both of them.

Her heart had cracked open even more at the soft way he took care of her. That night and every night.

The castle still felt empty without Brigid, Nell, or even Lia around. Not that she had ventured much further than the study or the bedroom over the past weeks while her body healed. She'd eaten most meals curled up in front of the fireplace with Lachie stretched on the floor alongside her.

They had all been in contact in their own ways. Lia and Fehrn had visited briefly—with hugs and threats passed on from both Niall and Rowan that they would skin them both alive if either ever attempted anything so foolish again—before their return to the Fae Dominion. Nell had sent a rather cryptic letter alluding to the fact she might be detained longer in the mountains than she originally intended. Not to mention that her letter had been hand delivered via an impossibly handsome, violet eyed vampire. And not even Lachie knew where Brigid had disappeared to, but he didn't appear overly concerned. It was common practice amongst Seers to vanish for periods of time should they be summoned by the Goddesses.

Although Brigid had secretly made a brief appearance, leaving a gold sealed letter slipped under their door during the dead of night from the mischievous elf herself. The letter had caused quite the commotion the next morning.

She had written to inform them—with great flourish—of Belle's new standing as Guardian of the Realm. As decreed by the Goddesses and ancestors. The blessing and ceremony would take place once her training for the role of Guardian had been completed.

Belle had ranted at Lachie, insisting he take her to the temple of the Goddesses in order for her to convince them they had made a mistake. He had simply laughed at her. She was now the most powerful witch across the realm. The role of Guardian had now passed to her.

And Lachie couldn't have been more proud.

Stars, if that fact didn't make her melt for him.

She wriggled back against his warmth. Maybe his arms wrapped around her was the second favourite way to wake up in the morning? Her actual favourite...

"Does my little Guardian need something?" Lachie's deep rumble pressed against her ear. Heat pooled low between her thighs. She could already feel how wet she was just from the sensation of him hard against her back.

The very... insistent length of him.

He dragged his palm across Belle's thigh, fingers pausing to squeeze into her soft flesh.

"Umm, it still feels strange for you to call me that." She worried her bottom lip. Her mind caught in-between guilt for replacing Lachie as Guardian and giving in to the freedom of this moment. Her body seemed to have no such concerns. Her hips moved of their own volition in slow circles to press back against him.

"And like I told you." He hitched her leg over his hip. "You are the rightful Guardian."

His fingers dipped down between her thighs.

"*Fuck.*" He breathed into the curve of her neck. "You're dripping, my fierceling."

Belle let out a moan as he circled her clit. Slow, lazy strokes that drove her into decadent bliss.

"So fucking perfect. *My mate.*" Lachie nipped at her shoulder before soothing the spot with his tongue.

A fresh flood of wetness came in response to those words.

Who knew matehood would unlock some new level of… intense arousal.

Belle arched back in need of him. Searching for his touch to brand her with that pleasure she craved. She couldn't get enough of him. Her mate.

"I need you." Lachie murmured in response. As though he could translate her thoughts through the slightest movement of her body.

He gripped her thigh and spread her further. His cock pressed against her slickness. With a groan he sank inside. Belle's body thrummed with pleasure at the slow, deliberate slide of him.

"Ohh." She let out a long gasp.

Lachie started to move, thrusting in unhurried motions. Fucking as though this was the only place he ever desired to be. And Belle knew beyond any shadow of a doubt she felt the same way. Their magic intertwined in a weaving, languid spiral. A perfect match to the rhythm of his hips against hers. Familiar gold orbs filled the air around them.

"I could get used to this." His fingers shifted from their hold on her hip. "Waking up to a taste of the Guardian experience." Lachie teased against the back of her neck. He threw her own words back at her with a playful growl. The sexiness in that moment caught her off guard. She clenched around his length. He bit out a rough curse, his voice muffled against her skin.

"Oh fuck." Belle moaned louder as he snaked his hand back around to tease her clit.

"You'll need lots of training, my fierceling." His cock thrust deeper. Voice gone raspy and intense. The sound of him against her ear had her slickness take him further. Fucking in slow, undulating strokes.

"Yes." Her breath hitched higher.

Lachie's fingers moved in light circles. Just the exact way he knew would set her entire body ablaze. Pressure coiled with the steady rhythm.

"I can see I will need to be... very... very... very... thorough." Each thrust punctuated his words. She spiralled closer to the edge.

"Please." Belle gripped the sheets. Pleasure, agony, and ecstasy all rolled into one inside her.

"Only if you're a good girl." Lachie rasped against her ear.

"Yes. Yes. Please. I'm—"

Electricity slammed through her clit as he pulsed magic from his fingertips. Perfectly timed with his cock hitting just the right spot deep inside. Belle cried out as she came, her orgasm tipped her over the edge into a shuddering release. Waves of pleasure kept coming.

With a groan Lachie's thrusts intensified. His own hot release following on the back of her own. His cock pulsed inside her until they both lay sprawled with gasped breaths and hammering hearts.

Belle's skin tingled as she felt his hands skim up and down across her skin. His hot mouth planted endless kisses across her nape and shoulder. He made no move to pull out of her and she exhaled a shaky breath at the anticipation of her mate's next move.

"Want me to stop, my love?" The low whiskey tone of his voice turned her stomach to a fluttering mess. She could already feel him getting hard again inside her.

Bliss tingled down her spine.

"Never."

CHAPTER 42

"I fucking hate these things." Lachie grumbled.

Belle elbowed him in the ribs as she flashed her brightest smile at the Queen of the Nymphs and her entourage. Their ethereal grace floated through the grand entrance hall amid hugs and air kisses.

This Winter Solstice celebration had doubled as Belle's first event in her role as Guardian of the Realm. Although she was still in training under Lachie's supervision until the eventual ceremony of the Goddesses.

He'd thought to tease her and wonder out loud how he might escape the pomp and ceremony of these events from now on. Especially since he was no longer the official Guardian. Belle had simply batted her long eyelashes and pointed out the finer details to him of all that encompassed being *mated*. Lachie had then reminded her exactly what it meant to be his mate while pressed up against the bathroom wall, over and over.

She felt her cheeks heat. Stars, the way this man's strong hands cradled her heart. One of which currently brushed over her lower back in a reassuring touch. With a deep breath she turned to ready herself for the next dignitaries to arrive.

"This will be good. Here comes Niall." Lachie's mouth brushed against her ear. A sinful smirk laced his tone.

Belle glanced up to the castle entrance. The soon to be crowned Queen of the Fae marched towards the door with her floor length gown in hand. A few paces ahead of where her bodyguard—a grim looking Niall—hung behind.

All Fae possessed a preternatural kind of beauty that Belle found captivating. Most chose to wear their hair in the traditional manner with one side of their long flowing locks shaved close to their head. It gave their delicate features a hint of raw magnetism. A subtle nod to the fierceness that belied a pretty exterior. While their people had lived in relative peace for millennia, Belle had read of their warrior origins. Fae kind notoriously had no tolerance for those who underestimated their power simply based on their looks.

The creature that walked towards them with shoulders thrown back and chin jutted out was utterly breathtaking.

She stood nearly the same height as Belle, perhaps a little shorter. Tanned skin and dark brown eyes framed her delicate pointed chin. Her long hair swept over one shoulder in shiny turquoise waves with a shaved strip curved down the right side of her head. Traces of floral patterns inked up her bare arms.

Her dress shunned the conventional attire of the previous Fae royals. Rather than soft pastel colours and floaty fabrics, this gown looked more like armour. The raven silk fitted tight against her figure and hugged the curves of her body.

"Your majesty." Belle dipped with a curtsey as the Fae neared.

"Please, call me Ruby. It is an honour to meet you, Guardian." Her almond shaped eyes held a hint of embarrassment at the formality as her gaze swivelled between Belle and Lachie. Instead she quickly reached out to grasp Belle's hand in both of her own before letting her hands drop. "Thank you for the invitation, and for your... generosity to our realm." An edge of something sharp bit through her tone.

Niall coughed into his fist where he stood at a distance behind her.

"It's Belle. And of course, anything we can do to help. I trust Niall will let us know if your Dominion requires more assistance?" She noted a tension stiffen in the Fae at the mention of Niall's name. "And my condolences for the loss of the King and his family." Belle continued.

It was unusual for Lachie's brother to be so... reserved.

"We've plenty of your finest Fae wine here your majesty, please enjoy our hospitality tonight." Lachie interjected. Despite speaking to the Queen, he kept his eyes pinned on his brother who stood with both hands clasped in front of him. Gaze firmly averted from where they stood.

The Fae's eyes widened a fraction. There was a pause before she let out a clipped reply. "Thank you."

Without acknowledging her bodyguard's presence the Queen nodded to Belle and Lachie and moved through into the ballroom. Niall simply shook his head with a scowl in their direction before following behind. Still he hung back with a few paces distance to separate the two of them.

"Don't ask." Lachie murmured when Belle raised her eyebrows in question. "Are we finally fucking done here?"

This year's celebration brought together only a small collection of dignitaries. Far less had been willing to travel under the new layers of concern for safety. Even though the occasion was joyful, the mood still held a sombre tone. Seeds of fear had been sown by the House of Elharean with great success.

But there had been no attacks since the assassination of the Fae royal lineage. No snatchers sighted. An eerie calm had descended since the night Belle had consumed Morçaeus' power. Since she had thrown her Aunt and Ceranthe alongside that vile monster into a portal to an unknown time and place.

There were many uncertainties to what the future might hold. For now all they could do was live for the moment.

Her emerald ring glinted upon her finger. Somehow the enchantment on the gem had contained the dark magic she consumed that night. But there was no denying her Ampher had connected her—seduced her into it's clutches. She felt the malice there in whispers during quiet moments. Only now she knew how to shield herself against it.

At first she had wanted to stop wearing the ring. Until Lachie reminded her that magic wasn't inherently good or bad.

There was no such thing as black and white in the gifts given by Source. The power lay in the intention of whoever chose to use that magic. Given time she might be able to learn how to wield the power now confined to the ring. But first they had agreed to focus on trying to uncover more about Ampher magic.

To take it one step at a time.

Plus, that ring now linked her to Lachie as much as it connected him to her. She might not be able to portal by herself yet, but with the ring it meant she could transport to wherever he was. Whenever she desired. Just as he could do the same to reach her.

And that had its advantages. Namely being able to surprise him with unexpected visits that invariably ended up wrapped in his arms.

Something caught Belle's eye and she gasped. Her hand grabbed Lachie, tugging him forward with ease despite only having hold of a single finger. She ran outside breathless.

"It's beautiful."

Snow fluttered and danced on the night air in fat crystalline flakes.

"You're beautiful. My little Guardian." Lachie wrapped a hot palm around her waist. His aquamarine stare captured hers. Her breath stalled in her throat.

"Lachie—" Belle slapped a palm against his chest with a giggle.

His lips brushed hers and captured a snowflake where it had settled against the plumpness of her mouth. The freezing air sizzled beneath his molten kiss.

"You are everything a Guardian is, and more." He rested his forehead against hers. "I was an idiot who was prepared to leave this all behind for selfish reasons. Yet you were prepared to leave it all behind for purely *selfless* reasons. To save us all. You are more than I—or any of us deserve."

Lachie twined his fingers through the loose curls where they drifted across her shoulder.

"It is an honour to serve you." The length of his body pressed against hers. Heat and magic spiralled between them. Orbs of light now floated and mingled with the snowflakes.

"I have a much better idea. I'd rather have you serve alongside me." Belle sighed against his neck. Bliss travelled through her at the delicious feel of her mate's fingers holding tight. Feeling the bond that threaded deep within each of their souls.

"Unless you're in our bed. Then I'll be having you beneath me over and over, my fierceling." Lachie's low rumble sparked a ripple of pleasure along her skin.

"Always."

EPILOGUE

"Will that be all for m'lady this evening?"

The severe planes of the lady in waiting—jailer—were outdone only by the woman's scrupulously swept back mousey hair. Each strand plastered against her head in a low bun. The witch stared down her angular nose. Chin held aloft with disdain thinly veiled as formality.

Has it really been two hundred years of this bullshit?

Fiadh's long nails rapped against the frozen window pane. The sheet ice held firm below her immaculate ebony manicure. Once long ago she might have seen beauty in the natural patterns and swirls of ice. Might have gazed with adoration where the crystal structures settled and formed. Only now all she saw was evidence of another layer to her confinement. A secondary seal over the window. Where only a faint pathetic glow of what might be considered daylight made its appearance.

She turned her dark head of hair with a hiss. "Yes. You can fuck off now."

As the stern features of her lady in waiting disappeared from the room a familiar weighty thunk of the enchanted lock on her door echoed across the marble flooring.

Another night locked in her tower.

Another night to plot her escape.

Two hundred years she had been held here, in the House of Elharean's mountain hide. In a godforsaken unknown realm. A formidable castle hewn from the very bedrock of this strange land. Where day and night melded into one long, ever-present twilight like a pallid death mask.

To all intents and purposes Fiadh had been encased below ground for the past two centuries. Held under by the force of dark sorcery... and her marriage vows. The kind of vows a foolish and naïve girl made that bound her Ampher to her so-called husband.

Him. The one who had found her. Poured poison into her ears. The House of Elharean prince who had groomed her.

Maybe she deserved everything? It had taken only a moment to sway her from her family. A good person surely wouldn't have been tempted at all. So perhaps this wretched existence is more than she should have hoped for after the terrible things she did.

Her uncontrollable rage had led to only death and heartbreak.

There was no redemption for witches with tarnished souls like hers. Blackened like the coal grates beneath fire embers. Charred and caked with the grime of the countless times she had set the world surrounding her into ash.

Oh yes, those perfect features had lured her in. The silken words and sympathetic ear. Dark promises of power and autonomy that quickly turned to the rotten and bloated carcass of her marriage. The soulless monster who tricked her into believing his words.

Once Fiadh realised the depths of his desire for her power, it was too late.

The blood vows already exchanged.

The rites performed.

The sacrifice endured.

Bitterness coated every bauble and ostentatious chandelier in the castle where she continued to live out her confinement. Or as it should be more aptly described—her *banishment*. The last she had seen of him had been years ago. It was hard to tell. When there's no distinction between night and day and the sky is made of granite, the mind loses touch with concepts such as time.

It had of course never been a *marriage*. That was merely a contract with foul intent. No sooner had she signed her life away in blood than she had been whisked here. Drained of her magic. Left in a state of hazy limbo. When she finally awoke she found herself trapped within this mountain. A prisoner who had been the executioner in her own twisted tale.

Now, her roster of wardens, guards, and captors—-all

loyalists to the House of Elharean and placed as servants into her life—kept her every move under close scrutiny.

Fiadh couldn't sneeze in this miserable lump of rock without it being reported to him.

Perhaps this is what I deserve for what I did?

And yet still she would search. Every day she luxuriated in what little freedoms she was permitted. Stepping into the cavernous library for hours on end. Surrounded by parchment and rough hewn rock walls. It felt more like an endless network of caves than a library. But it held a sliver of hope that had somehow never been extinguished in all this time.

What she searched for, she didn't exactly know. But somewhere in amongst the endless sea of scrolls, grimoires, artefacts, and spell books must be *something*.

A key to the ancient magic of Amphers who came before her.

Clues to the true nature of what she once was. Even if that power had long since been ripped from her. The answers she needed in order to burn to the ground everything and everyone.

She would tear the House of Elharean apart and make them regret the day they laid eyes on her.

Some feared the darkness.

Fiadh knew the darkness should fear her.

THANK YOU FOR READING

Want a Belle and Lachie bonus scene with a bit of extra steam? See Belle get her own back after Lachie's prank with the sigil. Download at https://www.elliottroseauthor.com/bonuses

If you enjoyed this book as much as I loved writing it, please consider leaving a review on your favourite book website. Reviews are crucial for any author and even just a few simple words can create incredible ripples of impact in helping this book and the Nocturnal Hearts series reach other lovers of paranormal romance.

Come join *The Cauldron*, my reader group for bonus chapters and other exclusives from the Nocturnal Hearts world!

Acknowledgments

It would be impossible to bring this Nocturnal Hearts series to life without a whole realm of magical help behind the scenes. I am ever blessed and grateful for the village I have behind me.

Lazz - The most incredible hype woman an Author could ask for. You are the coconut milk to my decaf and I wouldn't be here without you.

Dazz - Words don't do justice to the support you give my creativity. Thank you for loving my wild mind.

Inca, Shilo, and Bert - Belly rubs and cuddles all round.

Thank you to my incredible behind the scenes team who have helped bring this book to life. Kerryn Hewson my editor and Sandra at Maldo Designs.

To my beta, advanced readers, and PR magic-makers - You are so amazing. This world is so much richer thanks to your incredible input and cheerleading from all over the world. Thank you for your time spent with these characters, the way you love on their journey, and for sharing about this book. You are superstars!

And lastly, to you - the reader - thank you and I cannot wait to keep exploring more Nocturnal Hearts love stories with you.

ELLIOTT ROSE

paranormal Romance · nocturnal hearts Series

If you want to return to the Nocturnal Hearts world...

Keep reading for a sneak peek at the first chapter of

The Queen's Temptation - Niall and Ruby's story

Next in the Nocturnal Hearts Series

Book Three

~ The Queen's Temptation ~

He's her bodyguard, and she's committed to her crown.

Charmer. Rogue. Protector.

In his three hundred years Niall of Nocturne had never pretended to be a good man–or Witch for that matter.

It was meant to be a moment of hedonistic pleasure, until the beautiful Fae he met in the tavern that night ran away after just one kiss.

It should have been simple. Pure pleasure. No emotions attached.

No matter how gorgeous or captivating she was, he shouldn't

be thinking of her still. The mysterious woman he now can't get out of his mind no matter how hard he tries.

The one who just walked into the room wearing a crown.

His mission was supposed to be simple: act as personal bodyguard and magical escort to the *soon-to-be* crowned Queen of the Fae.

The problem is... now that he's had a taste of the forbidden, can he bring himself to let her go?

***

Fierce. Duty-bound. Queen.

Ruby inherited a crown dripping with the blood of her lineage.

A royal bloodline bound for eons by an ancient curse.

She was never meant to sit on the Fae throne.

While the alluring, roguish Witch might have easily seduced her that night, she came to her senses the moment their kiss was interrupted.

It was meant to be one last night of personal freedom before fulfilling her duty. A future sacrificed indefinitely to the crown and bound to an unwanted political betrothal.

Discovering her fated mate was never part of the plan.

Neither was finding her handsome stranger waiting for her in the Fae Court. The Witch now entrusted with being her *round the clock* protection as Queen.

Now temptation has left her no choice... the curse placed on Fae Royals will always claim its victims. She'll do everything in her power to ensure her *mate* never discovers the truth.

THE QUEEN'S TEMPTATION

A heady mixture of incense, Fae wine, and sex swirled in the air.

Hardly a surprise, considering the late hour and the tavern full of supernaturals looking for a momentary escape.

The atmosphere thickened with each seductive lilt of the music that wound through the crush of bodies. The promise of something dark and desirous intensified with every glass of golden liquor poured by the buxom Fae behind the bar.

Niall inhaled a deep pull on the spice between his lips where he sat in a dark corner. Alone. But if the night continued as he intended, that wouldn't be the case for long. Embers glowed as he sucked down on the rolled paper between his lips. Smoke billowed across his tongue leaving a trail of oak and plums in its wake before the plume drifted from his nostrils.

He rarely smoked—his preferred vices included hard liquor

and pussy—but since he'd been banished to the fucking Fae Dominion for the foreseeable future, he didn't care whether a lungful of spice was a good idea or not right now. The Fae produced the best herbs to smoke and he might as well live a little before beginning his mission as a full time royal bodyguard. With no apparent expiry date on this mission in sight.

Trust his family to offload this kind of shit heap into his lap. Niall of Nocturne's oldest brother might be revered as the Guardian of the Realm—the most powerful witch among them—but to his mind he would always be Lachie. A grumpy fucker with a bark that was definitely worse than his bite.

And Niall loved nothing more than to bait the beast.

It had become even easier of late to get under that frosty exterior since the arrival of a certain witch that his brother seemed unable to keep his eyes off.

There was nothing quite as sweet as the taste of mischief on Niall's tongue.

He and his brother were both due to appear together at the Fae Court within the next few days. A meeting to confirm Niall's new position as bodyguard to the soon to be crowned Fae Queen. Whatever stuck up nepotistic royal bitch that might be. Niall would make sure to take full advantage of the opportunity to rattle Lachie's cage some more. It might at least help pass the tedium of this assignment.

Another deep inhale drew the embers of the spice into a bright glow between his fingers. His eyes drifted across the darkened tavern. Bodies writhed against each other on the dance floor. Laughter pealed from the table of Fae gathered at the opposite end of the room where bodies lounged against one another. The low ceilings and flickering candlelight cast long shadows across the opulent decor and the couples wrapped in each others arms.

Nothing in the Fae Dominion could ever be described as lacking in aesthetic detail. These supernaturals prided themselves on visible displays of wealth and power. Even here, in a tiny tavern hidden in a modest village far from the Fae Court, the place dripped with gold and precious gems.

But the pretty package didn't fool Niall. The endless parade of women—each more beautiful and flawless than the last—didn't even make his cock twitch. His empath magic only saw the ugly truth beneath the gilded veneer. It made it impossible for him to enjoy anything in this realm when all he could see was the truth. The grotesque, callous, vapid truth where it lurked just below the surface.

Niall sensed the emotional frequency of every single being. His aura took it all in. Both the pleasant and the unmentionable. The light and the dark. Not only did he sense it, but his magic was tied to it. All witches could learn to command at least one element through their gifts from Source. While certain witches had additional powers bestowed upon them by the Goddesses. Niall and his siblings had each been given additional blessings—or so they were called. His empath magic was the entire reason he'd been tasked with this mission in the first place.

After the assassination of the Fae King and his entire lineage, he'd been requested to take up a permanent position in the Fae Court. To help ensure the House of Elharean couldn't deliver the same fate to the new Queen.

Being a witch with the ability to sense the emotions of every being in a room, in addition to his prowess in combat, afforded him a unique edge. One that the Fae Court were now desperate to secure. Only now he would end up tied to some precious royal princess every day and night until further notice.

Fucking great.

Lachie had his best spies and most trusted supernaturals on the hunt for the House of Elharean loyalists who had infiltrated the Fae Dominion. But so far, there had been no trace of those responsible for the murders. His siblings might see him as the sweet talking joker, but Niall knew times were serious. The threat from the House of Elharean's dark witches grew stronger. He'd just have to buckle down and do his duty.

Which was why Niall found himself in desperate need of a distraction.

One last night of whatever pleasure he could find. One last night to drink, smoke, and fuck himself into oblivion.

Obviously his brother didn't spare a thoughts for anyone else's dick but his own. This mission was going to be the driest of dry spells. One that no amount of charm and flirtation would get him out of.

Unless someone removed his head from his shoulders, he was practically immortal. Plenty of time to indulge in whatever vice he desired once this was all over.

He uncrossed then recrossed his long legs to rest one ankle over his knee. His large palm rested against his thigh as one finger tapped out a rhythm. The crowd was in high spirits, despite the recent assassination of their rulers. But as he exhaled another plume of smoke a single flicker hit him. Something new curled its way through the mass of bodies.

Fear.

Niall's finger stilled. His magic reached out to hone in on the source. Fear meant one thing and one thing only these days, there was a potential threat from the darkness the House of Elharean wielded with deadly precision. He needed to get a proper read on whatever supernatural had just entered the tavern. There were too many emotions muddying the waters where he sat in the darkened corner.

Was this being afraid due to something or someone... or were they fearful of what they had been tasked with doing?

The last thing he needed tonight was to endure a fucking blood bath. That would definitely spoil the mood.

Better to move now and get a proper read on the source.

Niall drained his glass and pushed up to stand. He strolled towards the direction of the heaviness where it had settled, spice gripped loosely between his thumb and forefinger. Close to the bar he sensed it pulse and flicker. Something more than fear threaded with the emotion.

Anger? He couldn't quite tell.

His long strides drew him to the other end of the polished gold bar where he leaned on one elbow. He'd look casual enough to the passing eye, but the position gave him an easy vantage point with his height. The large U shape allowed him to stand at one end and survey the scattered assortment of supernaturals where they nursed their drinks and chattered loudly.

The pulse of emotion hit his aura again. Strong and distinct. His eyes snapped to the source and his breath hitched in his throat.

It was her lips he saw first. A luscious plump pout captured his gaze as she sipped on a glass of Fae wine. A dark hood covered most of her face in shadow. Fae? Most likely in this part of the Dominion. His eyes roved down the trail of long turquoise curls where they extended below the material. Silken strands brushed across the swell of her breasts. Dark leather wrapped her curves in a sleeveless halter top showcasing an expanse of ink up her bare arm.

She looked ready for battle and Spirits if that didn't look sexy.

Fuck. She might be filled with fear right now, but he'd gladly replace that emotion… with pleasure.

It only took a moment to relocate himself to stand beside her. His heart hammered in his chest as he leant his elbows against the polished gold. She didn't look up as he filled the space, seeming lost in her own thoughts. Guarded against her surrounds with her hood—or now that he could see it up close, a dark cowl around her bared shoulders—still pulled low over her face.

The sounds of the tavern filled the air and yet he paused before speaking out loud. Was he nervous? When had he ever felt anything but at ease charming a woman?

He rolled the spice between the pads of his thumb and forefinger for a moment to gather his thoughts.

"Hey there, princess." *Fuck. Where did that come from?* Niall couldn't help but wince internally as the name more commonly used on himself by his own brothers fell from his mouth. Nearly three hundred years of slinging creative insults at each other, yet *princess* was always the one that stuck. Something to do with Niall being the only sibling with sun bleached golden curls as a child. Even if now he kept his hair short in a messy just-woke-up-like-this kind of fashion.

This wasn't the time to unpack why he'd just used his own nickname on the beauty beside him. Definitely not the time to try figure out why that had never happened in the past three hundred years.

She sipped her wine carefully. Slow and sensual. Her cool exterior belied the emotional response Niall could sense within her. She didn't shrink away or cower. Interest and awareness of his presence wove its way through her aura, even if she refused to show her hand just yet. He raked a hand through his tousled locks. No harm turning up the charm to full force. Even though he could easily manipulate her emotions— pleasure, euphoria, ecstasy, you name it he could influence others to feel it—he'd never do so without consent.

And in Niall's experience, once a woman knew how his magic worked they always begged him for it anyway.

His eyes raked across the woman stood before him. She hardly reached his chest in height, but that wasn't exactly where his eyes found themselves fixed. Now that he'd carefully manoeuvred beside her at the other end of the bar he took in her full form. Tight black leather hugged her legs... and round ass. Curves that he'd gladly worship from dusk til dawn had his attention pinned.

And there's still plenty of time left until dawn.

Also by Elliott Rose

THE NOCTURNAL HEARTS SERIES

Sweet Inferno

In Darkness Waits Desire

The Queen's Temptation

Vicious Cravings - August 2023

Brutal Birthright - November 2023

With more to come...

ABOUT THE AUTHOR

Elliott Rose is an indie author of paranormal and dark fantasy romance. She lives in a teeny tiny beachside community in the south of Aotearoa, New Zealand with her partner and three rescue dogs. Find her with a witchy brew in hand, a notebook overflowing with book ideas, or wandering along the beach.

- Join her reader group *The Cauldron* for exclusive giveaways, BTS details, first looks at character art/inspo, and intimate chats about new and ongoing projects.
- Join her Newsletter for all the goodies and major news direct to your email inbox.

Printed in Great Britain
by Amazon

26994707R00218